Dear Jane

You insp ... med
there is a bit dark!

Bloodstained Heart

Part One – Passion

Love Audrina x

AUDRINA LANE

DEDICATION

To all my amazing fans, especially Louise McKie, Miriam Baker, Jo Morris and Nicky Lee who all begged me to write this story.
I really hope it doesn't disappoint!

Also to Rita Ames who designed not one cover but two to distinguish the two parts that this is now split into.

Finally to my poet and friend Laura Diaz who has allowed me to use her poem at the start of this book and the next part.

ALSO BY THE AUHOR

The Heart Trilogy:

Where Did Your Heart Go?
Unbreak My Heart
Closer to the Heart

Companions to the trilogy:

Bloodstained Heart: Part One – Passion
Bloodstained Heart: Part Two – Revenge

Plastic Feeling

You are
Polluted
And
Convoluted,
Lost beneath
Your
Fake smiles
Whilst
Suffocating on
Plastic feelings
And
Denial
A slow
But
Violent death,
Poisoned
With elastic lies
Whilst
Crocodile tears
Fall out
Of your
Trustworthy
Eyes

CHAPTER 1

1978

She trailed into the room, staring at the ridiculous white dress her mum was wearing. As if anyone would believe she was virginal after already being married, divorced and with a daughter in tow. She gazed ahead at the tall, straight man waiting next to the registrar. He was wearing a smart suit, tie and his blond hair was slicked back. A younger clone of him stood to the one side, apparently his son (who lived with the ex-wife) but had been brought along to act as best man.

Dragging her wedged shoes, she was trying not to scratch the itchy, lace sleeves that flounced at her cuffs. The halo of flowers in her long dark hair was threatening to slip down over her fringe and into her eyes. Thankfully the congregation was small in the room. Her grandparents had refused to attend which just left her mum's best friend Cecelia and her husband Jed and another couple who Felicity didn't know.

She stood next to her mum and drifted off as they exchanged vows and became Mr and Mrs. Then it was back out into the weak April sunlight and an awkward car journey to the restaurant next to the silent son of the man her mother had married. He was her new stepbrother.

"So what's your Dad like?" she stammered.

"Rich," was his monosyllabic reply.

"Are you coming to live with us?"

"No chance, I'm better off with Mum." He turned away and stared out of the window.

Felicity fiddled with her cuffs and let her mind dwell on her new boyfriend Phillip. He had just started at the comprehensive and all the girls fancied him but she had been the lucky one. Her glossy dark mane of hair and shapely, developed figure had enticed him. She was still a virgin, having witnessed the car crash of her mother's first marriage due to their unplanned pregnancy! That was not going to happen to her, she wanted to progress, pass her exams and start earning money. Felicity Jennings was going to be somebody.

During the meal her new stepfather broke the news.

"So Felicity, while your mother and I are away on honeymoon for the week, we need you to start packing. You're moving into my house and will be starting at the nearby girls' school in a fortnight."

Her mother beamed at her across the table.

"Isn't that fantastic news, it's such a great school and only a short bus journey from our new home."

Felicity gaped at the proposal, too stunned to really take it all in.

"Why can't I stay at my college, I like it there, I have friends, I have exams soon."

His face was stony, the blue-grey eyes like slates on a roof.

"We're moving forty miles away so you have no choice in the matter. I pulled a lot of strings and made a huge donation to get you into that school. So I don't want any more moaning from you, young lady. You're my daughter now and defiance and disobedience have no place in my home."

He moved his eyes to her mother, gripping her hand tightly on the table top. It was like he was trying to reinforce this with her as well as her daughter. The rest of the meal passed in silence, but Felicity fumed. Her mother glowed and simpered to the man next to her. His son ate the food and then left to take a taxi home.

"I've booked a taxi for you Felicity, your mother and I will stay here for the night before our flight to Amsterdam tomorrow. She tells me you're a good, intelligent girl so I know this new start in your education will be for the best. A girls' school will rid you of the distraction of boys."

Felicity stared straight into his eyes, seething inside at the way he was talking to her. She wished her real dad was still around but he'd just upped and left one day, nearly twelve years ago. Her mum hadn't wasted time hooking up with several guys before Malcolm arrived on the scene and started taking her out to fancy restaurants in his flash car. She had hardly been at home over the last few months and now the wedding had completely uprooted her world.

Driving away from the hotel she stared out of the back window of the taxi, watching her mother wave until it left the driveway. Getting home she found a note pushed through the letterbox from Phillip.

"Can you sneak out, I've missed you today. I'll wait for you in our usual spot."

Inside she changed into her bellbottom jeans and jumper, then with a slick of lip gloss she left the house. Taking great pleasure in ripping the crown of flowers from her hair and flinging it into the nearby tree, it hung there looking like a late Christmas decoration as it floated in the breeze.

The park was empty apart from Phillip, sitting on one of the swings. A plume of smoke rose from the cigarette in his fingers. She skipped towards him in the dusk light. He was nineteen to her seventeen and over six foot. He stood up and waited to enfold her in his arms.

"I thought you'd still be in your bridesmaid dress."

"Ugh no, that peach concoction was awful, look it's given me a rash on my arms from the lacy sleeves." He let her go so she could push up her jumper sleeves to show him.

"Oh, baby." He stooped to kiss her elbow, before trailing more kisses down to her wrist. Her breath caught in her throat as her heart raced to his touch. They'd been together for nearly a month now and things were getting hotter between them each time they met.

"Hey, can I pinch a fag, I need it after the day I've just had."

He took her hand and they wandered along to the nearest bench. He lit one, took a drag and then passed it to her. Their fingers touched, striking lightning bolts of desire through her veins.

"Come on babe, it can't be that bad. Didn't you say your new stepfather was loaded?"

"Yeah, but I'm moving in a week's time, forty fucking miles away and to a new girls' school." She took a deep drag and then coughed on the smoke as it caught the lump in her throat.

She passed it back to him and smiled despite the despair she was feeling. The situation seemed hopeless before she'd even started to get to know the man who was now married to her mum.

They shared the cigarette and then when he stubbed it, she leaned back into his arms.

"Well, if your mum's on honeymoon, why don't I walk you home?"

"Ok, we can make out there instead of getting chilly on this bench."

At the door Felicity hesitated, remembering her mum's warnings about being home alone with a boy.

"Look, I'm not sure I'm in the right mood after today."

"I bet I could persuade you," he whispered, his lips trailing down her neck so that she arched back into him.

"Mmmh, ok just for an hour."

Felicity found a can of lager and they shared it on the sofa.

"This is better."

"Yeah, guess."

Phil ran his hand up the leg of her jeans and then beneath her jumper. His lips captured hers and she nestled down against the velour material. The weight of him upon her forced the breath from her lungs. His hungry hands slipped beneath her bra, feeling her nipples spring to attention.

"You're so sexy, please let me see you," he breathed as his teeth nibbled her ear.

"I'm not ready yet," she whispered.

"Oh I think you are. I can feel you beneath me."

His comment focused her mind onto the pressing cock that was straining beneath the confines of his jeans. She pushed against his bulk, hoping he would release her from his weight.

"Not yet, please."

She pushed again, as his hands grabbed tight hold of her breasts, squeezing them so tightly that it hurt.

"You're hurting me," she shouted, hoping to break him from the urges he was following. His mouth silenced her, his tongue forcing into her mouth, filling it and preventing any further sound escaping. She arched against him, but he took it as a sign that she'd changed her mind, letting his one hand reach to undo the belt on her jeans.

Something inside Felicity snapped and she jerked her knee up, knocking his hand away and catching his erection at the same time. It was his turn to groan as he let go of her breasts and collapsed back to cup his wounded member.

"You prick-teaser, you flirt, you can't just keep leading me on and then telling me no."

4

"Well, fine if that's the way you feel then get out, fuck off and leave me alone."

"I will." He stood up and stormed out of the lounge, as she pulled her jumper down, the cool air touching her sore nipples.

"Yeah, don't bother coming back, we're over, finished," she spat, as the front door slammed shut.

Then as the anger seeped away, she started to shake, the shock of the day's events catching up with her in one fell swoop. The house around her was silent except for the sobs she let escape. She climbed the stairs and snuggled under her bedcovers, her hands reaching up to cover her aching breasts that still felt as if they were in his vice-like grip. She caught a look at the photo on her bedside table, taken at her fifth birthday. Her dad holding her hand in his, a balloon in the other and a broad grin on both their faces. Happy carefree days before the fallout began. She missed him every day and knew that one day soon, she would find him again.

CHAPTER 2

Her mum and Malcolm returned a week later to find her bedroom piled high with boxes. School had been miserable all week; she couldn't stop looking at Phillip whenever their paths crossed in the corridors or playground. He just ignored her, cutting any attempts at reconciliation. Her best friend Jenny had been shocked to hear all the news, but they vowed to keep in touch and meet up every Saturday once Felicity had found the bus timetables.

The removal van arrived on the Sunday morning and picked up her boxes and those of her mother's.

"What's happening with the furniture?"

"It will just sell with the house," Malcolm declared, as they followed the van down the road. She watched the inner city of London fade into leafy suburbs before they turned into a gated driveway. Felicity's eyes widened at the red brick mansion before her. It looked huge in comparison to their old two-bed council house. Her mum glanced back and smiled.

"So what do you think?"

"Uh, it's massive."

"Yes, we'll all have plenty of room now my ex-wife and son have left."

Felicity almost opened her mouth to ask where they had gone to but the car stopped and they all got out. Malcolm grandly opened the front door and ushered them in, leaving the removal men to follow behind.

"Let me show you your room Felicity, I had it redecorated just for you."

"Thanks… Malcolm… I mean Dad, fuck what do I call you?"

"Less of the f-word please Felicity, you may refer to me as Daddy."

She followed him up the staircase, rolling her eyes. *For fuck's sake no swearing and Daddy!* Only babies referred to their parents in that way and she was practically an adult. She glanced back at her mum who just nodded and smiled, mouthing silently to her, "Just do as he says."

They passed three closed doors before they arrived at the end of the hallway and pulled open the last one.

"So here it is, go on in and take a look."

He stood aside but she still had to squeeze past him in the space he left. She felt his hand run down her back before patting her sharply on the ass.

"Settle in and then come back down for dinner at six. All the other rooms up here are locked, including the suite your mother and I will share. I have keys for all the rooms."

"Do I get a key for mine?" she asked.

"No, you will only lose it so all keys remain with me."

Before she had time to complain about wanting her privacy, he strode back down the corridor, meeting her mother at the top of the stairs. Felicity walked into a room that was definitely not to her taste. The walls were painted a salmon pink, the covers on the bed were white and trimmed with lace. There was a large wardrobe, chest of drawers and even a dressing table complete with mirror, and a double bed. Maybe she could hide some of the pink walls behind her posters when the boxes arrived. She looked out of the window onto the perfectly manicured gardens that surrounded the house. It felt like she'd just stepped into a fairytale.

She watched as the removal men carried in her boxes and she started to unpack. Her clothes first, though they hardly dented the space in the vast wardrobe that she could literally step inside. There were two shelves that she used for her books and her only remaining teddy bear, the last present her father had given her. He was almost threadbare now but she still loved him, his wise button eyes watching her arrange her make-up on the dressing table. Her mum knocked and then peeped through the door.

"So what do you think, pretty amazing and so big?" she said, sitting down on the bed as Felicity swivelled round on her stool.

"Yeah, but pink! Why pink, it's hideous and so not me!"

Felicity started to unfurl the posters of Marc Bolan and Jimmy Paige for her wall. The large expanse of pink beside her bed would soon be no more.

Her mum stood up and sighed.

"Just hold your tongue with Malcolm, he has a bit of a temper sometimes and I don't want you to start out on the wrong side of him. He's trying to make us his family."

"Ok, Mum. I'll try."

She reached over and ruffled Felicity's dark locks, so similar to her own. When she left, Felicity started to fix her posters up. It filled the time until dinner. The meal passed pleasantly but rather silently as the three of them got used to the new arrangements. Whenever Felicity looked up, Malcolm caught her eye and smiled. She returned it but felt a queasy sensation in the pit of her stomach.

"So ladies, make yourselves at home but I have to go to work," Malcolm said, standing up and straightening his suit and tie.

Felicity watched as her mum stood up and followed him into the hallway. She heard whispered conversation but nothing she could make out. Her mind was occupied with questions about her stepfather who worked nights but made lots of money. He didn't strike her as mafia, so what career paid for luxuries like this? It was still niggling away when she said goodnight to her mum and went up to her slightly less girly room now the posters were all over one wall.

After living in a suburban street for all of her life, Felicity found it disturbing that the only sound she could hear in the darkness was the breeze rustling the branches of the trees. Then the sound of her mother walking in the hallway to bed.

She must have slept because next thing she knew, it was dawn light slipping through the crack in her curtain. It took her a few minutes to remember where she was and that today was her first day at the girls' school.

Rubbing her eyes she looked around the room and saw a uniform hanging neatly on the back of her door, next to her dressing gown. It hadn't been there last night, so she hoped her mum had crept in and hung it up. The bathroom next door was huge and solely for her use as there was another at the far end of the house. Pulling on the knee-length navy skirt, crisp white shirt, which she left the top button open, she slung her tie on loose, like she used to at her last school. A crimson V-neck jumper was next and then she saw a blazer on a hanger, hooked over the doorknob of the wardrobe. This was seriously posh clothing and it all felt really stiff and new.

With her hair brushed out straight she applied her eyeliner and some lip gloss before stepping into some new navy court shoes that had found their way into her room. She saw a reflection that looked nothing like her. This was her chance to be someone new, not that the old her was bad, but she'd slacked a bit this last year. Her hormones had kicked in and she was getting glances and attention from not just guys in her year but older ones too, like Phillip. Her face fell for a second because she had liked him and his kisses had been the best so far, but her ambitions didn't include stupid mistakes like pregnancy!

She found her mum in the kitchen and sat down at the round table, much cosier than last night's meal in the dining room.

"Well, don't you look smart," her mum said, passing her a cup of tea. The toast popped up and she buttered it, letting Felicity spread her marmalade.

"It feels a bit stiff, but I guess I'll soon break it in."

Her mum tensed as footsteps echoed down the hallway and Malcolm stepped into the room. He was a tall man, over six foot at a guess. In his hand dangled a straw boater.

"Here's the final part of your uniform." He laid it on the table and waited for her reaction.

"Thanks."

"Have you forgotten the way to address me in such a short time?"

Her mum had turned to pour a cup of coffee and as she met his eyes, they were narrowed and menacing. Part of her wanted to rebel at this stupid term but she thought about her mum, so happy at the wedding ceremony.

"Thank you, Daddy."

"Good, Felicity." He placed his hand on her shoulder, giving it the slightest of rubs before he straightened up and accepted his coffee and a kiss from her mum.

"Malcolm will drive you to school and show you the route home so you can walk back."

"Yes, we need to leave in fifteen minutes."

The journey was silent and the road they travelled paralleled the path she would take home. He dropped her at the school entrance.

"I'd come in with you, but you're a big girl now."

He lay his hand on her knee, giving it a squeeze before leaning over and brushing his lips on her cheek. She pulled away and got out of the car. She still felt nervous but the feel of his lips were much more disturbing than joining a new school. Perhaps she was overreacting, perhaps if her real dad was still around and had kissed her, she wouldn't have minded. Taking a deep breath she walked through the gates and followed the path to the doorway.

After an induction with the headmistress Felicity was shown to her classroom and found an empty desk at the back. Part way through the lesson the girl at the desk alongside passed her a note:

"Nice to meet you, can we be friends, Laura."

Felicity glanced over and took in the blond girl beside her who smiled as their eyes met. Well that was a good start to the day, Felicity thought as she copied down homework for the week. Outside the classroom Laura linked arms.

"I'm fairly new too, started last week so it's good to have a comrade."

"Well, you'll know a bit more than me then," Felicity laughed.

"Not sure about that but let's compare timetables and see which lessons we share."

As luck would have it they were both taking the same classes so Felicity hung around with her new friend, trying not to let her private school accent slip. Her new posh persona was starting to take shape and her friend's plum tones were perfect for copying. School passed quickly and saying goodbye to Laura, they walked home in different directions. On the way she passed a bus stop and noted down the bus times for the inner city. She'd ask her mum if she could ring Jenny and arrange to meet that weekend. The walk was pleasant as she swung her hat along by its elastic and watched the expensive cars driving by. A few blasted their horns at her so she flicked the drivers her finger in defiance.

CHAPTER 3

Felicity soon settled into her new life and routine. School was great, she enjoyed learning and Laura was a good friend and ally. She missed having boys to flirt with and tease but it kind of meant she could concentrate more. Home life was strict under Malcolm's set routine, which included dinner every night at six and at the weekend, a shared breakfast together at nine, so no chance of lying around in bed. It was at breakfast a month later when Malcolm made his suggestion.

"So Felicity, I have an opening at my club for a cloakroom assistant on a Friday and Saturday night. I'm sure you could do with something more than your allowance?"

"Oh Flick, what a lovely offer."

"Yes Mum and thanks Da… Daddy," she mumbled the last word, still embarrassed at having to address him that way.

Malcolm beamed at her across the table.

"This way we can cut your allowance and you can make it up with good, old-fashioned hard work."

Felicity opened her mouth to complain but felt a tiny kick to her shin beneath the table. She guessed it was her mother so she shut it and instead picked up her cup of tea.

"I've got you the clothes you need to wear, I'll bring them by your room this afternoon. You need to be dressed and ready for five."

"Yes, Daddy and thank you," she replied, demurely.

The job sounded amazing and to be in a proper nightclub, underage – well perhaps her famine of male attention had just become a banquet.

She spent the day at home, finished her homework and then listened to the latest music on Radio One. Sitting at her dressing table she filed her nails and applied a deep red shade, which made them look like talons. She was so absorbed that she jumped to feel a hand on her shoulder.

"Sorry, I didn't mean to make you jump."

"I missed your knock Daddy."

"Oh, I don't need to knock, it's my house."

She watched his reflection in her dressing table mirror, his grey eyes dark and brooding. He let go of her shoulder to produce a hanger from behind his back.

"I've brought your clothes for tonight and a pair of shoes. Please make sure your hair is fastened into a bun."

He turned to leave but then looked back at her.

"Take that sluttish colour off your nails, if you have to paint them use clear. You're mine now."

Scowling she watched him depart and then looked at her nails. For fuck's sake she was seventeen and she would wear what colour she liked!

After a bath she slipped into the black pencil skirt, white shirt and fastened her long hair up. Then to match her nails she slicked her lips with crimson, her eyes defined with kohl. Her mum was at the front door.

"Hurry up Flick, he's waiting in the car."

She teetered through the door and across the gravel in her new black heels, a little higher than she was used to.

"Get in the back, we're late now," he barked.

She saw his gaze flash across her from the rear-view mirror, his eyes so hard to read. The journey was silent as they drove into London and parked behind a large, opulent building. They entered through a door at the back, walked along a dark corridor and into the foyer. Malcolm turned on the lights and she watched as crystal chandeliers spun kaleidoscope patterns over the flocked wallpaper. Maroon purple on beige in swirling paisley patterns, a thick pile carpet matched the maroon. She stood with her hands behind her back, worried about her disobedience.

"So Felicity this is a very exclusive gentleman's club. Everyone through the door will have a membership card which they will show you. It has a number on it so all you need to do is find the coat hanger with the same number. Hang their coat or jacket on the hanger, say hello or thank you but keep talk to a minimum."

Felicity nodded as she followed him into the booth.

"I will bring you water through the evening and there is a staff toilet at the back but try not to use it between seven and eight when most clients arrive or between eleven and midnight."

Felicity settled on the stool behind the desk and that was when he saw her red nails. He loomed over her, his frame almost cutting out the light from behind him. It looked like a strange halo around his hair.

"This is your only warning, do not disobey me or I will be forced to…"

A knock startled them and he stepped back and went to open the door. A group of six young women stood waiting.

"Hi girls, do go through." He smiled and motioned them to the far door. Felicity saw their painted nails, in brighter shades than hers and pouted. Her anger simmered beneath the surface of her skin. Her teeth were gritted beneath her painted red lips when he turned to face her, a false smile on his face.

During the hour before opening another four girls arrived, plus two heavy-set men in black suits who took up position on the main doors. Other staff who didn't loiter just rushed through the door beyond. Felicity pulled her magazine out and waited. Malcolm appeared just before six, passed her a glass of water and then motioned to the men to open the doors.

"Felicity I'm going to be here for the first half hour checking that you are doing the job to an appropriate standard. So stand up, put your magazine away and be polite."

She nodded and silently obeyed. Every man through the door seemed to be of a similar age to her stepfather. A few were younger and many were older, grey-haired, pot bellies straining beneath their smart shirts, tucked into their trousers. They were all polite and restrained. She said nothing more to any of them bar "good evening" and "thank you".

Malcolm left as promised after half an hour and she was alone. The stream of men dried up so she sat back down to her magazine, her favourite column the problems. The security men stared at her but stayed mute despite her attempts at conversation. Then when eleven chimed on the grandfather clock in the recess, the men filtered back out. A few were more vocal, slurring their words from the alcohol. Most had loosened or lost their ties as Felicity handed them their jackets. A few leered and attempted to flirt with her but she ignored them and they all gave up when Malcolm appeared. He stood beside the desk, laughing and joking, pressing his palm into theirs or clapping them on the back.

Then after an hour watching the cleaners scurry around, everyone had left and it was just Felicity and Malcolm.

"You did well." He praised on the walk to the car.

"Thank you, Daddy."

"At least it will keep you out of trouble over the weekend."

Once more the car journey was silent but sitting in the passenger seat, she didn't have to endure his constant stare. At home she paused in the hallway.

"Good night, Daddy."

He grabbed her hand and pointed to his cheek. She shrugged and on tiptoes aimed at his cheek. At the last minute he turned and they pressed lips.

"Good night Felicity." His voice sounded hoarse and not his usual assured tone.

She crept into her room, wiped her make-up off and left her clothes abandoned on the dressing table stool. She guessed most children kissed their parents on the lips, but what about stepparents? Shivering from the chill of the sheets she turned the light off and started to drift. A noise in the hallway made her peep from beneath the covers. Malcolm stood in the doorway, staring at her. Closing her eyes quickly she waited, trying to control the thumping of her heart. She waited for an age but when she peeped again, he was gone.

***

Felicity settled into her new life; school in the week and normally some shopping on a Saturday with either Laura or Jenny. Then on a Friday and Saturday night it was work with Malcolm. After nearly six months they returned home on the Saturday and she was about to say goodnight when he stopped her.

"Would you like a drink?" he asked.

"Yes please, Daddy," Felicity replied, thinking he meant to make her a soft drink. Instead she followed him into the lounge and he went to the sideboard that held his crystal decanter.

"So it's your birthday soon?"

"Next week, I'll be eighteen."

"Well I think it is time to start your next education. A young lady should understand how to hold her drink, and not just that common lager."

She watched him pour a whiskey into the glass and then reached for the Martini, pouring it into a tall glass before he passed one to her.

"You'd better not tell your mum about this," he said. "It will be our little secret."

"Thank you, Daddy."

Felicity took a tentative sip. It tasted a little sour and she wondered if she should ask for some lemonade. From beneath her eyelashes she saw him watching her so she smiled.

"Never dilute your drinks with mixers; they are always better straight or on the rocks."

Malcolm finished his drink in a gulp before refilling his glass. She swallowed the rest, feeling it burn on its descent into her stomach. Standing up she swayed and almost lost her footing. A strong hand reached out and steadied her, at the same time enfolding her in a hug.

"Daddy really has been naughty, giving you alcohol," he sniggered.

She could smell the oak fuelled liquor on his breath as his lips brushed her cheek.

"I won't tell, Daddy," she whispered.

His hand slipped to pat her ass, hard enough to sting slightly.

"Off you go to bed now Princess. I'll see you in the morning for breakfast."

"Goodnight, Daddy."

He released her and watched as she left the room. He strained to hear her heels on the staircase. On his way to bed he paused and opened the door to her room. In the dim light from the hallway he could see her one leg uncovered. He itched to stroke the smooth skin.

CHAPTER 4

Her birthday fell on a Saturday this year and she had already been granted permission to have the evening off work. Stretching in bed she opened her eyes, wondering if being eighteen was better than seventeen. She dressed and went down for breakfast to see a mountain of parcels by the chair where she always sat.

"Happy birthday, Flick," her mum said, turning from the stove to smile at her daughter.

"Happy birthday, Princess." Malcolm wandered into the kitchen. "So what plans do you have today?"

"I'm going to spend the day and then sleepover with Jenny."

"Mmh, who is this Jenny, have I met her?"

"She was my best friend from my other school."

"Oh."

Silence reigned as he poured his coffee and then offered her one. Her mum placed a cooked breakfast in front of them both and then carried hers over.

"Let's eat first before you open your presents."

Felicity nodded but when she smiled at him, his stare remained stony. What had she said to upset him she didn't know, but she knew his temper from the club. She often heard him bawling out members of staff and one girl the other week had left in floods of tears. As they ate Malcolm rustled his way through the *Times*, sometimes stopping to read them a headline or comment on the state of the country.

"Why don't you open your cards?" her mother suggested.

The first one was from her and Malcolm, *sweet daughter* emblazoned on the front. The next was from her grandparents, who despite cutting ties with their daughter, wanted to keep in touch with Felicity. She also opened some from her classmates at school.

The first few presents were clothes from her mum, some fabulous red corduroy flares that she had been lusting after for weeks. A beatnik style polo neck in black and a beret too. Some new albums to add to her collection, including the new band that all her friends were raving about. Marc Bolan brooding on the front cover. The last present was a small box and she watched Malcolm lean forward, his newspaper discarded.

"That one's from me," he said.

Inside was a jewellery box and then, a bracelet with a charm hanging from it. She held it aloft, it was beautiful. The silver shone in the lights and she fingered the small heart-shaped lock and the first charm was a silver teddy bear. Slightly schmaltzy she thought but it was obviously expensive.

"Thanks Daddy, it's beautiful."

"Here, let's put it on and see how it really looks." He moved round the table and she held her wrist aloft. Once fastened he pulled her hand up and planted a kiss on it.

His ominous mood had passed as he moved to kiss her mother before he left.

"He chose it himself," her mum said. "He's really taken with you."

Felicity nodded and smiled. "I'm going to get ready now, try on my new clothes and pack my bag."

"Off you go, enjoy your birthday."

She watched her mum return to the chores around the house. In her room she put the album on her small record player. She loved the crackle at the start before the needle connected with the grooves. The opening cords of *20th Century Boy* filled her room. The clothes fitted perfectly and she was soon out of the house and on her way to the bus stop.

Jenny met her in town and passed her a small gift of some bubble bath. They hung around in the town centre and she saw Phillip staring over at her from within his crowd of friends.

"Thought we would go to youth club tonight, you know shoot some pool and dance to the juke box," Jenny said, as they wandered through the park back to her house.

"Sounds all right."

"Everyone misses you, they're going to dig your new accent."

"Oh, you mean this new accent," Felicity said, putting her best posh voice on and sounding like Laura.

With nails painted, hair done and make-up in place, the two girls tottered down the road. Felicity had teamed her black boots with a brown suede skirt, white blouse and a crazy waistcoat she loved. A hair band slung into her long hair completed the look. Jenny went for her long floaty floral dress and both girls attracted attention as they entered the youth club. A few of their girlfriends walked over to join them. From the corner of her eye Felicity saw Phillip, leaning over the pool table. He straightened up and his eyes channelled straight to hers. Like an invisible fishing lure, she reeled him in.

She left the group of girls and met him by the vending machine.

"Hey, Flick you're looking hot."

"Hi Phillip, mmh are you a sight for sore eyes."

He pulled a can of coke from the machine and offered it to her. She left her red lipstick stain on the metal edge before passing it back to him. The tips of their fingers touched and she felt the fizzle between them.

"So it's my birthday today."

"Is it now?" He dug in his back pocket and pulled out a small parcel. "Jen told me and that you'd be here tonight. I've really missed you Flick, I was a swine to you last time."

She pulled open the paper and found a set of hoop earrings inside.

"I can get Jen to pierce my ears for me now."

He swept his hand up her neck, pushing aside the strands to view her ear. Gently his breath swept over her skin before he nipped the lobe gently. He knew how much it turned her on and took the opportunity to push her back against the cool glass of the vending machine.

"Will you forgive me, can I make it up to you?" he whispered in her ear. She needed no further words to agree, letting him move her head so she looked into his eyes. She nodded before his lips touched hers, gently at first before she allowed his tongue to rub against hers. His smoky, familiar taste tugged at her heart.

"Lovebirds, can ya both move, I need a drink."

They stumbled away and left the building for the quieter ground to the side of the building. Phillip lit a fag and they both sat down on the steps for the fire escape.

18

"So what's it like living in the suburbs?" he asked, passing her the cigarette.

"Fucking big house, it's too quiet at night, sometimes I can hear birds singing."

He laughed at her comment, silencing her giggles with another deep kiss. The metal of the steps was cold on her bare legs and she shivered.

"You cold?"

"Yes, any suggestions?"

"My brother lent me his car, it's in the street. We can drive out, find somewhere quiet."

Felicity paused for a second then stood up.

"I'll just let Jen know that you'll drop me back at hers for midnight. That's our curfew."

Skipping into the hall she saw Jen in the corner with Phil's mate Brian, indulging in a spot of silent conversation. She coughed and they sprang apart.

"I'm just off for a drive. Meet you back at yours later?"

"Lovebirds back together then?" Bri chimed in.

"Yes, let's just say absence makes the heart grow fonder."

Jen laughed and then sighed as Brian ran his finger up the skin of her arm. Felicity grabbed another can of coke from the machine and a bar of chocolate and found Phil waiting for her. He draped his arm over her shoulder and they walked towards the street and the car.

He came to a stop in a deserted industrial estate, parking beneath one of the still-lit streetlamps. Many of the others were broken and a burnt-out car marred the high rise cityscape. They crawled over into the back seat and Phillip produced a small bottle of vodka.

"We can mix it with the coke," he said, taking a long draw from the can and then topping it back up before passing it over.

"Malcolm says I shouldn't mix liquor. It's better straight."

"Oh, and who is this Malcolm?"

"My stepfather. I work at his club on a Friday and Saturday evening and he's teaching me all about different drinks."

She took a sip, feeling the warmth of the alcohol in her throat. Not as potent as the Martini of the other weekend.

They shared half the bar of chocolate and most of the vodka and coke before Phil took it from her fingers.

"Let's go back to where we left off on the steps."

He ran a finger up her thigh to the hem of her skirt as his lips touched hers.

"Slowly," she breathed, opening her mouth to let their tongues collide. Slipping and sliding over their teeth and gums, igniting a flicker within her.

Her skin felt hot beneath his fingers that were inching up over her skirt to pull the shirt from the waistband. Lying back beneath him she sighed as his fingers slipped over the outside of her bra. He paused, his breath hot on her cheek.

"Can I?" Was his tentative question. She nodded as he slid the fabric aside and squeezed her nipple between his thumb and forefinger.

"Ahhhh," she gasped, this time his touch just right. Not too hard or too soft. Spikes of desire ran deliciously through her body. She arched against him so that he moved his lips down her throat. Her fingers fumbled to open her buttons so that her hot skin met the chill of the evening air trapped in the car. His head slipped lower, bestowing kisses onto the valley between her breasts. At the same time he pushed the wire of her bra upwards to let her large breasts loose.

He paused and admired them with his gaze as his hands struggled to contain them in his palm.

"You're stunning, so beautiful Flick."

He pulled his t-shirt over his head and she marvelled at his developing muscles. She let her nails run over the ridges and heard him moan. His mouth covered her nipple, sucking on it and making her breath come in staccato moments. This was all so new and exciting, a throbbing red heat seemed to radiate from between her thighs. She rubbed her legs together trying to heighten the feel with friction. Phillip knew she was excited as he dropped his weight back on top of her. One hand firmly on her cushioned breasts, the other trailed down and beneath her skirt.

Felicity opened her eyes when his fingers delved beneath the elastic of her knickers. She screamed as two eyes stared back at her from outside the car window. She scrambled against Phillip who took the scream as pleasure not fear. Then the cold night air entered the car from both sides. Still screaming Felicity felt hands hook under her armpits and haul her from the vehicle.

"Get off me," she yelled, her exposed breasts there for her assailant to see in the dim streetlight. The man was silent, his strength immense as he carried her to another car and threw her in the back seat. He shut the door and after pulling her shirt closed she tried the doors, both locked. In a second the two men were back in the front of the car, and turning the engine over, they sped off. Felicity stared out of the back window. She could just make out a human shape sprawled in the road. She choked back her tears, and stuck in her throat was a single word, "Phillip."

CHAPTER 5

After persistent questions to the silent driver and passenger, Felicity sunk back against the plush leather seats, shaking with shock as her mind replayed the image of Phillip. Who were these men? Were they kidnappers about to hold her for ransom? Her mind raced as they travelled through the night, coming to a stop outside a place she knew. It was Malcolm's club. As the interior light lit up the inside of the car she looked at her assailants and recognised them as the doormen. Her mouth was so dry that her gulp sounded like a croak. She could see Malcolm waiting. Opening the door the two men grasped her roughly by each elbow, propelling her quickly towards her fate.

They let go and she smoothed down her skirt, rage bubbling inside her like a churning cauldron of poison. In her mind attack was the best form of defence.

"What the hell do you think you were doing?" She screamed into the dark night. The man beside her pushed her through the doorway and Malcolm grasped her wrist. His grip was tight and hurt as she tried to twist out of his hold.

"Answer me!"

Malcolm did, his other hand slapping across her face, knocking her backwards and against the corridor wall. Tears stung her hot cheek, the pain immense. The shock had made her teeth bite down and the bitter, metallic taste of blood pooled on her tongue.

She scrambled against him, fighting with her free hand to scratch her nails down his cheek. She didn't get a second chance to inflict anything more serious as his other hand stopped her. She was now pinned against the wall, his full weight squashing the breath out of her.

"Stop struggling, calm down or you'll get another slap." His voice was low and menacing. "I don't want to hurt you Felicity, I was just trying to save you from making a big mistake."

"Your big mistake was sending your bullies in to beat him up and scare the shit out of me," she spat.

Her chest was heaving and pushing against the firmness of his body. She felt claustrophobic in the tight gap between her stepfather and the wall. Blood rushed around her body and she started to drip cold sweat. Then the room began swimming and she shut her eyes.

Opening her eyes later she gazed up at a ceiling, painted midnight blue. She was lying on a chaise lounge in a small room. She looked across and found mirrors on every available wall, making her dizzy to look at her swollen face. Struggling to sit up, the door opened and Malcolm strode in, carrying a mug.

"Here, I've brought you a cup of tea. You fainted." He smiled, his face changing from its earlier incarnation.

"Thanks, Daddy," she said, her hands shaking as she grasped the mug. He also held a towel wrapped around something.

"Ice for your cheek. I'm so sorry I struck you like that. I have a bit of a temper sometimes."

Felicity was mute, so unsure what to say or do next. She was frightened of his chameleon guise. Instead she cradled the mug and let him stoop beside her and apply the cold towel to her cheek.

"It shouldn't bruise but I guess we need a story for your mother," he murmured.

"What do you mean a story?"

"Well, we can't tell her the truth. She's confided that she hopes you don't make the same mistake she did and finding out you were half naked with a guy will surely ring alarm bells."

Mistake, was that what her mum considered her to be? Red blooms of indignation stained her pale skin as she swallowed the last of the tea. It burned her throat but she didn't care anymore.

"I love you like I would my own daughter, Felicity, I want you to succeed and not throw your life away with the first boy who shows some interest in you." He sat back on his heels, his expression open and honest. She smiled at him, watching his smile crease his features.

He reached to take her hands in his, he squeezed gently and she returned it. All her fear seemed to melt away, leaving just a bitter resentment of her mother.

"We'll tell her that you felt ill so you rang me at the club and I came to fetch you, it will help to explain your pale skin."

"Yes, Daddy."

He helped her up and they left the club for home. The drive was silent until they almost reached the driveway.

"Daddy, will Phillip be all right?"

"Yes, but I think you might be best breaking all ties with your old life. Remember onwards and upwards. Your friends there will only try to drag you back to their level."

She nodded and he turned slightly to look at her in the back seat.

"That's my girl."

In the end they found the house in darkness, her mother already in bed.

"Another drink, calm those last few shivers," he said.

"Why not." Felicity couldn't think of a better way to finish her eventful birthday night.

"Cheers and happy birthday." He clinked his glass against hers and drained it down, replacing the liquid with a second large measure.

Felicity gulped hers down, but it met the nerves in her stomach and she struggled to keep it from coming back up. Backing out of the room she fled to her bedroom, stopping to throw up in the bathroom next door. Pulling the sheets up high she stared at her ceiling. Too many thoughts and worries were streaming through her head. She heard his tread on the stairs and he came and stood in her doorway.

"Can't sleep?" he enquired, seeing she was wide awake.

"No," she mumbled. He stepped into her room, pulling the door closed behind him.

"Can I try something, it's what my mum used to do with me when I was a child and couldn't sleep."

"Yes, Daddy," she whispered, wondering what he had in mind. A bedtime story?

"Close your eyes and roll onto your belly."

She felt him bunch the covers up from the bed and push them down, revealing her nightgown. Softly his hand touched her back, rubbing in small circles up and down her spine. He moved upwards to her neck, still stroking and rubbing, then crossed to her shoulders. She relaxed beneath his touch, which felt so soothing. The patterns he made followed back down the line of her spine, stopping at the base.

"Does that feel nice?"

"Mmmh, yes Daddy." She was struggling to stay awake.

"Well, if you're a good girl perhaps I can do it again another night."

He pulled the covers back over her and then dropped a brief kiss into her sleek black mane.

"Goodnight Princess, don't worry about your mother. I will sort it all out."

He was greeted by small snuffles. Felicity had dropped off to sleep. He let his hand run through her hair and over her body.

Back in his bedroom he found his wife, waiting in her usual manner. Peeling off his suit he found the handcuffs to snap over her wrists and ankles. She lay sprawled naked and spread-eagle before him on her stomach.

"My Master, you have returned."

"Yes, so how have you disobeyed me today?" His erection strained against the confines of his y-fronts. He had been fighting it ever since Felicity had arrived at his club.

She ran through her list of incomplete chores, each garnering a spank on her ass. His hand felt the heat increasing with every touch of his skin on hers.

"Your daughter has been disobedient too," he growled, "so this is for her, she is too young to punish yet!"

This time he reached for the riding crop he kept hanging on the back of their bedroom door. She whimpered and mewled as he ran it up the crack of her ass before four well-turned thwacks left their mark. He freed his cock and walked around to kneel by her head. She strained against her cuffs to take him in, sucking hard in the way she knew he loved. He closed his eyes to find the image of Felicity there, her shocked look at the moment after he had slapped her cheek.

Drawing out he walked back down the bed and loosened the cuffs at her feet so she was kneeling before him.

"Does kitten want a wash?" He asked the words he always used but again, his mind flashed an image of untouched flesh. Smooth, pink and virginal. His tongue lapped at the juice seeping from her lips, mingling with the smoky aftertaste of his whiskey. She ground onto his face, groaning as he deliberately refused to touch her clit. Then he pushed inside her, grabbing her hair and pulling tightly so that the metal cut into her wrists. Each slam brought him nearer to release, now he pleasured her with his finger until she was sagging against him.

"Come now, come for Daddy," he cried, filling her with hot burning spunk. She slumped down on the bed, spent and satisfied as he withdrew. She adored their Saturday night role play, but the Daddy word was a new one for him. He usually referred to himself as Master.

He removed the cuffs and gently bathed her sore skin before she snuggled into his side. She was asleep in moments but Malcolm remained awake, his thoughts on only one person.

CHAPTER 6

At breakfast Felicity was late down. A small bruise had developed on her cheekbone but she had covered it with concealer. Her mum looked up and smiled.

"Malcolm told me about last night, what a shame to feel ill on your birthday."

"Thanks Mum, still feel a bit shaky this morning." Her stomach was gurgling over her larger than average intake of alcohol and her head throbbed.

"How about scrambled egg on toast and then you go back to bed?"

"Thanks Mum." Felicity watched Malcolm appear in the room and take his usual seat.

"Are you all right, Princess?"

"Still feeling a bit yucky, Daddy," she said, his eyes running over her face. She hoped he wouldn't see the hint of yellow beneath her foundation.

She finished her homework first before lying back on her bed, her mind still full of last night's events. She closed her eyes but all she saw was flashbacks from the back of Phillip's brother's car. The way her body had responded to his touch had been out of this world. She let her hand sneak beneath the hem of her t-shirt, creeping inside her bra to find her nipples peaking against the fabric. Marc Bolan's voice sang to her as she tried to recreate the feelings. It slowly started to work as the heat flared around her body and between her legs, making her jeans feel uncomfortably tight. She pulled them off and slid under the covers.

Lying on her front she pushed a pillow between her thighs so that it rubbed against the gusset of her knickers. Fuck, this was starting to get her off. She rubbed up and down, her pace quickening as she let her fingers play over her nipples at the same time. With her eyes closed she imagined Phillip beneath her. Oh god, it was happening. Breathless from the exertions of playing with her body, she gasped and moaned as her orgasm wrenched through her.

From his study next door Malcolm was enjoying the obscured view of his princess. The peephole he had cleverly installed could not be seen from Felicity's side or from here in the office unless you knew where to look.

As she started to moan and shake he let his hand wander beneath the waistband of his trousers. He was hard again and needed release but would his hand be enough? He looked at the clock, it was nearly dinner time. Felicity did too and stepped out of bed to climb back into her jeans. The back view of her ass hiding beneath the fabric of her panties took his breath away. Then she wandered out of the room, past his locked door and down the stairs. Stealthily he straightened up and stepped into the hallway – he still had time. It didn't matter if he was late at his own table. Inside her room he could just smell the musky sweetness of her in the air, wafting around just under the cloud of her perfume.

He picked up the pillow and inhaled the potent scent of her orgasm. It was damp in places and he resisted the urge to run his finger over it. Shutting the door he locked it from inside and pulled down his trousers and pants. His hand closed around his shaft as he played back all his images of Felicity, mingling slightly with those of her mother who could almost pass as her older sister. Faster and faster he went until he groaned and let go, letting it fall upon the pillow, splattering around but hard to see against the white pillow case. With a satisfied smirk on his face he tucked himself back in. Then he placed the pillow beneath her other one and with a chuckle wondered if she would smell him as she slept.

Downstairs his two girls waited patiently at the dining table.

"Sorry I'm late, I had an important letter to finish," he declared, sliding into his seat at the top of the table. Felicity watched her mum stand and start to scurry between the kitchen and dining room. A traditional Sunday roast graced the table as Malcolm stood up to carve.

"A little less well done next time Martha," he said. "I like a little blood."

His mind almost slipped back into his festering Felicity fantasy. Oh there would be blood when he broke her.

"Roast potatoes, Daddy?" Felicity's voice broke him free and he nodded.

"Thanks, Princess. How are you feeling now? Better I hope?"

"Yes, I must be because I'm hungry," she replied.

He stopped in mid-spoon of the carrots and glared at her.

"Oops, sorry Daddy."

The meal passed without any further incident. They watched some television together before Felicity excused herself.

"Think I'm going to read in my bedroom. Goodnight Mum, night Daddy."

"Night Flick," was her mum's response before she went back to her crochet.

"Night, Princess."

Malcolm watched her leave the room, once more admiring the twin curves of her ass. He grinned as he remembered the little present he had left in her room. However if she was truly still a virgin perhaps she wouldn't know the scent.

Pulling out her copy of *Lady Chatterley's Lover* Felicity huddled beneath the covers. Her one pillow still felt damp but it only made her smile to think about her orgasm upon it. That pastime could become addictive unless somehow she could find a new boyfriend or secretly get back in touch with Phillip. However now she knew that Malcolm was watching her, both of those options seemed out of reach. Feeling tired she closed her eyes and thought about all the men who frequented Malcolm's club. Few were young enough to pique her interest, maybe the odd one. An image of Malcolm's silent son popped into her mind. Mmmh she was sure there would be family occasions for him to be at.

The next couple of weeks passed in the usual routine. At school she had her O-Levels to study for and she was determined to excel. Malcolm was friendly towards her and she enjoyed their working nights out on a Friday and Saturday night. Laura was now a firm friend and she enjoyed her Saturday in town, shopping, gossiping and staring at cute guys. Once or twice Felicity attempted a conversation with the lad at the record store. He was sporting a similar look to her idol Marc Bolan and she thought she was getting somewhere until the following weekend he blanked her. A look of pure terror flashed across his face.

Sitting in the café with Laura, Felicity suddenly spotted her friend Jen wandering up the pavement. She was glancing around as she walked so Felicity ran out and shouted.

"Hey, Jen… over here."

"Flick, thank goodness I've found you. I was grounded over your Saturday night disappearance but Mum's let me out now."

Her face was pale as Flick dragged her into the café and bought more coffee for everyone. She waited as her friend took a sip, the worried look not leaving her face.

"What happened that night?" Jen asked.

Laura finished her coffee and sensing Felicity's reticence at opening up, she stood. "I've got to meet my Mum at two, so I'll catch you at school on Monday."

"See you Laura."

Now it was just the two of them, Felicity cleared her throat. She took a glance around at the other people sitting near them. One was a single guy in a black woolly hat that kept looking over at the two of them.

"I didn't feel well so I got Phillip to run me to a bus stop and I caught the last bus home. My stepfather came to meet me," she lied, in case the guy was eavesdropping for Malcolm.

"Well, I'm so pleased you're ok, Phillip was in a right state. They found him on this deserted industrial estate, beaten up and left for dead."

Felicity paled at the words and looked across at the lone guy still there, looking like his chair had moved closer to their table. Dropping her voice she leaned closer to Jen.

"Is he ok?"

Jen shook her head. "The doctors say that he'll be paralysed for the rest of his life from the waist down. Whoever it was really went to town on him, possibly with an iron bar. It was just lucky someone found him when they opened up one of the units on Sunday morning, otherwise…" Her voice trailed off and they both shuddered.

Felicity sat open mouthed, the shock had stunned her. But what to do next? She had to speak to Malcolm, he had a lot to answer for now and she was not going to give in this time. A chair scratched over the linoleum and the silent man stood up. Felicity watched him leave, wondering if he was about to report back to her stepfather.

"He's still in hospital at the moment, he keeps asking about you, claiming you were there and that whoever beat him up took you away. I guess that hitting his head might have made him forget about dropping you off."

"Guess so," was her strangled reply.

Her thoughts and anger simmered gently for the rest of the afternoon and as she got dressed for the club, it grew deeper.

"Princess, are you ready?" he called from the bottom of the staircase.

"Coming Daddy," she replied, spitting out the last word.

Her mum waved her off as she got into the car.

"Think we're going to have a busy night tonight," he said, his conversation starter.

"Yes, Daddy." She stared straight ahead, not wanting to look into his eyes. She hoped he wouldn't guess what she was thinking.

"Did you have a nice day in town?"

"Yes, I caught up with an old friend, plenty of interesting gossip."

She caught his eyes as they looked in the rear-view mirror at the same time as hers. Did she detect a sly look?

All evening her rage bubbled and churned. Malcolm brought her a coke out later, tipping her a wink at the same time.

"My men are talking about you, telling me what a stunning stepdaughter I have."

"Thank you, Daddy."

When they filed out at the end of the night she felt strangely tired. Her eyes swam as she bid the regulars goodnight. Slumping back on the stool she closed her eyes. She could catch a few winks whilst the cleaners scurried around.

CHAPTER 7

When she came to she was gazing at the same midnight blue ceiling again, lying on the chaise longue.

"Daddy," she shouted.

"Princess, I'll be with you in a moment," he replied from the room beyond.

"Why am I lying here?"

He strode in the room, his tie loosened, and he had a swagger to his step.

"You fainted, honey," he said, kneeling down to place his cool hand on her forehead. Her head felt muzzy and thick, her skin warm and clammy against his coolness.

"Lie back again, take a moment."

Closing her eyes she felt his hand stroke softly down her arm; it brought goose bumps to her skin and in a strange way her heartbeat increased. She wanted to still feel angry with him but somehow her mind was floating away. The fingers on her arm moved down to brush the curve of her waist and then onto the top of her thigh. She moved slightly but he squeezed instead. He trailed downwards, until he found the bare skin of her legs.

"Lie still, beautiful. You need to know how it feels to be touched by a man."

"Huh?" Her voice sounded faint and faraway, like she was not really there.

"Relax, my princess… Daddy loves you." His voice was calm and soothing. Her eyelids seemed too heavy to open as she sank further into the molasses. Perhaps she was dreaming.

His hand seemed to have moved again, travelling back up her body, glancing across her breasts, her nipples pushing against the thin material of her bra and tight shirt. Three buttons were undone as his hand wandered onto the skin before slipping between the lace that covered them. She arched into his delicate touch, feeling the worn semi-rough skin of the pads on his forefinger and thumb. In her mind she was back in a car with Phillip. Lips touched her throat in a series of kisses that ran upwards to alight on her mouth. Hungry and devouring she was helpless to respond. The tongue probed and delved deeper and she choked to find the breath she needed.

She reached to grasp the wide shoulders of her lover, memories assaulting her from all angles, swimming together in a shoal that just would not desist. Clinging tightly she felt the dream slipping from her grip, the hands and tongue withdrawing. Blackness engulfed her throbbing body, if only the fingers would come back, release her from the longing urges, surging through her blood. Flaming heat hid between her thighs and she squeezed them open and shut, needing satisfaction.

Waking up in her bed, the bright sunshine hurt her eyes, and pain throbbed behind them.

"Mum," she croaked, her throat dry. She felt rough like she was suffering from a bad cold.

"Muumuu…"

"Hush, honey. You're sick," her mum soothed.

She placed a cool, damp towel on her forehead.

"Malcolm's really worried about you… said you fainted at the club last night."

"I don't remember, Mum."

"You don't need to remember honey, thank goodness you were in safe hands."

The voice of her mum disappeared again. Hands… hands, yes she remembered hands. They were on her body, on her breasts last night. Shaking her head she moaned at the pain and snuggled further beneath the warm covers. A hot water bottle was on her feet, bringing warmth up her legs and thighs. Thighs, yes hands were there too, she remembered the throbbing between them. Hours slipped by before Felicity heard a noise and the bedroom door opened, the light behind it blocked by Malcolm.

"Hey, Princess. I've brought you some soup and a tea." He balanced the tray on her bedside cabinet and then sat on the edge of the bed.

"Why can't I remember?"

"You're delirious honey, don't worry Daddy will look after you."

His hand pulled down the covers so that she was able to sit up against the pillows. Her nightdress clung to her body, sweat soaked through.

"I feel all sticky," she said, and her voice shook.

"I can run a bath for you."

She nodded and reached for the mug. He guided her hand before he stood up.

Sipping the hot tea her throat started to feel less dry, her mind clearing slowly. Malcolm returned and smiled.

"It's all ready for you, I even snuck some of your Mum's expensive bath oil in the water."

He held out his hand and helped her up from the bed. Felicity's legs felt shaky, like she was learning to stand for the first time. Clinging to her stepfather she was thankful for his strength and guidance. He paused in the doorway of the bathroom. He watched her struggle to pull her arms from the sleeves and remain standing.

"Let me help, that's what daddies do."

He whipped the gown over her head before she could protest. He watched as she took the few steps between him and the edge of the tub. She staggered and he rushed to coil an arm around her waist. She sagged against his bulk and he simply picked her up and lowered her into the scented water. The smell was her mother, so she smiled and sank lower beneath the surface.

"I'll come back in a bit and help you out," he said, turning to leave.

He didn't want to leave; the drugs had made her so compliant last night. He had wanted to do much more but he wanted her awake, not drugged. He wanted her to demand his touch, yearn and plead for it just like her mother did. This was just the start, gaining her trust.

Relaxing in the warm water Felicity felt the clouds clearing from her head. The way Malcolm was just seemed so wrong, but was it? She dredged her memories for those containing her father. He had bathed her once, blowing bubbles into her eyes, and she had thrown them back at him. Her mother had told them both off for making a mess of the tiles and soaking the carpet. He had just laughed, infuriating her more. Wrapping her in a soft towel and carrying her into the bedroom. With the water cooling and with it her temperature, Felicity got out and dried off. When Malcolm returned she was back in bed, a fresh nightie on and her stomach growling.

"Can you heat up the soup please Daddy?"

"Feeling better?"

"Yes Daddy and thank you, that bath did me the world of good."

All the way to the kitchen Malcolm lamented taking too long. He had wanted to dry her glorious body off with the towel, imagining the fabric rubbing her nipples. Feeling her respond to his touch like she had last night, like her mother always did.

"Martha, can you do some fresh soup, Felicity is hungry," he said, feeling a different hunger welling in his loins.

He watched her open the can and pour the tin into a saucepan. The flame on the stove was forgotten as he pushed her against the worktop. His hands found her naked beneath the dress she wore, just how he liked her. Ready and waiting for him, he just dropped his trousers and pushed inside her, no foreplay required for this pussycat. Grunting he pushed, feeling her grip him tightly.

"Harder baby?"

"Harder," she gasped, feeling the first blow of his palm on her behind. His balls beat a different rhythm against her slit. Grabbing her hair in his fist he slammed her facedown onto the granite. The pain shocked and excited her even more as she gyrated against him.

"Now," she screamed, "let me feel you Master."

She pulsed onto him, letting him fill her. He withdrew and it ran down her thighs. She followed it to the floor, her body limp and wasted.

"Clean me off," he demanded. She opened her mouth and sucked him clean. Then as if nothing had taken place he pulled up his trousers and left the kitchen.

Felicity was pleased to see her mum enter the room, soup and a slice of bread on a tray.

"Malcolm says you're feeling better?"

"I think so."

Balancing the tray on her lap Felicity tucked in, the chicken soup just what she needed. By the evening she ventured downstairs for dinner.

CHAPTER 8

"I'm leaving," Laura whispered, as they huddled together in the playground the next day.

"Leaving?"

"Yeah, my dad's been posted overseas so we have to go too."

Felicity was being abandoned once more, this time by her best friend. The only saving grace was the fact that they only had three more weeks at school, then study leave and exams.

"What about your exams?"

"I'll take them on the base. Do you want to keep in touch? We can write each other."

"Yeah, why not."

Malcolm had already told her that once she passed her exams she could work the bar in the club and he'd start to teach her the business. He had been full of praise for her school grades and work in the cloakroom. Felicity wavered between liking him and still festering her knowledge of what the bouncers had done to Phillip. Revenge was a dish best served cold – she'd heard that saying and loved it. In fact she was tempted to get a tattoo with it on.

Her exams went well and instead of having a summer stretch ahead of her, like some of the other girls who were going back to start their A-Levels, Malcolm had told her they weren't necessary to his plans for her. Business acumen was best taught on the job, he said. Before they started work Malcolm had plans – they were off on holiday to Spain. Felicity had never been on holiday before, let alone a plane.

"We're meeting Anthony at the airport as I need to spend time with my son."

Felicity pouted at the thought of sharing a fortnight with her stepbrother. He'd hardly been talkative at the wedding so two weeks of silence was sure to put a dampener on things.

On the plane she sat on the edge of the row, Malcolm and her mum on the one side and Mister Sulky just across the aisle.

The villa they walked into was smaller than their house but no less sumptuous in its design and fittings. Felicity gasped at the small outside pool, just for them to use. Then standing on the upstairs balcony she could see the sandy beach and sea. Her mum and Malcolm had the largest room with a bathroom attached, this meant that she had to share the other with Anthony. Once she had unpacked her clothes Felicity slid into her swimsuit and grabbing a towel to lie on, she wandered to the pool.

It was deserted, her mum had gone shopping for some basic food items with Malcolm and she had no idea where Anthony was. Stretched out on her towel she picked up her latest novel by Jackie Collins. She knew Malcolm wouldn't approve so she had wrapped the cover of a Charlotte Brontë novel over it. Grinning as the action between the hero and heroine heated up she was distracted by the noise of water. She turned and peeped over the top of her book. Anthony was in the pool, ploughing up and down in a monotony of lengths. Shading her eyes from the sun glinting on the surface she admired his body as he stepped out and slung a towel around his hips.

Then he was walking towards her to take a seat on the next lounger.

"Hi, you swim well," she stammered, feeling a blush spreading over her cheeks.

"Thanks... oh, what's your name again?"

"Just call me Flick, I prefer it to Felicity."

"Flick it is then, just call me Tony." For a second a grin crinkled up his features and she smiled back. Perhaps this holiday was shaping up nicely.

"So what do you do?" she asked, her paperback discarded as she moved onto her side and leaned on her elbow.

"I'm a lifeguard, but hoping to one day run my own pool."

"I can't even swim," she replied.

"Well, why don't I teach you, it will give me something to do instead of playing golf with Dad."

They heard the car pull into the driveway and silence fell between them. Felicity could see the fear in his eyes as Malcolm stepped onto the patio area.

"Drinks anyone, come on we are on holiday," he beamed, crossing to take a seat on the third lounger.

Her mum appeared with a jug and glasses on a tray, filling each of them and handing them around before she sat down. Felicity couldn't remember a time when she had seen her Mum in a bikini and realised that their bodies were so similar in build. Hiding behind her paperback she took peeks as Malcolm spread suntan lotion onto her mother's skin.

So intent in her peeping, she jumped as the cold lotion hit her warm skin.

"You might need some to stop your shoulders burning," Tony said, flashing her a bright smile that she couldn't resist returning.

She languished under his fingertips, sliding over the back of her neck. Something about the touch made her close her eyes and try to imagine if it was his lips instead. Her nipples were peaking against the rough surface of the lounger and moving even slightly made them tingle from the friction. She missed him when he withdrew and hiding back behind her paperback, she cast furtive glances at his body, spread out next to her.

"What are you reading?" Malcolm's voice cut through her reverie.

"*Jane Eyre*," she replied, smugly.

"I'm impressed, keep up with the classics, much better than those trashy novels."

"Yes, Daddy," she murmured, then blushed when she saw a frown cross Tony's brow.

A peaceful afternoon passed as the four of them basked and didn't really talk. Malcolm dived into the pool a little later and tried to cajole her mother to join him. She laughingly refused and giggled like a school girl. Tony stalked into the house to get showered and changed. When her mum stood up Felicity followed suit as they were going out to eat in one of the local tavernas. The bathroom was empty so she wandered in and locked the door. The water from the shower pattered on her warm skin and she emerged rather more glowing that she liked. Pulling on her long floral sundress she left her hair loose, enjoying the feel of it cascading over her pink shoulders.

Malcolm had booked a taxi and the three of them squeezed onto the backseat whilst he directed the driver from the front. They headed away from the coast along narrow tracks that hardly seemed wide enough for the car. A low white building greeted them, swathed in dust from the tyres. The owner knew Malcolm as he greeted them all like long-lost friends. Felicity stared at him, he looked vaguely familiar, perhaps a member at the club? The food was sublime and Felicity took advantage, trying the various dishes that were brought out. Her favourite were the prawns, succulent and dripping in a tomato sauce.

The sangria in jugs was plentiful and when they hit the air outside Felicity staggered, the dizziness making her realise she had over-indulged. Tony grabbed her elbow and helped her into the cab, while Malcolm seared her with his disapproving look. Her mother was giggling and red-faced, the booze making an impact on her too.

"Think I'll just go to bed," Flick said when they arrived back at the villa.

"Here, take some water with you." Her mum offered her a glass and she wandered to her room.

"I'm gonna retire too," Tony said, following her up the stairs.

In the hallway she paused.

"Do you want to use the bathroom first?" he asked.

"Thanks, I'll tap your door when I've finished."

"Can I do the same tomorrow morning, I could give you your first swimming lesson before Dad gets up?"

"Sure, just not too early."

Under the covers later Felicity felt too hot in her nightgown so she slipped it off. The cool covers and the breeze from the window helped to soothe her sunburn. She fell asleep to the words of Jackie Collins whose heroine had just succumbed to the charms of the hero.

CHAPTER 9

Felicity woke to an urgent but light tap on her door.

"Flick, you awake," a whispered voice called.

"Ugh… what time is it?"

"About nine, it's lovely outside… come on."

"Ok, I'll meet you down there," she said, staggering out of bed.

Her head felt like it was filled with cotton wool, while her bleary eyes took in the rays of sunshine peeping through the filmy drapes on the window. Feeling daring she put her bikini on, then the nerves kicked in and she wrapped her beach towel over it.

Tiptoeing past her mum and Malcolm's room, she heard snores resonating from within. She was glad she was the furthest room from theirs otherwise this would have kept her awake. Tony was in the pool, so she stopped to enjoy the view of him crawling up the length, before he flipped over at the end to return to the shallow water.

"Come on now, it's just the right temperature this morning."

He scooped some water up and threw it in her direction. She laughed and stepped back, dropping her towel on the nearby lounger. She didn't catch his expression of desire, darkening his pupils to deep black. He turned away and did a leisurely breaststroke up the pool and then back.

Felicity had dipped her toes in and sat dangling her legs into the water, feeling apprehensive at taking the plunge.

"It's not deep," he said, standing up in the water.

She watched beads of water trickle over his well-defined chest. Her face flamed at the thoughts she was having. He was much fitter than Phillip, her only point of comparison. Well unless she counted seeing her stepfather yesterday. She shuddered and slipped down into the water, glad when her feet touched the bottom and she was only waist deep.

"See it's not that bad."

"Yeah, so what now?" She shivered slightly, not from the water but fear.

"If you lie back I'll support your shoulders and you will just float."

She nodded but remained stock-still.

"Just think of it as a big bath," he encouraged, moving to stand behind her.

With trepidation she started to let herself fall, knowing he was behind her. The scent of him was so tantalising and fresh in her nostrils. She gulped for breath, this time not from fear. Her blood pounded around her body so quickly, moving from the tips of her toes straight to her head and back. The burning ache between her thighs was scalding despite the cold water. Juxtaposed on the verge of falling, should she take the chance? She fell. His hand held her, not tight just balancing on the skin that he had covered in suntan lotion the previous day. Then she was staring up into the sky, his face just on the periphery of her vision. He lowered his hands and the strands of her hair floated on the invisible currents, whipping across his knuckles.

"So if I let you go now, don't panic. The water will cradle you."

His hands left her and she panicked, sinking below the surface. Tony quickly pulled her up, but she coughed and spluttered out water. Aware that his hands now held her securely around the waist, her skin registered the alien touch of his.

"Ok, let's have a rethink. You need to feel happy in the water." He nodded, affirming her feelings. He let go of her waist and sank down so that he was kneeling on the bottom of the pool. His shoulders and head remained above the surface.

"I'm going to hold my arms out and you're going to lie across them on your stomach. I won't let you go until you're ready."

Biting her lip she looked to the side, wondering if she should just give up now. Then she turned her gaze to him and saw his sweet, gentle smile. So different from his father's, his was like that of an eager little puppy dog.

He moved so that his hands grazed her belly before he reached for her hands. He was now in front of her, his face just a few inches from hers.

"You're floating."

She beamed, letting the water lap around her, feeling happy in its caress.

"Ok, now I want you to start to flex your feet, move them up and down. This will make you move forward. I'll keep hold of your hands."

She felt him squeeze her fingers, the simple flex sending spikes of cold shivers right through her. Like little pinpricks of ice that somehow turned to intense fire. Tony towed her across the pool, his eyes locked on hers. At the side they turned and went back across, and each time he loosened his grip on her hands a tiny bit.

"Breakfast is nearly ready," her Mum shouted through the door.

Her voice shattered the peaceful swell of the pool between their bodies. Standing up in the water Tony pulled her up, not letting go until he knew her feet were touching the bottom.

"That's enough for today, same time tomorrow?"

"Yes," Felicity breathed.

Just the proximity of his body was having a profound effect on her, one she'd never felt before. The sun hit her body in waves, warming the cold parts, but still she shivered.

"Have I got time for a couple more lengths?" Tony shouted.

"If you're quick, or unless you like your bacon extra crispy."

Felicity hurried inside, the towel feeling rough on her drying skin. Malcolm was on the stairs but moved aside just enough so she could squeeze past.

"Morning, Princess… don't take too long in that shower." He tapped her butt and then let her pass.

After a quick shower she opened the door to find Tony waiting. She smiled and let her eyes drift down to where his towel was tied at the waist. He had a light wisp of blond hair covering his chest and then running in a line that she just itched to follow with her finger. Turning red she fled to the safety of her room, taking more care as she dressed. She wanted Tony to see her as more than just a stepsister, or a teaching project.

After breakfast Felicity and her mum wandered down to the beach together while Malcolm and Tony took the short drive to the golf course. Felicity enjoyed the beach, people watching behind her shades. Olive skinned local lads with dark hair flirted with blonde European girls. All Felicity could think about was Tony and the feel of his firm touch on the skin of her waist this morning. Then… the smell of his fresh scent over the chlorine of the pool as he rescued her from drowning. Closing her eyes she saw his fine physique as he ploughed up and down the pool, watching the water droplets run over the firm muscles of his chest and abdomen.

The next few days passed in the same leisurely manner, except she was waiting and ready for his knock every morning. By the third morning she had learnt to float unaided on her back. The strengthening sun crept over her face, bathing it in warmth, or was it just hiding her blushes every time he complimented her?

"So what next?" she asked, feeling her confidence growing.

"Well, I guess you need to learn a stroke, how about backstroke to start?"

His face loomed into her vision, blocking out the rays of the sun.

"So stay in this position then?" She smiled up at him.

"Well in a minute, it will be easier for me to show you a length first."

Letting her feet touch the floor she stood up and shook out her hair. The slick weight of it clung to her shoulders and she reached to smooth it off her forehead. All the time she was aware of his stare, the intensity of his cool grey-green eyes. She lounged against the side and watched him lie back into the welcoming water.

"So your legs just do the usual up and down flipper motion. Your arms need to move like this."

He pushed away from the side and each arm raised up and back into the pool. His palm cupped to sweep aside the water and then disappeared into the depths before the other arm did the same. She sighed to watch his fluid style, catching her breath when he flipped over at the end of the pool. His body twisted to turn as he broke the surface. Slowly he returned to touch the side of the pool, so close to her body.

He stood up and ran a hand casually through his blond hair.

"Think you can do it?"

"I'll give it a try."

"Perhaps you should start with the legs first. Just keep your arms still."

Lying back she did exactly that, the length of the pool seeming shorter on the way back.

"That was great, now try the arms," he encouraged, a slow smile turning up the corners of his mouth. After the first two lengths which were a bit messy and uncoordinated, the third was better. By the fourth she was getting the hang of it and feeling brave.

"Race me," she shouted, kicking off from the side and splashing water in his face with her feet.

She was halfway up the pool when he caught up with her and then made his pass. He was hanging onto the side of the deep end when she reached out and grasped it.

"Not bad, not bad at all," he praised.

"Are you sure?"

"Well, it's a start. You need to keep practising and that will improve your technique. Show me your hand."

She held it out to him and he curled his round the outside of it. "See if you curve your hand slightly it will cut through the water easier and you'll get quicker."

The patio door opened and Tony dropped her hand like it was a burning stone.

"Hey, early birds how's the water?" Malcolm asked.

"It's good Dad," Tony replied before he kicked off from the side and crawled back down to the shallow end. Felicity turned onto her back and did another length of backstroke.

"Your mum sent me out to say that breakfast is almost ready."

"Thanks Daddy." Felicity beamed, standing to take the steps out.

Tony had swam back to the deep end and was just turning to return back down the pool. He loathed the way his father was treating Flick, she was far too old to be calling him Daddy.

CHAPTER 10

Malcolm and her mother had been invited out to the golf course dinner on the Saturday night, leaving Felicity and Tony to fend for themselves.

"Shall we wander down to the seafront, I think there's a place that does burgers," Tony suggested, once their parents had left the villa.

"Sounds great, I'll just run and get changed."

Pulling on her sundress and smoothing out her hair she fastened it up with a hair band. A slick of pale lip-gloss finished the look as she tied her espadrilles and went back downstairs. Walking along together she itched to take his hand but he seemed distant with her.

The evening was warm and Felicity paused to take in the path of the moon as it sparkled atop of the waves meeting the shore. She felt like she was in one of her favourite novels, the hero playing hard to get. Could she step into the role of seductress? Was Tony interested in a schoolgirl just turned eighteen? The promenade was busy with families, couples and the locals. Many of the girls were taking quite an interest in her companion, after all who wouldn't with his shock of blond hair, startling eyes and his skin tanned to perfection.

She felt his hand on the small of her back, guiding her off the path and into the restaurant. The waiter hurried to seat them and she watched as Tony ordered drinks and burgers for them both. His fluent Spanish was a shock as when they were out with his father, he normally remained silent.

"You speak Spanish?" Felicity gasped, as perched on stools they waited for their drinks.

"Yeah, when you've been coming here as long as I have you pick it up quite quickly."

"Perhaps you can teach me a few phrases?"

"*Si, Signorita.*" He laughed as they were interrupted by the waiter returning. Two bottles of beer and two succulent burgers with fries were placed on their table. Seated in the window they ate and Tony watched the girls parading by. Felicity watched him, wishing she were older and not his stepsister. Tony drank another couple of beers, but Felicity couldn't keep up and found her head swimming by the middle of the second.

Outside in the cool night air the effects of the alcohol felt worse as she swayed slightly. Tony caught her elbow and she smiled up at him.

"Shall we walk on the sand for a bit, I love the feel of it on my bare feet," she murmured.

"Yeah, why not," he agreed as they stepped off the sidewalk and into the soft sand. Flick sat down to untie her shoes while Tony kicked his off and then picked both pairs up.

"This feels great," Flick said, running down to the tidemark. The sand was firm, wet and cool as she skipped in and out of the waves.

"Hey, when I'm a better swimmer I can go deeper," she laughed.

"You'll get there, perhaps by the end of the holiday, you seem to be a natural."

She smiled at his compliment and feeling brave reached out and took his hand. He hesitated for a moment, his eyes flicking left and right like he was searching for something or someone. Relaxing he closed his fingers around hers, his grip firm but soft. They wandered back to the villa and as it was still empty of their parents, Tony grabbed another beer from the fridge.

"Want one?"

"How about we drink this instead?" Her hand gripped the neck of the brandy decanter on the sideboard.

"That belongs to Dad, I don't think we should."

The alcohol and the closeness of Tony made Felicity brave and reckless.

"Are you scared of him or something?"

Tony took a long gulp of his beer, afraid to admit the truth in front of this young girl, his alluring stepsister.

The clock ticked midnight as Felicity poured two fingers, sloshing the amber liquid onto the wooden worktop.

"Bottom's up." She laughed, tipping the glass against her lips and swallowing it all down in one mouthful. The liquor hit her stomach and curdled against the beer and burger from earlier. She held it down and levelled her gaze on Tony who'd been watching intently. He blushed and looked away, he too downing the brandy in one. Its smooth taste burned on the back of his throat.

"One more and then we'll be good children and go to bed before our parents come home." She fluttered her eyelashes in a provocative manner. Catching the red rash spreading over his neck and deepening in his cheeks, her hand shook as she poured the next measures into their empty glasses.

"Flick, please stop… you don't know what he's capable of." His voice was a mere whisper.

She giggled, passing him the glass. "Come on, let's live dangerously. I know a secret about your father that I can use if I need to."

"What secret?"

"Ah, now that would be telling," she said, knocking back the second glass and slamming it empty upon the counter. She swayed and stepped back, unsteady on her feet. Her knees found the arm of the sofa and she fell back upon it. Her hysterical giggles filled the empty villa. Tony sighed and then picking up both the glasses he swilled them off in the sink and put them away.

"Tony," she slurred. "Tony… kiss me. I know you want to."

He walked over to the couch and quickly picked her up.

"You need to get some sleep Felicity," he said, carrying her up to the bedroom. She clung to his broad shoulders, which stirred in her a memory of his father. He climbed the stairs with ease and then tried to untangle her upon the bed.

"Stay."

"I can't," he muttered.

He prised her fingers from their grip and left her stretched out on the bed. When he returned with a glass of water she was asleep. He softly pulled the sheet over her sprawled body, trying to ignore his yearning to touch her thigh. He backed from the room and pulled the door closed. Turning he bumped into his father, standing silently on the landing.

"Downstairs now," he growled.

Tony gulped and followed his father back downstairs. They squared off to each other across the tiled floor.

"What the fuck were you doing?"

"Sh… she fell asleep on the sofa so I carried her up to bed."

"Yeah, right," he snarled. "I should never have left you both alone."

Malcolm stepped forward, shortening the distance between them. He was still taller and bigger than his son.

"She's mine," he hissed, now nose to nose with Tony. The spittle hit his face and Tony longed to wipe it off. "I'm watching you… one false move and you're on the next flight home."

The tension eased between them as Malcolm stepped back. Tony scurried past but then Felicity's words echoed in his head.

"You'd love to have me out of your life wouldn't you? Free to be this Daddy person you so want to be… but never to me."

He hurried upstairs, aware of his father watching his every move.

Malcolm moved to his decanter and stared at the level. He'd obviously drunk more than he thought as he opened the cupboard. Reaching for the first glass he noticed a smudge of pink lipstick on the rim. He poured a double and swallowed it down. The anger for his son still bubbled there but beside it was the seed of an idea. Leaving the glass on the side he climbed the stairs, staring at the shut doors of the other two rooms. He longed to take a peek at Felicity but knew Martha was waiting for him.

He had a quick wash down in their bathroom before he entered the room. His submissive was waiting, prone and face down on the bed. Her underwear was carefully chosen by him before they had gone out. Dark stockings clung to her legs, while the pale skin of her upper thighs was marked by the tight suspenders that bit into them. Her black G-string disappeared up the crack of her tight ass. The hollow of her back before the strap of the bra was just revealed beneath the long straight dark hair that cascaded down.

"Master is here," he declared. "Your safe word is Daddy."

He smirked as the choice tumbled from his full lips.

"Yes Master," she acquiesced, closing her eyes and waiting for his first touch. He ran the feather duster up her one leg, it was so soft. She knew that this was just the start, smothering her face in the pillows. Martha knew that with her daughter so close by that silence was demanded tonight.

Malcolm pulled aside the thin fabric of her gusset and left the feathers there. He knew that every move she made would press her sex against them, driving her wild. He undid the catch on her bra and she arched so that he could pull it free. His hand slid beneath her to catch and tweak the nipples, each time a little harder until she stifled her cry into the covers.

"More?"

She nodded and sighed, watching as he pulled the paddle off the side table. It was her favourite toy as she wriggled and felt the feathers brushing her sensitive clit. Moaning softly she felt the first sting on her ass, the pain deepening with each smack, heat radiating through to her swollen nipples.

She felt the dibble of warm oil running over the mounds of her bottom. It edged down as his finger reached to rub it into her dripping folds and crack. She knew where he was heading tonight. Anal was not her favourite but she endured it for him, for her husband, her Master. His fingers one at a time invaded her, pushing her open to allow his cock easy entry into the tightest confines. She panted with each push, her mind resisting the pain, her body embracing it. He started to push, grunting with the effort of holding back when she could feel him pulsing and ready to explode.

"Where do you want it?" He groaned, on the brink whilst she was hardly satisfied at all.

He pulled out and rolled her over, the feathers now gone, leaving her exposed. His rough finger pummelled her clit, rubbing it red raw until she throbbed uncontrollably onto it, her whole body spasming. Her hand reached for his cock to pump it and return the gift of her burning orgasm.

"You want it baby."

"Yes Master," she gasped.

He splattered her all over, but she failed to close her eyes quickly enough and felt the sting of the droplets running down her cheeks. She opened her mouth to lick a few that had landed there, salty on her tongue. He sat back watching her for a few minutes, his face calm and puce coloured from the effort. His eyes black and dangerous. Then he stood to get the wash cloth, running it gently over her body. He kissed her nipples gently and then moved down for a few tender licks of her raw clit that despite the pain, stirred again for him.

CHAPTER 11

Felicity tapped on Tony's door the next morning. She had woken in the night, drank the water and her headache was a manageable dull thump.

"Tony... Tony," she whispered. She tried the handle and opened the door to find his bed empty. Hanging onto her towel she closed it again and scurried downstairs. Her eyes blinked against the bright sunlight of the morning sky streaming through the patio doors. She pulled it open to find Tony thrashing his way up and down the length of the pool. The water was slick on his skin, his hair flat and wet on his head.

She stepped out of her towel and dropped it onto the lounger. She sauntered to the steps at the shallow end and tested her toes into the water. It was cool but welcome on her warm skin. Tony eventually stopped as he saw her painted toenails in the water ahead. His eyes climbed her thighs before he broke the surface and stood up.

"You never knocked me," she pouted.

"Sorry, I forgot," he mumbled, turning away to hide his embarrassment. When he looked back his eyes immediately jumped past her to the house. He saw Malcolm at the upstairs window, staring out upon the two of them. He raised a hand to his son, a smile on his lips, but beneath it the dark glare of his eyes.

Felicity followed his gaze and seeing Malcolm she waved gaily. His smile broadened and his eyes lightened.

"Come on then, I want to learn a proper stroke," Felicity said, her hands firmly on her hips.

"Ok," he relented. "We'll start with breaststroke."

Felicity giggled at the name, watching as he looked down at her emerging breasts, bobbing just on the surface of the pool.

"Do a couple of warm-up lengths of backstroke and then I'll show you." He leaned back against the side, wiping his hair from his forehead.

Felicity duly completed two lengths of the pool and then he nodded and she did another two. Each time she felt stronger in the water. They swapped position and she watched as he dropped into the water and did the breaststroke up and down the pool.

"That looks complicated," she said.

"Here, come closer and we'll break it down. Arms first as you kneel on the floor of the shallow end."

With the arms mastered she held onto the side and struggled with the legs.

"Here, let's try this," he said, after trying hard not to laugh at her flapping legs. "I'm going to hold both your ankles and move your legs in the correct way, then when I let go you keep going."

Stretching her legs out she waited to feel his firm grip around her ankles. His touch was electric and making her shudder. She was so aware of him stationed between her legs, guessing he was staring at her ass as he moved her legs in the frog-like action required by the stroke. When he let go she continued and felt her thigh muscles working against the resistance of the water.

"Ready to go for a length?" he asked. "I'll hold your arms first so you can concentrate on the leg action."

"Yes boss." Her blue eyes looked into his steel grey-green ones.

Tony towed her up and down the pool, watching her critically and with admiration. Either she was a fast learner or he was a good teacher, he guessed a bit of both.

"Ready to go it alone?"

"Yes, I think so." A slight tremble ran through her body but she held her fears down.

Very slowly she pushed off from the side and tried to coordinate both arms and legs. With barely two strokes completed she was sinking. In fright she opened her mouth to shout and swallowed a mouthful of water. Her coughs turned to chokes as she tried to stand up. Strong arms lifted her from under her arms and allowed her to stand, water spluttering from her lips. His hands slid down to rest on the curve of her waist and her chest heaved but not from fear, which had been quickly replaced by lust.

"Are you ok?"

"Yes, just struggled to get them going in the right rhythm. Can you show me again?"

His hands left her skin and she stepped back against the side of the pool. Her hand slicked down her hair as she tightened her ponytail.

Tony set off very slowly up the pool and then back down so she could understand and see the way that his arms were stretched, so were his legs.

"I know you can do it Flick," he assured, "I'll swim alongside you this time."

He let her push off ahead of him, knowing that with his height and speed he'd be next to her in one stroke. With the image of him firmly in her head she completed her first length of breaststroke. She paused at the end of the pool and then turned to return. By the time she'd done six lengths she had mastered the basics of the stroke and marvelled at the way she covered the distance quicker than before.

"I think we'll leave it there for today, but you're a natural in the water," he breathed, his voice husky and low. She was about to plant a small kiss on his cheek when he turned and swam away. A shadow loomed over the pool surface.

"Morning, Princess," Malcolm said, shading his eyes against the glare from the sun on the pool surface.

"Morning Daddy, it's a lovely day," Felicity said, upset that he had turned up at the wrong moment.

"Your mum could do with a hand in the kitchen," he motioned, "if you've finished your lesson?"

Tony had climbed out at the deep end of the pool and was on his way into the house. He never even acknowledged his father and Felicity wondered what had soured their relationship. She climbed up the pool steps and Malcolm passed her a towel. His gaze travelled her body before he stepped from his robe and entered the pool.

Felicity helped her mother with the cleaning and washing before they stretched out on the loungers by the pool.

"Where's Tony?" Malcolm's voice boomed. "He's not in the house."

"I think he went into town," Martha replied, immediately on alert.

"Fucking hell, that boy has no manners."

Felicity lay still as Malcolm stormed back into the villa, followed by her mother. Despite the closed patio doors Felicity could hear the argument erupting inside. Then silence. She tried to dive back into her book but the heroine had lost her admiration by giving in to the desires of her leading man. In her mind she vowed that no man would hold sway over her mind or body.

She was just debating going inside for a shower when Tony sauntered through the gate at the side. He froze when he saw her and then hid it with a smile.

"Hey Flick, are you home alone?"

"You'd better be quiet, your dad's really angry at you. He wanted to know where you were this afternoon."

"Fuck, perhaps I'd better leave before he sees me."

"Yeah and you'd better apologise to my mum, he was shouting at her so loud but now it's been silent for the last fifteen minutes."

Tony pulled off his t-shirt and shorts to reveal his perfect body clad only in his trunks. He tossed them on the lounger and smiled smugly at her. She narrowed her eyes against the glare of the sun and something in his look piqued her curiosity.

"Why the look?"

"Ah... you're too innocent for all this," he murmured and as his words hung in the air, he took a couple of steps and dived into the pool.

Abandoning her book Felicity felt anger rising at his snub. Too young? Fuck it, she was eighteen and she needed to know. Rising from her lounger she walked to the shallow end. She watched as he thrashed up and down the pool, his stroke jagged and raw, a far cry from his naturally smooth style. He slowed when he saw her legs and feet beneath the surface.

Tony wanted to ignore them but knowing what was to come this evening or within the next few days, he didn't. Gripping her ankles he tugged her off her feet, dragging her under the surface. He knew she wasn't expecting it but he ran his hands quickly up her legs and thighs, his body pressed above hers. He enjoyed the fear in her gaze, her mouth opening to the water and the surprise. So he clamped his mouth over hers, his tongue revelling in the heat of her as he tasted her fear. Her nipples were rubbing against his chest and he longed to hold her down for longer.

Knowing her limited capabilities he released her to the surface, feeling her struggle from his grip. He surfaced for breath watching her scramble and fall to sit on the steps. He ducked back under and part of him wanted to swim away, but the rebellious part prevented this. If he was going to get into trouble then it might as well be big style. Her thighs were parted so he slid his body between then and let his fingers slide beneath the cup of her bikini. With one push up she was free and her breasts bobbing in the water, her nipples hard to his first touch. Her struggle against him had lessened, more so when his mouth latched on briefly to suckle and tug. She arched against his lips and he sucked harder before he had no choice but to surface.

Her wide eyes greeted him, wide with shock or desire, he guessed a mixture of both. He glanced again towards the house but it remained silent, the patio doors shut and reflecting the glaring sun.

"Wh… what were you doing?" she gasped.

Her bikini floated on the surface, still fastened around her neck. Her nipples were cramping at the feel of the cool water surrounding them.

"What you've been waiting for me to do," he said, his voice hoarse, but deep like his father's.

"I want more," she pouted, her tongue just protruding between her pink lips. He bowed his head and let his lips slide over the other one. He could feel her hands running through his hair, holding him there as he sucked hard. She moaned this time, throwing her head back. She knew that he was experienced in his touch.

Pulling away he turned and swam back to the deep end, leaving her wanting more. She was about to unhook her bikini top completely when the slide of the patio door made her sink deeper. She pulled her top back on and fumbled to tie it as Malcolm stepped onto the slabs. His eyes fixed onto the pair of them in the pool.

"Tony, I need to talk to you right now," he commanded, his voice bouncing off the walls that surrounded the grounds. Tony was rigid at the deep end of the pool, his knuckles white as they gripped the side. Felicity needed no second warning. She hightailed it up the steps, grabbed her towel and fled to the safety of the house.

CHAPTER 12

Pushing out of the pool Tony's mind reeled. How much had his father witnessed? A quick slap on his cheek stung but he stayed mute, staring up at his father.

"I don't like disobedience."

"I'm sorry Dad, I just needed my own space for a while."

"Sit down, we need to talk."

This was a departure from the normal punishment, so Tony obeyed. He took the seat on the lounger by his clothes. Malcolm took the lounger Felicity had been on, sweeping aside her paperback so that it landed on the floor. He'd pick it up later when he was finished.

From her bedroom Felicity watched the two men chatting by the pool, it was not a heated conversation as she could hardly hear them. She picked up her dressing gown and in the hallway saw her mother leaving her bedroom.

"Are you ok Mum?" she asked, moving closer and now aware of the red staining her cheeks.

"Yes, just go get your shower," her mum muttered. From the doorway Felicity watched her mum step toward the stairs, a look of pain flashing across her features. What the fuck had he done to her? Locking the door she remembered the slap he had given her that night at the club. It had left her reeling, but had Malcolm been doing the same to her mother?

The hot water hit her burning skin and she turned the temperature down. The cool droplets helped but also irritated the feelings that Tony had awakened with his touch in the pool. She couldn't wait until tomorrow's lesson, would he make another move?

Letting her fingertips play over her body she closed her eyes, tweaking her nipples and thinking of the way his eyes had held her. She reached between her thighs, feeling a film of silkiness there that was thicker than the water. She started to rub when her reverie was shattered.

"Hurry up Flick, I need a shower as we're going out in less than an hour."

Feeling bereft of her touch she rinsed off and stepped out of the shower, wishing she'd been bold and left the door unlocked.

"Come in," she said, reaching to release the catch.

She held her towel loosely, letting it only part cover her body. Tony stepped in and then immediately backed away.

"Get out now, before he sees us," he hissed, shielding his eyes from her nakedness.

"Just shut the door, lock it… he'll never know we're both in here."

Felicity stepped forward, closing the gap between them, dropping her towel.

She closed her eyes, feeling both bold and nervous in his presence. He bent down and picked up her towel allowing a longer look at her slim body, the curve of her hips from her waist. Then up to the dark hair plastered wet on her shoulders and partly obscuring her breasts. He wanted to sweep it away, to latch onto the sweet nipple he had suckled before in the pool. To taste her for real and not with the added chlorine. He glanced back down to the dark, downy hair that covered her pussy, it looked neat like she'd trimmed it. The urge was overpowering as he tightened the towel around his waist, hoping the tenting wouldn't show if she opened her eyes.

"Look, I can't… not here… not now… but maybe…" He slipped past her, putting the towel into her hand. Her skin was tinted red as the shame of rejection washed over it. She wrapped the towel around herself and stalked to the door.

"You know I could just scream," she intoned, loud enough for him to hear the vicious intent. "But I won't."

Wriggling her ass on departure from the room, Tony slammed the door shut and pulled the catch. She was a demon, a bewitcher of men and he felt powerless to resist. He couldn't resist now, not after his talk with his father. The warm water pounded his head, sliding down to catch on his erect cock. He knew she'd seen it with the little upturned smirk of her smile as she left. Letting his hand rub in the soap suds he paid particular attention to his grip and rhythm. Leaning against the cold tiles he tugged his cock, slowly to start with but then in time with his quickening breath. His mind ran riot at all the things he longed to do to Felicity, all except the ultimate. Splashing the tiles with his seed it clung to his hand before dripping, wasted onto the shower tray. The water removed it with ease, the pressure inside him easing now.

In her room Felicity dropped face down on her bed, annoyed, angry and upset by Tony's seeming rejection. He could have taken her there, she had been more than ready after their time in the pool. She burned all over and thought of his words, *maybe... maybe*. Perhaps he needed to be more like his father. As calm washed over her she dressed and did her hair, tying it back with a simple hair band. A slick of lip-gloss was all she required as the golden glow of her tan was enough. Downstairs she found them waiting for her.

"At last, I thought I'd have to send Tony up to drag you down," Malcolm joked, clapping his son on the back. A look passed between them of words spoken earlier. Her mum looked glorious, her black hair tumbling over her shoulders in a wild abandonment Felicity had never seen before.

"Come, let's walk into town, there's a great restaurant overlooking the harbour."

Felicity watched him guide her mother with his hand placed on the small of her back. Tony held the door open for her and the two of them trailed along together. The silence was palpable but necessary to keep Malcolm off their case.

The evening was pleasant enough, food and sangria plentiful. Malcolm played best friends with the restaurant boss and bought drinks for other diners around them. Her mum giggled and laughed, pressing against his side in a girlish manner. Felicity was careful not to drink too much while Tony was silent. She crept a hand beneath the table and across to touch his thigh, slyly looking sideways at him. He flinched but didn't bat it away, instead when he'd finished his steak, he placed his hand on top of hers.

"So how are the swimming lessons?" Malcolm asked, taking a slug from his tumbler of whiskey.

"Good thanks Daddy, I've been learning breaststroke." She couldn't stop the giggle that threatened to break out so she coughed.

Tony looked away, lost in his thought of her hard nub of a nipple slipping between his lips.

"You wanna learn the crawl, much faster stroke," he boomed. "You'll cover the distance so much quicker."

"That's next on the list before we go home, Dad," Tony replied.

"Well, you've got two days to impress me with your teaching skills." He smirked.

Back at the villa, Malcolm turned to Tony.

"Come on then, how about a race in the pool to show the ladies?"

"Dad, I'm tired."

"Nonsense, you're only worried that I'll show you up." He swaggered into the villa and the emerged in his trunks. Tony knew it was no use to resist and followed suit.

"Martha, you can start us off and Felicity, you can see who wins over one length."

"Only one length, that's barely time to warm up."

"Ok, make it three."

The two of them slipped into the pool and took up position by the side in the shallow end.

"Ready, steady… GO!" her mum shouted, then burst out laughing as the water sprayed her from their flailing limbs.

Felicity watched at the deep end, Tony clearly fitter than her stepfather, as they turned and pushed off again. Malcolm was not far behind as they turned a second time and started the final length. When they neared the end Tony hesitated and Malcolm was the first to touch.

"Daddy wins," Felicity exclaimed over her mum's clapping.

"Better luck next time son."

Tony nodded and pulled his body from the pool. Water glistened on his skin in the pale moonlight.

"Night Dad, Martha, Felicity."

"I think I'm going to do the same, night Mum, night Daddy."

Felicity wandered into the house and upstairs. From the pool and patio came shrieks followed by a splash. Felicity looked through her window and saw her mother was now in the pool. Staying hidden in the shadows of her curtain she watched them frolic.

Malcolm had her pressed against the side before he lifted her from the water, leaving her legs still dangling. She was naked.

Flick knew she should move away from the window but something held her. Malcolm looked up to the house and his eyes seemed to find hers. He smirked and held them, his hand grasping her mother's breast. He squeezed it tightly as she yelped but arched towards it. She was about to turn away when she felt a hand wrap around the back of her neck. Tony was right behind her as his breath swept her cheek. She wanted to turn into him but he pushed her closer to the window ledge.

"Watch them, it's what he wants."

"But I don't want to."

"Oh, I think you do," he murmured, his other hand moving around to cover her own breast. He massaged it through the thin material of her sundress before slipping his fingers down through the neckline and beneath her bra.

"Tell me what they're doing."

"What?"

"Just do it or I'll stop."

Felicity gulped, her mouth dry with a mixture of fear and longing. The moon was high and bright and left no shadows. She watched Malcolm pinch at her mother's breasts, turning them a deep black colour in the faded light of the night.

"He's pinching her nipples."

"Hard or really hard?"

"I don't know," Flick sighed, the sight of her mother and Malcolm compelling. Tony was tight against her now, his hand tweaking and pinching the tight nipple. His hand moved across and did the same to the other until it reached a peak.

"Now what?" His voice was hoarse and croaked over the words.

"His hand is between her thighs, pulling them wider apart."

Flick could hardly believe what she was witnessing; she wanted to stop but she didn't. Tony moved behind her, dropping down onto his knees. His hand left her breasts but they were still tingling and aching. She wanted more.

Her long sundress swept the floor but he moved his hands beneath the fabric, pulling her feet so that she stood legs apart. The scent of fear and excitement on her skin was intoxicating to him. He knew he could only go so far with this, he knew there were hidden cameras in the villa.

"His fingers are inside her, he's jabbing them in and out," Flick gasped, feeling his hand running lightly up the skin of her leg. She was trembling beneath his touch. Was he really going to touch her? Delve into her pussy like his father was doing to her mother?

Outside her mother lay with her legs so widely stretched, her pussy bucked up to every downward push of his fingers. He now had two inside her. She saw him gaze up to the window to check she was watching. This is what they had planned.

CHAPTER 13

Felicity felt his fingers grip the elastic of her panties, pulling them down in a single stroke. She was shivering now as the cool night air from the villa struck tiny touches to her warm skin. Outside Malcolm's head had taken the place of his fingers, his nose breathing in the scent from her innermost folds. She was slick and dribbling for him as he let it feed his parched tongue. In his mind he wondered if she tasted the same as her daughter. He had seen Tony's shadow fall across the window and knew the plan was in action, and this was only the first part of it.

"Keep talking Felicity, keep telling me so that I can do the same," he murmured, his breath short and tight.

"He's licking her."

"Where?" Tony grinned; he loved asking the question.

"Her pussy."

His fingers had just returned to her inner thigh, tantalisingly close to her own pussy. He would be the first to touch her.

"Is this your first time?" he softly asked. He guessed it was.

"Yes," she whispered, glancing away from the window to look down at him.

His finger ruffled her fine hair, searching for the slit and finding her clit peeking out for him. The edge of his nail glanced over it so lightly that she almost didn't feel it. But her body did, sending a blaze of hot flames licking around. Her nipples ached to be touched again and she brought her one hand up to do the honours, sliding her palm and fingers between the lace and her skin. She was throbbing now, and it resonated through her skin, beating in time with her quickening pulse.

"Was he doing this?" Tony asked, a single finger sliding into her wet hole. It was tight and clamping around him strongly.

"Breathe," he murmured. "Relax... let me in."

Felicity did as he said and found the pinprick of discomfort leave, his other finger joining the first. He was stretching her little by little, his thumb grazing her clit in a sweeping motion. Her thighs were trembling and her breath was so fast now. He loved it when they responded like this, so eager, so pliant. His cock was pushing the fabric of his pyjama bottoms now, wanting to take the place of his fingers.

Felicity looked back out of the window, the head of Malcolm still firmly between her mum's thighs, her legs now tight against his head. Like she was trying to force him in there. Through the glass of the window she could hear the moans, drifting on the breeze of the night.

"Is he still finger fucking her?"

"No..." Her response escaped in a light breath. "His mouth is there."

Tony chuckled, his fingers still slowly probing her sticky depths.

"Take your dress off, be naked like your mother is." His voice was lilting and hypnotic so Felicity obeyed, pulling the material up over her body, unhooking and releasing her breasts. Her skin shone in the moonlight spilling through the window. Tony gasped in wonder, looking up at her full glory before he wriggled into position between her open legs.

The scent from her was overpowering, sweet, fresh and musky. He knew that his first taste would be the most perfect. This would be his reward for doing as his father wanted.

"Stay where you are, you're perfect."

Then the heat from his mouth met the folds of her sex, tentative at first. One small lick around the outer edges. She gripped the windowsill, seeing her mother had dropped into the pool so she could no longer see what they were doing. But the water around their entwined bodies was creating waves that crashed against the sides and rebounded back. He let out a breath and it tickled and sent more flames running through her body. Part of her wanted to sag onto him as his next few licks touched her core. She wanted to grind onto his mouth, gyrate above him as strange ripples formed and began to spread.

"More?"

She whimpered her assent, finding her shaking legs spreading further, opening wide to him. A small stream of juice irritated as it slid down her thigh. He alternated between darting into her hole or taking it up to draw out her clit. It thrummed on his tongue and she moaned loudly.

"Just let go, let out your frustrations, and be free and alive," he murmured before he took a tiny bite, his teeth nipping gently but pushing her up a level.

"Do you feel it?"

"Yeeeeeeessssssssssss," she wailed, throwing her head back so that her hair brushed the base of her spine. Tony's hands held her ass cheeks firm as he frantically licked at a dizzying speed, almost unable to breathe as she shuddered and came on his tongue. The ripples spread to capture his wet lips as she throbbed and sobbed at the same time. Her legs shook so violently that she crumpled and he lowered her to the floor so she sat opposite him.

Her pupils so wide with desire, they obliterated the blue of her eyes. Her mouth was part open in shock at what she'd just felt.

"Fuck," she breathed. "Fuck, fuck… FUCK."

She leaned forward and pressed her lips to his, tasting the tang of her on them, wanting something more for him. Terms of endearment, words of love. Was this what love was like? All consuming, burning desire to feel that heat inside her again. Like an addiction. Tony gently pushed her away and stood up.

"Goodnight Flick."

"What… is that it?" The flush of her orgasm faded to anger at his attitude.

"It's all I can offer you Flick."

Before she could ask any more questions of him he fled the room, banging the door shut. The tiles on the floor were cold on her bare skin and slowly she stood up. She drew the curtains across her window, the moon now shining on an empty pool. Shaking from the cold she pulled on her nightgown and huddled beneath the covers. Her body ached in a pleasant way, as small aftershocks still rocked through her skin. She reached to touch her nipples, still hard and begging for more. Closing her eyes she replayed the scene from the pool and her room but as memories became dreams, Tony was still with her.

In the hallway Tony rushed into the shower, swilled off and then bumped into his father between the door and his bedroom.

"I did as you asked," Tony said.

"Good... she was responsive?"

"Yes."

"So this won't be such a hard job for you to get your inheritance early."

"Guess not."

"Just keep her sweet, she has a quick temper."

Tony nodded and left his father in the hallway, closing the door of his bedroom.

Malcolm hesitated, partly wanting to look in on Felicity but knowing he shouldn't. In his bedroom Martha waited for him, so he slipped into bed bedside her and pulled her close.

"Everything is going to plan," he said, planting a kiss on her upturned lips.

Martha turned on her side, closing her eyes and knowing what was still to come. It was the price she paid for comfort, security and a life of submission. She just had to keep her guilt in check and arrange a trip to the doctor's for her daughter when they got back. His arm stretched across her, resting just below her breasts that were still throbbing from his earlier ministrations. The time in the pool had been great fun, even though she shivered at the thought of her daughter being made to watch.

Malcolm smiled as he drifted off to sleep. He never guessed how easy it would be to coerce Tony into helping with his plan. There was no denying the spark between him and Felicity, he had witnessed it when he watched them in the pool. But her virginity was sacred, it was his and his alone. All he required from Tony was a couple more moments with her, a little training with regards to pleasing a man and then bam... she would be his. Tightening his grip on Martha, his thumb stroked the underside of her breasts. They were similar in size to Felicity's but marred and sagged from childbirth. Felicity's would be firm, ripe and good enough to bury his face in.

CHAPTER 14

The next morning Tony knocked softly on her door.

"Ready for a swim?"

"Mmmh... guess so," she mumbled back.

He could hear the edge to her voice, irritated with his quick withdrawal last night. He had spent a sleepless night, part of him eager to get his hands on the money and break away from his father's tyranny. The other felt guilt that he was doing this to an innocent young girl, too young to really understand what was going on. She was being groomed and Tony was an accessory to this. He knew there was something his dad wasn't telling him but perhaps that was for the best.

He dropped his towel on the lounger and picked up the discarded dress and underwear that belonged to Martha. He laid it over the spare one and then turned and dived into the water. He moved smoothly through the water, easily a better swimmer than his dad, but over the years he had also discovered the best way to keep him sweet. After ten lengths he paused and heard the slide of the patio doors. He watched her saunter towards the pool, dropping her towel to reveal her gloriously nubile body. One he'd had the pleasure of last night.

"Hi Tony," she said, her voice quiet, "or are we not talking anymore?"

"Hi Flick, look sorry about last night. I suddenly got cold feet, Dad didn't really know I was in your room."

She breathed a sigh of relief and stepped into the water. He glanced at the house and all was silent so he held open his arms. She filled them and looked up at him, her blue eyes sparkling like a reflection of the pool in the sun.

Leaning down he kissed her lightly on the lips.

"So you do like me?" she whispered, wrapping her arms around his broad back.

"Yeah... but you know we kind of shouldn't. We're stepbrother and sister, isn't that forbidden?"

"Well, so what if it is... I can keep a secret if you can," she replied. "Anyway forbidden sounds dangerous and exciting, just like in my Jackie Collins' books."

With another quick kiss they parted and she smiled up at him.

"Come on, let's get started on the front crawl, I have a point to prove before the end of the week."

Flick nodded and started with her usual warm-up lengths of backstroke, swiftly followed by breaststroke to show him she hadn't forgotten.

Pausing in the shallow end he demonstrated a length and then explained.

"Front crawl is the same as backstroke really." She was only part listening as she watched a bead of water trickle down his chest before hitting the surface. She yearned to touch him, follow the line it had taken but continuing beneath the water. He felt her hot gaze on his skin and smiled. He had her just where he wanted, pliable to his every need and whim. The power surged through him and felt more exciting than desire.

"Ready for a go?"

She nodded and pushed off from the side. This was much easier than breaststroke. After four lengths he pulled her up and showed her some refinements and she was off again, getting faster and faster.

"Brilliant, we can maybe practice again this evening before we go out?"

She lounged in the crook of the shallow end corner, resting her arms along the length of the side.

"Teach me how to swim under the water like you do."

"Well, that's easy, it's more about learning to control your breathing. Oh and the water resistance is stronger so each stroke will take more effort to complete."

"Show me."

Tony took a gulp of air and ducked beneath the surface, pushing off from the side. Smoothly he did breaststroke to the deep end, turned and returned before he surfaced. He made it look easy.

"Start by just ducking under and seeing how long you can last."

Felicity nodded and took a couple of deep breaths in and out. Tony watched the rise and fall of her breasts, itching to reach out and hold them, trying to contain them in his palms. Then she ducked under but discovered that she kept rising to the surface.

"How do you stay under when the water is so buoyant?"

"Come under with me, I'll hold you until you need to take a breath."

He took both her hands and counted to three before they sank. The thrill of his touch threw her and she lasted barely five seconds.

"That was crap, try harder."

"And if I do, what reward will I get?" Flick playfully demanded.

"Well good girls might get a treat," he replied, arching his eyebrows.

After another count of three they descended into the depths, Flick shut her eyes and tried to control her slight panic. The water was snug around her as her body fought to breathe. Her lungs were burning and her chest heaved for a few more seconds and then she broke hold. Reaching for the side she gasped and caught the air, sucking it in like her favourite drink. As her pulse rate slowed she felt a hand on her ankle, the fingers sliding up her skin that reminded her of the previous night. Then both hands held the mounds of her ass before taking in the curve of her spine. It felt like molten fire inside her, fighting to heat the colder water. Flick turned as he broke the surface and captured his green-grey eyes with hers.

"Was that my reward?"

He shook his head, flicking droplets from the ends of his blond hair. His body pushed her into the side before he twisted his hand into her long ponytail. He coiled the hair around until tight so he could pull her lips to his. Crushing against her she lost the ability to breathe once more. She opened to his insistent probing and let his tongue slide against hers. Her nipples were tight and hard against his chest. She felt his erection against her thigh and longed to touch it. She was sure it was bigger than Phillip's when his had pressed against her. But she was ready now, she wanted it… she wanted him.

He broke apart as the patio doors slid open.

"Morning early birds," her mother said. "How's the swimming

lessons?"

"Good thanks Mum." Flick felt her face flaming red, wondering how much her mother had witnessed.

"Breakfast will be ready soon so don't be too much longer."

"Thanks Martha," Tony shouted from the deep end of the pool. "Just a few more lengths to do."

Flick got out and tried to steady her legs, still shaking from their brief encounter. Pulling the towel across her body she rubbed dry before stepping into the house. Malcolm looked across from his seat at the kitchen table.

"Morning, Princess."

"Morning, Daddy," she replied, feeling his stare drop from her face to the flushed skin of her neck and chest. She dashed up the stairs and straight into the bathroom, shutting and locking the door.

She showered and pulled on her denim shorts and a fringed vest top before seeing Tony emerge from the bathroom. He glanced across and smiled, pulling his finger to his lips in a ssssh motion. Flick giggled and blew him a kiss as she wriggled past him and down the stairs. Tony and his father left for the golf course after breakfast and Flick spent the rest of the day by the pool. When it got too hot she jumped into the pool and practised holding her breath. She wanted to surprise Tony later when he got back.

The men strolled onto the patio mid-afternoon, sweat beading on their skin. Tony hid his hair beneath a baseball cap which he flung in the direction of the spare lounger.

Flick looked up from her paperback and shot him a small smile. Her mother got up and fussed around getting drinks for them.

"Fancy a dip in the pool?" Felicity asked, directing her enquiry at Tony.

"Yeah, I'll just go grab my towel and trunks."

With everyone in the villa Felicity walked to the steps of the pool and into the cool water. Such relief on her warm, sticky skin. This was her last chance to practice holding her breath. It felt like she was under for ages but a splash at the deep end startled her to the surface. Streaking down the pool was Tony, who ignored her, turned and then did a further two lengths. He slowed and flipped over so that he was lying on his back.

"How was the golf course?"

"Hot and boring, especially when you always have to let the old man win."

She giggled and glanced at the house. Her mother and Malcolm were nowhere to be seen. It was like Tony had read her mind.

"I think they've sloped off to bed."

Flick turned red as memories flooded her mind. Tony roared with laughter.

"You're such an innocent."

"Well, I'm sorry about that… what are you gonna do about it?"

He grabbed her wrist, pulling her roughly towards him. She banged into his chest with force as he changed his grip to her waist.

"This," he said, pushing her lips apart with his. His tongue invaded and she had to push him back to catch a breath.

"See you're not ready," he laughed, swimming away.

Still red faced but angry now, she pushed off from the side and tried to catch up, but he was waiting at the deep end.

"Bastard," she shouted, grasping the side.

"You women are all the same, lead us on, and make us think you want it but you can't really handle the full force."

"Well, fucking give me a chance… you know I'm a quick learner."

She leaned in, this time her lips grazing his cheek. Soft, as if walking through cobwebs, that Tony hardly felt it. But she pressed on each little touch getting closer to his waiting lips. Then she went for the kill, her soft lips parting his, her breath fresh and her tongue tentatively probing. He reached to reel her in closer, their bodies touching again. Feeling bold in the cover the water provided, her finger traced a path down his defined chest to the waistband of his trucks. She longed to touch him like he'd touched her. But he caught it and yanked it away. His mouth unlatched to whisper in her ear, "Tonight, *mi amour*."

Then he ducked past her and swam slowly back down the pool. Catching her ragged breath, Felicity smiled and followed.

CHAPTER 15

A small urgent knock woke her in the middle of the night.

"Get dressed now," Tony whispered in the darkness. He stood in the doorway, silhouetted in the moonlight from the window. She pulled on her mini sundress and was about to open her drawer for some knickers when he caught her hand.

"Just as you are."

Then still holding her hand they silently crept down the stairs and out of the house. Slipping her flip flops on Tony tied the laces of his trainers and they walked along the pavement towards town. She noticed he had a rucksack flung over his shoulder. They were just on the outskirts of town when they took a small path off to the left.

"This way," he said, keeping tight hold as she followed him down the small track. The clear sky and full moon lit the way. The path wound its way so that on the last turn the ocean and a small beach came into view.

"Oh wow this is amazing Tony," she breathed, kicking off her shoes as they filled with soft sand.

"It's our little secret," he said, but she wondered how many local girls had been here with Tony. She brushed them from her mind, after all he was teaching her what he liked and wanted. He found a nook in the dunes and pulled a couple of towels out, laying them on the sand. He patted his hand and she sat down next to him. He pulled a bottle of tequila from it and cracked the top off. Taking a small swig he passed it over to her and she did the same, grimacing as it burned down her throat and warmed her from within.

He shrugged his t-shirt off and lay down next to her, gazing up at the moon and stars scattering the dark sky above them. The waves broke against the shore in a settled rhythm that soothed his mind. She turned and ran her index finger down over his chest, following the grooves and the contours like she'd done earlier in the pool. His breath quickened as she neared the waistband of his shorts, but before she could slip beneath he grabbed it, twisting her arm so that she fell back onto the towel. Looming over her his lips tugged on hers, parting them easily to allow his tongue to rove within.

She sighed into his mouth, feeling her nipples peak the material of her dress, longing for his touch.

"You want me so bad, don't ya?"

"Fuck yeah," she gasped, the words breaking on her tongue.

"Well, I think you have some learning to do." He sat back, taking another mouthful of tequila and standing up. His hands hooked into the waistband and she watched open mouthed as his shorts fell to his feet.

"Take a good look at your first real man." He planted his hands on his hips, proud of his fine physique and his manhood not even fully risen.

"Think I might go for a swim first." He turned and ran down to the shoreline. Felicity pulled her sundress off and followed him, glancing around to ensure there were no further prying eyes. Tony bounded easily into the sea and then dived straight into the oncoming wave. Felicity wavered at the shore, her toes feeling the nip of cold kissing them. She'd never been in the sea before but as Tony swam further away from her she took more steps until she was waist deep. Her breath was coming faster now, scared by the power of the surrounding water. She turned and a large wave loomed behind her, knocking her forwards and sucking her under. The sand had disappeared as she scrambled to gain her footing, the salty water starting to choke her. This was it, she was going to drown a virgin!

She was about to close her eyes and give up when strong arms pulled her to the surface, much like he'd done the first time in the pool. He lifted her up and carried her from the waves as she coughed and spluttered the sea water from her mouth. He pulled a third towel from his bag and wrapped her in it, feeling her shivers shaking through her skin.

"I didn't mean for you to follow me you idiot," he chided, rubbing her through the towel.

"So… sorry," she sobbed, feeling stupid now that he'd rescued her.

He whipped the towel from her body to dry his own, as Flick sat back down on the others and reached for the tequila. The alcohol warmed her from the inside and her breathing calmed. She held out the bottle and he took it, dropping the wet towel into the sand.

The moonlight served to highlight his firm torso, the shadow and light making his body glow white like a Grecian statue in her gaze.

"Sure you're ok? We can go back if you want." His hand swept his wet hair from his face and some trickled down to nestle in the blond line of hair that led to his cock. It twitched as she stared and blushed, feeling equally scared and wicked at the deep desire flowing in her blood.

"Come closer," he said. "Stay on your knees, you'll be just at the right height."

She shuffled along the towel until he placed his hand on her head.

"So just begin by stroking him first, feeling him in your palm like this."

Flick watched as he grabbed his cock, slowly wrapping his palm around it and tugging it upwards. Within a few strokes he let go and it sprang to attention. Her mouth dropped open at its sheer size and girth.

She swallowed against the dryness in her throat before she reached and let her index finger take the first tentative touch. It was smooth and velvet at the head, and running down she felt his every twitch through the arteries and veins that were just beneath the skin. Then the curled pubic hair at the base as she cupped his balls.

"Squeeze them lightly if you like," he murmured, finding her touch light but at the same time arousing.

"Like this," she asked, closing the two globes in her palm, rolling them around a little before letting them drop. This time she reached around his shaft with her hand, moving it up but feeling it falter against her dry palm.

"Spit on it," he said, lifting it away and pulling it up to his mouth. He licked the salty taste off her palm and moistened the pad. He guided it back down to his head, moulding her into place, keeping his hand there to guide her into his favoured rhythm.

Flick felt him quicken and strain in her grasp, smiling up at him to see the pleasure etched onto his face, his eyes closed. Just as she was getting into the swing, he stopped her. "I think you should use your mouth now, it's just like sucking on a lollipop."

He stepped closer to her and wrapped his hand around the back of her neck, forcing her closer. Nervously she licked her lips before opening her mouth to his invasion. Her tongue licked first over the end before he pushed it in, but she gagged and he pulled out.

"Slowly, please," she pleaded, spitting bile and sea water onto the sand.

"Ok, why don't I lie down next to you instead," he replied, feeling pleased at the amount she'd taken with his first push.

Tony stretched out on his towel and watched the blanket of Flick's hair hide her face. She lowered her mouth onto his cock, fighting the urge to gag again when the tip touched the back of her throat. She struggled to take him all in as she sucked her way up and down the part that she could. She felt his hands on her shoulders, gripping her tightly as he started to buck to match her mouth.

"Keep going, Flick," he urged, his own throat tight. "I want you to taste me when I come."

His hands reached around and scooped up her breasts, trying to squeeze as much of them into his palms. He pinched her nipples and felt her pause and gasp at his touch.

"Don't stop now, baby," he moaned, as she matched him thrust for thrust. She didn't dare stop despite her jaw aching from the forced position.

Then her mouth filled with hot, salty liquid that leaked down to the back of her throat and she pulled out and turned away. Spitting it out onto the sand she coughed and spluttered against the taste on her tongue. Tony had his eyes shut as the last few droplets clung to the tip, opaque and sticky.

"Ugh… that was vile," Felicity said, wiping her mouth on the damp towel. Then she picked up the tequila and took a long swallow, revelling in the taste that was a hundred times nicer! Tony looked up and grabbed the towel, wiped his cock and watched as it wilted.

"You'll have to do better next time, I love a woman that swallows."

He reached for the bottle and winked at her while he swallowed. He saw the flame of embarrassment on her skin. She turned her back on him, hunched over at her failure.

Tony reached and pulled her back against him, wrapping his arms firmly around her shivering body.

"You were pretty good for a virgin but we have one more night tomorrow for you to get it right."

"What do you mean, get it right?"

"Swallow it, that's what guys want, me included," he chuckled, the sound vibrating in his throat. Flick turned and pressed her face into the crook of his neck, breathing in his masculine scent. His hands moulded against her breasts, squeezing them tight. She clenched her thighs together in the same rhythm that his hands were employing.

"You like this," he murmured. She nodded, resisting the urge to reach down. It was like he could read her mind. "Do it, touch yourself... I like to watch."

Felicity hesitated, shy once more after her last attempt to please him had failed. Tony moved one hand to capture hers, leading her down to the throbbing that lay between her thighs. The tip of her nail caught the edge of her outer lips.

"Where shall we start," he whispered, confidently circling the outside and making her squirm.

"Tony," she gasped, leaning back into him so that his lips could latch onto hers in a deep kiss. His fingers drew hers closer to the itch within before they both glanced across the nub of her clit.

"There, just there," she breathed, aware of the ache pulsing upwards from every pass they made.

"Show me how."

He released his grip and her fingers alone played over the sensitive spot, each touch sending a shudder up her spine and an ache into each of her breasts. Tony sensed this and started to pinch each in turn, every touch slightly stronger than the last. She groaned as her finger slid into the slick that was forming before rubbing furiously on the point above.

"Go baby, do it for me," was his guttural cry.

"I need you," she cried. "Do what you did the other night."

He chuckled at her request before releasing his hold and letting her fall back onto the towel beneath them. He crawled round to find an open invitation between her spread legs. The scent of sex invaded his nostrils like expensive perfume, intoxicating.

Felicity watched his blond hair as he moved in. She was powerless to resist when his tongue took a sweeping lick of her sex. His breath trailed after, a cooling breeze on the heat he ignited.

"More Tony… I want more."

He curled his tongue into a point that teased out the tip of her clit into a pinnacle of passion. With every little lick or nip that he bestowed she whined and demanded more by pushing into him. He feasted on every part of her folds, his finger pumping in and out of her in a rhythm that matched his tongue. Her nectar spread over his lips and dripped down his throat, each drop he savoured as she demanded more. Felicity gave herself up to the intensity of the vibrations that pulsed in her blood. This was heaven as she squeezed and released, each orgasm more powerful than the last. The waves consumed her in their violent grasp as she gripped his hair, holding him, drowning him.

Tony gulped down the last of her juice which had poured into his mouth like a waterfall. He'd heard about women ejaculating but had never witnessed this until now. This was more than he could have hoped for as his cock reared up again, longing to enter the tight, wet hole his finger was plugged into. However, the image and words of his father were enough to subdue the sudden urge to pierce her very core. Felicity had gone beyond the point, he watched her eyes roll before her body went slack. For a few seconds she forgot to breathe, passed out and all was silent.

"Flick… FLICK… can you hear me?" His shout awakened her and she opened her eyes.

"Fucking hell. There's no need to faint, I'd thought you'd died."

Her eyes took in the pale tint on his cheeks, highlighted by the moon's white light.

"Oh… I thought that was meant to happen," she murmured, pulling him down to crush her body beneath his. Blissful peace made her facial features soften. She looked even younger that her years.

Tony rolled away and lay beside her, the shock enough to subdue his second erection. A solitary cloud blanketed them in darkness for a moment and he took a deep breath.

He was falling for his stepsister. Love was an alien feeling to his heart and it made it ache with despair. If he failed to deliver his father was capable of cutting him off completely, but if he did perhaps there was still a chance that he could win Felicity at the same time. When the moonlight returned he rolled over to find her staring at him.

"We'd better get back before they find out we're missing."

"Yeah, I guess," she replied, her body still sensitive to even a voice. "Did we do it?"

He smiled, still in awe of her electrifying reaction to just his finger and tongue.

"Now that would be telling," he replied, standing up and pulling her with him.

They dressed in silence and with the towel Felicity wiped away the liquid still running down her thighs. She felt like a woman now, but also an addict wanting more.

CHAPTER 16

The final day of the holiday dawned. Felicity for once was the last awake. She stumbled into the kitchen feeling like last night was written all over her face.

"Morning baby, the guys have already gone to play golf," her mum said, placing a coffee down on the table. Flick sat down and wrapped her fingers around the heat and waited for her mother to bustle around. But she didn't and instead with her cup in hand, she sat across from her.

"I guess we need to talk," she said. "I've seen the way you look at Tony and probably other boys and I don't want you screwing up your life with an unexpected baby."

With the words hanging in the air, Felicity took a gulp as the words of her stepfather joined them. The anger simmered away inside her at the memories of the words, words that had hinted her mother never wanted her.

"Maybe, but I'm not like you Mum... maybe I'm smarter... maybe I have plans," she spat, seeing the way her words pierced her mother, watching her recoil.

"Oh, but you were planned honey, I loved your father but he just wasn't as ready for parenthood as I was," she stuttered, turning her eyes away from the glare across the table.

"Well..." She was about to mention the words Malcolm had said but she held her tongue. The explanation of that night was not somewhere she wanted to go. Her gaze flitted to the window, the reflected light of the sun sparkling brightly on the pool. Her mum noticed this and scrapping her chair on the tiles, she stood up.

"I've booked you in at the doctor's on our return, humour me and your stepfather and go. He really wants the best for you, he finds Tony a disappointment."

That comment stung her heart, the heart that now beat faster whenever she thought about Tony, let alone heard his name.

When the men returned Flick was hiding behind her paperback, almost at the end – but Jackie had lost her power now that the real thing had entered her life.

"So Princess, Tony has told me about your swimming lessons. I'd love to see."

Blushing, Felicity put down her book and stretched her limbs. Tony hid behind his father and tried to ignore the way his eyes longed to roam over her elegant shape. She brushed past him, almost close enough to touch, making the hair rise on the back of his neck. He watched her step into the water and wait.

"Let's see your breaststroke," Malcolm said, snickering over the word breast. He watched the way the water lapped against her cleavage, constrained beneath the bikini top.

Concentrating, Felicity took a small breath and pushed off from the side. She still struggled with the legs being co-ordinated but she wanted to prove that Tony was not a disappointment.

With two lengths completed she paused at the side.

"What do you think then, Daddy?"

"Let's see the front crawl and then I'll tell you." He sat down, removed his shoes and dangled his feet in the water. Tony was still behind him, stock-still and hardly breathing.

"Ok," she said, taking off before she had the chance to add daddy to the end. Breathless she reached for the side and swept the hair back from her face.

"Did you forget something?" he asked.

"Daddy," she gasped, her cheeks red from the exertion and shame of uttering the words.

Malcolm turned to his son.

"You've done well Tony, very well," he said, getting up and clapping a hand on his back. "Think we'll celebrate tonight."

With a mere glance that sent Martha scuttling into the villa, he took a look back at the pool, his lips curling into a snarl of a smile. Felicity watched him close the patio doors and then turned her gaze on Tony, still stock-still.

"Tony... Tony, are you coming in?"

He shook his head, turned and ran back through the gates into the street. Flick climbed out of the pool and grabbing her towel, ran to the front of the villa. But he was nowhere in sight. Her shoulders slumped and she shuffled back to her lounger. She longed to go inside for a shower but knew that she might disturb them. Picking up her book she finished the story and then lay back and stared at the clouds. One more chance tonight... but would he knock?

Tony slunk back in an hour before their dinner bookings. The taxi ride was silent and only broken when they alighted at the restaurant from their first night. Inside Malcolm held court as the place seemed to be filled with his golfing cronies. Every time Flick tried to capture Tony's gaze from across the table he avoided her. She drank down her sangria but this time it had no effect.

Back in the villa they all went to bed, they had to be up early for the flight. Felicity lay there, watching the hours tick by from midnight to one. In the end she slunk out of bed and tiptoed into the hallway. Lightly tapping Tony's door she paused but hearing nothing, she opened it. His bed was empty so she walked quietly downstairs.

The moon was high and bright again as she took a walk down the street, every sound making her jump and look behind. She almost missed the entrance to the path but she followed it and let the sound of the sea on the shore guide her. She paused before rounding the corner, suddenly scared that she would find him there with another girl. But he was alone and emerging from the breakers, like Neptune the ruler of the ocean. Her breath caught in her chest and started to quicken as every step brought him closer. Stepping from the shadow of the dune he looked up and saw her. The wind was gently blowing her loose hair, tossing it in waves over her shoulders. To him a siren, she needed no song to draw him near.

"Tony," she called, running the short distance through the sand. Her hands slipped on the wet skin of his chest taking in the ridges of his muscles. She snaked them around his waist and pushed into his body, wishing she'd thought to remove her sundress first. She wanted her skin to touch and mould with his. Tony felt her longing as he swiftly found the hem of her dress and tugged it over her head. Then they were touching, the full length of each of them, the heat drying the last cool droplets of water. His desire palpable in the quiver of his skin.

"Why, why did you come?"

"Because I love you," she declared, looking straight into his eyes. Her lips touched his before he could reply and he let her tongue invade his mouth as their saliva mingled to make a heady cocktail.

The stumbled together across the sand to the same little nook of the previous night. His towel was there to catch their fall in a jumble of locked limbs. He ended up beneath her and she wasted no time in kissing a path down his body. In her mind she knew she had to accept the taste of him, on the hope he would accept her. Without a second thought her mouth accepted his full length, straining against the need to heave as it tapped the back of her throat. Her slow rhythm built as his hand tangled in her hair, pushing and pulling in time with his thrusts. Her tongue tasted the first few drops but she kept going until he filled her mouth. Pulling up she looked down on him, a trickle dribbling from the corner of her lips. Felicity swallowed the rest, keeping a fixed smile in place despite her revulsion.

"I did it, I did it for you Tony," she breathed, watching him shrivel beneath her gaze. She lay down beside him, resting her arm over his chest. Flick needed no return for her act of pure love, she just smiled up at the moon.

"We need to get back." Tony's voice broke her from the reverie. "We have to be up at six, ready to catch the flight."

"When can I see you again?" she murmured, afraid to break her hold on him.

"It's my birthday soon, perhaps I can persuade Dad to let me take you out to dinner."

"Like a proper date?"

"Yeah, guess." He prised away her arm and sat up. Standing up he pulled on his shorts and t-shirt then ran the short distance to retrieve her sundress from the sand. Shaking it out she put it on, some sand rasping against her nipples that were already engorged from his closeness. He saw her wriggling and reaching out, he gripped the cloth covering them. Palms pressed against the swell of the fabric, he looked down upon her, then pushing the material lower he latched onto each one for a brief suckle. Felicity arched and sighed, just happy to accept anything he could offer in this brief moment in time.

Then he tucked her glorious abundance back inside the dress and took her hand.

"Come on, we'd best get back, I don't need Dad on my back again."

Felicity nodded and tried to ignore the throbbing within her. She would wait for their date. Creeping into the villa they parted on the landing with one brief kiss, afraid to try anymore lest they were discovered. In her room Felicity dropped onto her bed, putting her pillow between her thighs so she could finish what he had started.

In his room Tony stared at the ceiling, in turmoil. The plan was set, his father would allow the date to take place and he would then lead Felicity to her fate. His mind was set, his inheritance money just a month away now. His heart thumped loudly in his chest, pumping his yearning for her through the arteries of his body. A single tear slid down his cheek and soaked into his pillow, adding to the others that had fallen through the years. All of them caused by his father. The next morning they sat together in the backseat of the taxi, unable to touch more than the occasional glance of their fingertips. On the flight they were separated by the aisle and then on touch down, she waved goodbye to Tony as he took his cab and they took theirs.

CHAPTER 17

A month passed before Felicity was called into Malcolm's study.

"I've just been talking to Tony and he'd like to invite you to his 25th birthday dinner."

Felicity's mouth dropped open at his age, he was older than she'd guessed. She straightened her expression and smiled.

"Can I go then, Daddy?"

"I can't see why not. I'm so pleased the two of you became friends on our holiday."

"It's a Saturday night, so you can take the evening off," Malcolm continued. "Oh and if you let me know where you're going, I'll put a tab on the bar for him. It will be our secret until you tell him." He grinned before turning back to the papers on his desk.

Felicity ran back up to her room, hugging herself with the thought of a romantic dinner. Her mum had snapped a few photos of them while they were on holiday and Felicity had one on her bedside table. She stared at it every night and now she had something to look forward to.

Working with Malcolm had been a real eye-opener, he expected perfection and also for her to grasp everything first time. To start with he had her in his office, doing the filing and general membership subscriptions, renewals and reminders. She had then progressed to taking down his letters and had persuaded him to send her on a typing and shorthand course. So once a week she was out on her own at the nearby college. It was the only time she felt she could breathe without being scrutinised. So with her dinner date only a week away, she tripped out of college and took her time to look around the shops. The only advantage with working was the money and she'd been saving since she'd started.

Her dress was easy, she'd been staring at it for the past week every time she went out of the office for lunch. It was the centrepiece of the window display. Walking into the shop she approached the assistant and asked for the dress in the window in her size. It was scarlet red and once she slipped it on over her shoulders, she knew it was perfect. The top was flounced, small spaghetti straps, but then the rest off the shoulder, revealing the top of her chest to perfection. Cinched in at the waist with a silver belt and then flaring out and finishing just below her knees. She twirled around in the changing room and held her hair up to survey the look in full. How could he possibly resist her in this?

Grasping her bag she wandered into the nearest shoe shop, only red shoes would do. She was wandering the aisles when a male voice interrupted her.

"Felicity, is that you?"

She turned and looked at a middle-aged guy who looked vaguely familiar. Was he a regular at the club? She just couldn't place him.

"Honey pie?" he whispered and she was straight back in her old house, a fluffy teddy bear in her arms.

"Dad... Dad, is it really you?" She barely managed to get the words from her lips. Dropping her shopping bag she tried to move but he covered the short distance faster and wrapped his arms around her. He was only slightly taller than she was, his dark hair long and resting on his neck. Unwrapping her he held her at arm's length. "You've grown!"

The moment of joyful reunion had passed as Felicity narrowed her eyes, taking in his leather jacket which covered the t-shirt with a band logo emblazoned on the front. He wore flared jeans and boots beneath.

"Where have you been? Why did you leave?"

"How about I take you for a coffee and explain, since you've only heard the one side of the story." He held out his hand to her.

Just before they reached the door Felicity saw the shoes that she needed.

"Hang on Daddy, I just need to buy these." She plucked the sandals from the shelf and strode over to the counter. She was about to hand over her money when the girl paused and stared at her dad, her mouth dropping open.

As he counted out the cash the girl behind the counter turned beet-red and pushed a piece of paper and pen across the counter.

"Who should I sign it to?" he asked with a wry smile.

"Katie-Jane," she stammered.

Felicity had just grasped it, a memory from her past of a guitar hanging up in the lounge. They left the shop and turned into a small side street and a bar.

"You are old enough now, right?"

She nodded and they found a table and bench seat in the far corner. Her dad returned with a beer and a wine. She watched as he gulped half of his back and signalled to the bar man that he'd have another.

"You're famous, you're in a band," she said, taking a small sip of the sharp white wine.

"Yeah, I guess you don't remember hearing me play the guitar... you were too young at the time."

"No, I just remember all the arguing and shouting."

"I'm sorry, it was the hardest decision for me to make, the band started going places and I was torn. Your mum didn't want me to go either but it was stay and keep struggling on the little money I made or try the big time."

He finished his pint and walked over to pick up his second, ashamed that he'd not been back in touch with her sooner.

"So how did you know where I was?" she asked.

"I didn't, it was pure fluke that I saw you across the street and wondered if it was so I followed you into the shop and I knew when you turned around that my hunch was right. You have my eyes, the same beautiful ice blue," he murmured, his hand reaching across to rest on hers. She let it remain for a few moments before withdrawing as the anger of abandonment washed through her.

"Well, you could have tried harder to stay in touch. You knew where we lived."

"I sent you postcards from around the world, didn't you get them?"

Felicity shook her head. "They never arrived," she whispered.

She realised her mum must have thrown them away. He finished his second pint and could still feel the shakes coming on, needing his fix.

"Look Honey Pie, I'm here for the rest of the weekend I'm staying at the hotel on the corner. I'd love to chat some more." He stood up and Flick left the rest of her wine.

"Dad, don't go," she whimpered, feeling like an abandoned puppy once more.

"Come over tomorrow, lunchtime if you can," he said, enveloping her again in his embrace. His arms held her tight and she breathed in the scent of his aftershave which mingled with alcohol, leather and sweat. They walked back out into the street, rain starting to lightly kiss the pavement.

"Bye, Dad and thanks for buying my shoes."

"Bye Felicity," he said, as they parted on the corner. She watched him disappear into the hotel before she ran to the nearby bus stop. All of a sudden she was aware of time slipping away and she needed to get ready for tonight.

At home she didn't mention meeting with her dad, after all her mum had kept secret the postcards that he'd sent. Under the water in the bath she seethed with resentment of all the lies her mother had told over the years. Perhaps tomorrow she'd hear the real story from her dad, her famous dad. Carefully she swept the razor over her legs and armpits before she towel dried and lathered on her moisturiser. With scissors she trimmed her pubic hair and then took a long look in the mirror. She preened and turned to take in all the angles of her body, letting her hands sweep down from her waist and over her hips. Her nipples were erect just at the thought of Tony as she encased them into her bra.

From his office Malcolm watched and salivated over her supple skin, pert breasts and the virginity that awaited. Tonight was going to be the best night ever at the club. His erection rose in his hand as he tugged it casually, feeling the blood pumping through it. Part of him wanted release but the other part was waiting, waiting for later and his son's arrival.

Felicity pulled on her new dress, the red fabric brushing against her sensitive skin. Her heart pounded in a rising cacophony of desire for the only one that mattered in her life… Tony.

CHAPTER 18

Descending the stairs she found her mum and Malcolm waiting at the bottom.

"You look beautiful sweet pea," her mum breathed.

"A real princess, just make sure my Tony looks after you," Malcolm said.

"Yes, Daddy."

He held her coat open and she shrugged it on, the September evenings were starting to draw in and a light mizzle of rain hung in the air.

"I'll drop you off in town," he said, as she slipped into the passenger seat beside him. Malcolm hoped she wouldn't detect the tension in his body, increasing as his nostrils caught the scent of her perfume. It was the same one Martha wore and it never failed to mask the musk of desire beneath the surface.

She pecked him on the cheek before she got out, leaving a stain of red lipstick there. Her heels clipped along the pavement almost as fast as her heart was beating within her. Tony watched her approach and drew in a breath, she looked older with her hair tied up.

"Flick, it's so good to see you."

"Hu… hu… hi Tony," she stammered, talking difficult as her breath was swept away in his warm embrace.

"Some of my friends are already here, the others will be shortly," he said, guiding her inside the restaurant with the palm of his hand on the small of her back.

Others… OTHERS? He never said there would be a group of them! She gulped down her surprise, replacing the feeling with nerves at having to compete for his attention. The shine of the evening had been tarnished.

She accepted a flute of champagne and put her best mask of sophistication on. Tony introduced her to the various couples and a few single guys and girls. She enjoyed the looks that she received from the men but the women glared at this interloper. A blonde called Mandy slunk over and coiled an arm around Tony's waist.

"So who's this then?" she asked, casting her critical gaze over Felicity.

"This is Felicity, my stepsister."

The two women faced off to each other, each with an equally false bright smile on their painted lips. Tony knew he had to be careful, he couldn't risk the plan failing. Before anything more was said they were shown to the table and Felicity secured the seat next to Tony, across the table from a guy called Leo.

The food and wine were plentiful and Felicity was glad that she had learnt to limit her intake a little after the holiday. She wanted to be in control later when she would make sure she was alone with Tony. Luckily much of the talk revolved around music and films of the time and Felicity enjoyed the admiring looks as she talked with enthusiasm about Marc Bolan, T-Rex and her love of rock music. Most of the girls at the table preferred the charms of The Osmonds who quite frankly left her cold. As dessert was served she felt a hand on her skirt, and a sly look to her right confirmed it was Tony. He leaned in and whispered, "Make an excuse to go to the ladies', I'll meet you there."

Felicity nodded and beamed, the evening was back on track.

In the subdued lighting she waited, but when his hand caught hers, he pulled her into a small alcove just across the corridor.

"I've been dying to do this all evening." He bent his head to lightly kiss her exposed shoulders, working a teasing line of kisses up her neck and to her lips. Each kiss was more devouring than the last so that when he withdrew Felicity was panting for more, her body shaking with delicious bubbles of desire waiting to burst.

"So what's the plan? How do we lose all your friends?"

"When you get back to the table say that you're not feeling well and I'll offer to take you home."

With a last, long kiss he wiped his mouth of the red stain she'd left. Flick watched him swagger up the corridor and enter the dining area. She ducked into the ladies' and waited until the pink flush on her skin subsided.

She walked slowly back in and staggered a little as she neared the table, prompting Leo to stand up and rush to help her.

"Are you ok?" he asked, letting his hand run down her back, guiding her to the table.

"I'm not feeling so good," she muttered.

Tony was now at her other side.

"Leo, I'll take it from here. Can you get the waiter to call a cab?"

Back in her seat he poured her a glass of water, which tasted funny but she drank it down. As they waited Felicity started to feel the room spinning, she really was feeling unwell and not just faking it. She reached and grasped Tony's hand.

"Come, we'll wait outside," he said.

Her hearing seemed intermittent as she waited for him to apologise to his friends, telling them he'd meet them all later at their usual haunt.

A black cab pulled up to the kerb and they got inside.

"Lie back, close your eyes," his voice soothed, cutting through the fading sounds in her ears. She eased her head onto his lap as the car engine thrummed into life beneath them. When the car slowed she opened her eyes and gazed up into his.

"Feeling better now?" he asked. "Because for my next surprise you need a blindfold on."

She nodded, her limbs still a bit heavy, but she sat up so that he could fasten the dark velvet scarf over her eyes. As he tied it at the back he moved around to whisper in her ear, "I want you to feel everything first, touch is so much more powerful when one of your other senses is knocked out."

"But what if I want you to stop?"

"Oh, I doubt you will," he murmured, his voice so low she struggled to catch it. He left a kiss on her cheek before she felt cool air as the car door opened. Hands reached in to take hers and she wondered how Tony had got out of the car so quickly. Her ears strained to pick up any sounds but it was eerily silent apart from the clip of her heels on the pavement. Then that stopped and she guessed that she was inside and on carpet.

Tony gently pulled her coat from her shoulders and allowed the warmth of the surroundings to turn her skin pink.

"Tony, I'm scared," she whispered, her chest rising in an ever-quickening pattern. She felt his arms wrap around her and then his lips pressed onto hers, opening them with a quick flick of his tongue. She tasted of the chocolate dessert from the meal, sweet and tempting. With every long kiss she settled into his embrace and let her body come alive to his touch. He took her hand and she heard a door close so she guessed she was in a room now. Soft music was playing but it was nothing she recognised.

"I'm going to slowly undress you and then lie you down on the bed."

She nodded as he turned her around to find the zip on the back of her dress.

CHAPTER 19

Felicity trembled as her dress swept over her skin on its fall to the floor. Tony gasped as he revealed the red underwear she wore beneath, the lace bra failing to contain her breasts which were confined within its wire and shape. Her panties gave glimpses of the dark hair beneath and a suspender belt held her black stockings in place. He knew she'd done all this for his benefit. The skin at the top of her thigh was highlighted pale and beautiful in the dim light. He ran his hands over the nylons on the way down to the floor, where he knelt down so that he could grasp her shoe.

"Hold on, Flick," he said, feeling her hand rest lightly on his shoulder. With both shoes removed he stood up and again marvelled in the view while it was still his alone. He hesitated for a moment. If he left now he would take no further part of this plan outlined by his father but equally, he would have to wait another five years for his money. He remembered her words from the beach... he was playing with her feelings but he was powerless to resist her charms.

Scooping her up into his arms he walked to the bed and laid her upon it. Then he quickly unbuttoned his shirt and dropped his trousers onto the floor. He heard the music go up a level and knew that his father and selected friends were arriving soon. He stepped over to the bed and let his hand trail down over her curves, then on the way back up he slipped his fingers under the wire of her bra and she gasped as he grazed her nipple. She arched up to meet him and in a swift move, he pulled the garment loose, letting her spill out onto his palms, one in each. He moved across to straddle her and after a quick squeeze that made her moan and her nipples point upwards in hard little nubs, he ran his hands under her arms. Upwards they moved until his hands circled her wrists.

"I think a little restraint may be just the thing I need for you," he murmured, a small low laugh resonating in his throat as he tied the restraints into place. It stretched the top half of her torso nicely and despite a small struggle against the straps she lay still, pouting.

He let his hands wander through her hair, pulling it from the band and pins that had kept it in place. It tumbled though his fingers like silken twine to entice him further. Then his lips marked a path from her forehead, to the tip of her nose, and removed the last remnants of red lipstick from her skin.

Felicity although tied didn't feel restricted without her hands, although she longed to run them over his chest like she'd done on the beach. So far this was beyond her wildest dreams or all the images she had read in her trashy novels. This felt like she was the centre of his attention to be pampered. Tony moved further down her body, his breath quickening as he bit lightly at her nipples, darkening them from pink to deep violet red and engorged now with the blood pumping beneath her skin. He trailed his lips down the valley between and over her smooth, flat stomach.

Tony reached the elastic of her knickers and hooked his finger beneath them. She obliged and lifted her hips upwards. The scent of her sex filled his senses and he breathed in deeply, guessing she was damp and ready. Letting his finger trail through her nicely trimmed bush to the folds hiding beneath, the little hood of skin covering the centre of her pleasure, he glanced across it and was rewarded with a deep guttural moan from her lips. He touched his lips to her clit lightly, memories of the first lick filling his mind, relishing that he'd been the first to feel her like this. The door behind him glided quietly open. Knowing his father's love of stockings, he left them on and ran his hands down to restrain her ankles in the same way as her wrists.

"Relax, my beauty… this is where the fun begins," were his parting words. He turned to see the black desire on his father's face at the sight of Felicity before him. He stood alone and Tony wondered where the others were. The couple of times he'd witnessed this in the past he'd shared the experience with his three trusted friends and investors in the club.

"Tony," she cried and both men froze.

Malcolm motioned for Tony to approach the bed and answer her.

"Yes?"

"Can I take the blindfold off now?" she asked. "I want to see what you're doing."

"Later," he whispered. "Just enjoy, but if you want me to stop just say the word... Daddy."

Picking up his clothes and shoes he walked past Malcolm. At the door he paused and watched his father still drinking in the sight. This time was different, he didn't want to stay and join in. An acrid taste filled his throat and he swallowed before leaving the room. He knew that the others waited next door, able to view all the action through the two way mirror and see his father's signal to enter. A brief look of puzzlement flashed over Malcolm's features. Usually his son stayed but he couldn't speak or the game would be blown and he wanted his moment of enjoyment first.

With the door closed again Malcolm advanced towards his step-daughter, waiting to enjoy the forbidden touch and taste. He stopped at the head of the bed and ran his fingers through the strands of her dark hair, breathing in the scent of the same shampoo used by his wife. She sighed and trembled at his touch before his hand grazed the side of her cheek. His lips followed afterwards and as she couldn't touch him, she was unaware that it wasn't Tony. His lips feasted on hers and after a small start, she responded.

Felicity wondered why Tony now tasted of whiskey but she imagined that he'd taken a sip before starting his enjoyment of her. His kiss delved and devoured her mouth, his skin rubbing against hers. She wanted to speak and ask him to drop lower, to go back to where he'd been before tying her ankles. She could feel a warm trickle of her juice on the top of her thigh and she wriggled to try and dislodge it.

Malcolm watched her squirm within the confines of the restraints and smiled, smelling the scent of desire in the air. His mouth latched onto a firm nipple as his hands cupped and compared mother to daughter. In this department daughter won. His tongue continued the journey over her smooth, supple skin, taking in the curve of her hips and then over the lace of her suspender belt.

He paused and stood back a moment to look at her spread legs and the delights between, covered with a light fleck of dark pubic hair. Inhaling the scent springing from her body he allowed it to swirl around in his head, producing a heady mix of desire and power within him. He took another sip from the glass of whiskey he'd brought into the room. Then with it still warm on his tongue, he moved to kneel between her thighs. Felicity felt his weight on the bed and knew that he was at last back where she wanted him. She longed to arch her hips upwards to catch that first buzz his tongue and lips gave her.

"Please do it," she whimpered. "Like you did on the beach."

Oh so that was where Tony did all his romancing when they were at the villa. He trailed his little finger up from the top of her stocking to the edge of her outer lips. He could feel her trembling beneath his touch as he gently moved in a circular motion... until he couldn't resist. The slick film of her desire coated his finger and he pulled it away to lick off the taste, truly delicious. He bent down and took his first full taste, letting his tongue take in all her folds before moving up to her clit, which was erect and waiting for him. He flicked over it and relished the sounds of her sighs and groans as he sucked hard.

"Daddy," she gasped and he smiled.

His son had done well and earned his money this time.

He moved away and let his finger push inside her. She gripped him tightly and he knew that he needed to loosen her up to take his full length. Felicity felt his mouth move back onto hers and sighed in satisfaction. She was close to release and wanted to suck him first in case she passed out from the sensations. She was throbbing all over as his tongue slid against hers. When he pulled back again she took her opportunity.

"Let me see you, let me suck you."

Malcolm let out a low laugh at her request before he straddled her chest and guided the tip of his cock to her lips. She opened wide to take him, this time not choking as he hit the back of her throat. She'd been practising at home with a banana and hoped he would appreciate her efforts. She let him control the pace and kept her mouth wrapped around him. He was struggling to hold back so he withdrew and pressed a light kiss to her forehead. He heard the door open and knew his friends were entering the room, two positioned by her head ready to remove her blindfold. The other one had brought one of his girls into the room and was letting her administer to his needs as she knelt before him. He moved back down between her legs and again started to lick her, letting her arch and grind onto his tongue in wild abandon.

Felicity mewled as her first orgasm ripped through her from the force of his tongue, but this time he didn't let up, and his tongue increased the pace as she felt two fingers inside her.

"I want you, please Tony... I'm ready," she sighed, the words almost lost in her gasps for air.

Very slowly Malcolm came up for air, her juice dripping down his chin. He kept his finger pressed onto her clit, rubbing it softly with her juice, feeling it thrumming for his touch and ready to shudder again. He nodded at Simon and Will who knew that once he was inside, they needed to remove her blindfold. He inched the head of his cock into her opening, feeling it start to tense. He pushed on through as her scream escaped into the silence. Virgins were never really prepared for the feel of a man inside them.

"Tony... I mean Daddy, please stop it hurts."

He gave the signal and his friends pulled off the blindfold. Felicity blinked at the subdued lighting of the room before she focused. She couldn't believe this was true! It wasn't Tony inside her... it was her stepfather...

CHAPTER 20

She started to writhe beneath his bulk but the straps kept her imprisoned as his body loomed over her. He was pushing hard now, sweat beading on his forehead.

"You're mine Felicity; it was all part of the deal."

What deal? What is he talking about? The pain of him within her had started to subside as she then clocked the two men on either side. *Fuck, this must be some sick joke. Where's Tony?*

She closed her eyes tight, hoping the dream would fade, but her body was being a traitor. Her hips now bucked against his, her thighs tightly stretched to allow his bulk to lie there. Hands were touching her hair, lips kissing the tears from her cheeks. This was not how she'd imagined her first time to be as she gritted her teeth, wishing she could fight back, tear his hair out... oh, and what she'd do to his cock!!!

"Hold her tight everyone, think she needs to know who's boss," Malcolm commanded.

Each of the men in turn unstrapped her but held her tight so she had no chance to move. Her body was trembling and her legs unsteady as they turned her over, strapping her back down. This time her knees were bent as she knelt with her ass in the air. The two men near her head reached over to cup a breast each, twisting her nipples between their fingertips and making new bolts of desire run rampant through her body.

"Hey Lisa, why don't you give her a taste of pussy," Malcolm sniggered, watching her stand and walk around to the head of the bed. Felicity stared up at the girl. They'd spoken so many times in the past although never about what her job was at the club. Felicity knew that's where they were.

"Help me, make them stop," she begged, fresh tears running down her cheeks. Lisa smiled and bent down.

"Just enjoy it, I only had two guys on my initiation, you've got four and me," she said, before her lips touched Felicity's in a soft kiss.

Felicity was just starting to enjoy the soft touch of her lips when she felt fingers and tongues on her pussy, slowly sucking and licking up the juice that was dribbling down her thighs. The next cock slid inside. It wasn't as large so she guessed it was one of the other guys taking his turn. Malcolm strode round and into view.

"Come on Lisa, I'll help you into position, we want to see some girl on girl action and Will at the back likes his balls fondled."

He yanked Felicity under the arms so that Lisa had room to slide beneath before her pussy was directly beneath her face.

"Daddy, no," Felicity beseeched, pleading with her blue eyes.

"Just be a good girl and try it... you never know, you might enjoy it."

He leaned down to kiss her lips but feeling her teeth grinding, he pulled back.

"Do it for Daddy, otherwise I'll have to make you."

She watched his fingers pry apart the folds and run his finger around in the wetness there, then pulling out, he smeared it on her lips. It was sticky and wet as she opened her mouth and poked her tongue out in the general direction. She had no idea what she was doing, hardly able to concentrate as she was pummelled from behind. Then lips and a tongue tickled over her clit and she sighed again as the heat rose. This touch was more slow and gentle and realising that if she co-operated it might be over sooner, she let her own tongue do the same. The taste was nicer than spunk as she licked her way around the folds, letting them unfurl. She heard Lisa sigh beneath her as her painted nail reached down and rubbed a little at the tiny nub at the head. Felicity took this as her cue and let her tongue touch the same spot, licking slowly as it rose within her mouth. If this was what Tony had done to her, it seemed unfair for her to not do the same with her only possible ally in the room. Malcolm's fingers were pumping in and out, the squelching sound only overshadowed by Lisa's whimpers as Felicity grew bolder and sucked her in, letting her teeth nibble.

"I'm getting close now," Will grunted, his pace almost frantic as

Felicity orgasmed around him at Lisa's fine touch.

"Cum on her back," Malcolm said. "Lisa loves a spot of spunk to clear up." His fingers withdrew from Lisa but were replaced by another set as she continued to grind against them whilst keeping Felicity's mouth on her clit.

Warmth splattered over her ass as Will pulled out and slumped back at the end of the large bed.

"Fuck, she's good. Your turn now Tom," he breathed as another cock rubbed at her entrance, coating its head in her juice before sliding inside.

She felt buffeted and bruised from Malcolm and Will, but she guessed she had to endure one more, or was Malcolm going to get a final go?

Tom was slow and steady in his pace and it gave Felicity a chance to slow down. Sweat was running from her body, her tongue was tired and sticky with juice. Lisa wriggled out and Felicity watched from the corner of her eye as she lay down on the bed beside her. Malcolm then pushed inside her. The final guy seemed to be working on himself, then he walked round to her face.

"Shall I?" he asked.

"Do it," the other men chorused, obviously used to the routine of these evenings.

"Close your eyes sweetheart," he laughed, then she felt warm spunk splatter her cheeks and forehead. It ran down her nose and settled on her lips and chin. Felicity nearly heaved from the thick heavy globules that ran over her lips. There was no way she was going to lick it off. She hated the taste of Tony so this would be much worse.

"Hey, Malc get over here, I think she's a squirter," Tom laughed.

Felicity knew something had been building inside her, she'd lost count of how many times she'd come yet her body it seemed, kept wanting more. Everyone switched as Lisa moved onto all fours and let Tom enter her. Malcolm ran his hand casually over Felicity's pussy, relishing the feel of it throbbing and jerking as his finger entered her.

"Daaaaaaadeeeeeeee," Felicity wailed. He was twisting his finger inside her and it seemed to be pulling a stronger feeling from her body. She was squeezing down so hard, her hips grinding in serpentine loops. With a couple more pushes she let go, feeling liquid squirt from her. Her face was red in mortification. Her head was spinning at the sensations as she tried to slump down.

"Untie her legs," Malcolm said, seeing her droop as the spray covered his fingers and dripped onto the sheets. It was lightly pink in colour and he knew he'd broken her, well almost. She lay motionless beneath him, eyes closed and passed out like before.

They untied her wrists and she still lay there, prone before them all. Lisa took the time to wipe her face with the end of the sheet. She felt sorry for this poor girl.

"Stay still, this might burn a little," Malcolm said.

He held a small poker type item in his hand. Felicity could hardly move let alone speak as pain seared her right buttock. She smelt burning skin but amid the other sensations still within her bloodstream, it seemed insignificant, like a cigarette burn on your skin when you weren't careful.

They rolled her over and Malcolm loomed into view.

"Last thing Princess, then I'll take you home and look after you," Malcolm said.

Hands held her loosely but she had neither the inclination, will or strength to move. He pumped away on his cock, up by her face. She listlessly watched a bubble of cum start to appear from the end.

"Open wide," he said, and squashed her cheeks between his free hand and forced himself inside her mouth. He didn't need her to suck as he came immediately, a long stream of spunk filling her empty mouth and slowly trickling down her throat. She wanted to throw it all back up over his smug face.

They helped her up, resting her back and head against the pillows.

"Here, drink this." Lisa offered a glass of water, now swathed in a black silk dressing gown. The other men wore similar, it was only Malcolm that remained naked. His hands were on his hips, back arched and shoulders wide, like an arrogant King of all he surveyed.

Felicity was tired, so tired. She gulped down the water, letting it wash away the vile taste on her tongue. She longed to slip into a hot bath and just scrub her skin raw to rid it of the awful memories it now held. The light in the room seemed to be fading into blackness but she embraced it. Darkness meant escape from the reality.

"That's good stuff Will, so pleased you're a vet and can get hold of these sedatives. How long will it last?"

"She'll probably be out of it until tomorrow morning, possibly longer… midday…"

"Then she'll not remember anything, right?"

"Not sure, you'll have to wait and see on that score. But she's going to find the brand at some point."

Malcolm grinned, he loved the brand. All his working girls had one and now Felicity could maybe join their ranks. The secrets his club held were long and his clientele exclusive and that's what kept them coming back and the activity behind the doors so sought after. The London Club had a reputation to uphold.

Wrapped in blankets the security guards placed Felicity into the back of the car.

"Is Tony still here?" Malcolm asked. "I was hoping he was going to join in."

"No, he said he wanted to go back to his birthday party crowd so I gave him the envelope as you requested."

"Excellent, I'm sure he'll give me a call tomorrow to say thank you."

Malcolm signalled to the other guard.

"Get her home, Martha knows what to do," he said.

He watched until the tail lights turned the corner into the busy street. Then he swaggered back into the club, needing a drink after that session and a comfy armchair to rest in.

Leaving the club Tony didn't feel in the party spirit so with his envelope shoved deep into his pocket, he hailed a cab and went back to his flat. He poured a drink and sank down on his sofa, pulling the envelope out and gazing at the figures on the cheque. It was dirty money and part of him wanted to rip it up. However lying open on the coffee table was his dream and it was up for sale. Monday morning he'd be in the estate agents purchasing his career and his move away from London and his father.

"Cheers, Dad." He held his glass aloft in the empty room and downed the whiskey. It felt bitter as it gushed down his throat and heated his insides. Shutting his eyes all he could see was the image of Felicity tied to the bed, unable to escape from his father's clutches. Their relationship had always been difficult when he'd been growing up. Tony had always been trying to be good and clever at school. His father had high hopes of him becoming a lawyer or something like that. In the end it was his love of sport that threw the spanner between them. His father couldn't see the opportunities and despised him for then not wanting to take a more active part in the club. He shuddered as he remembered the beatings and when he'd been old enough to fight back, Malcolm then took it out on his mother. He wanted happiness, he wanted to make new memories and move away from the darkness that lurked in his soul.

CHAPTER 21

Bright sunshine shone through the chink in her curtains as groggily, Felicity opened her eyes. Her body felt bruised and numb as she searched her memory for last night. A cold cup of tea was on her bedside table but with her mouth so parched, she drank it down. *What happened last night?* She remembered leaving college and buying her dress. She needed the loo so she staggered out of bed and pulled her dressing gown on over her nightdress. Her legs felt stiff as she took the few steps from her door to the bathroom. It felt like she'd run a marathon, her thighs were still burning. She rubbed her hands over the skin, trying to soothe them and that's when she saw the two bruises. Large and deepening from a yellow stain on the edges, to deep purple-black in the centre, one on either side of her inner thighs.

Shaking now with fear she turned the tap on for the bath. Watching the water fill, a film of scented bubbles on the surface, she stared into the full length mirror. Her hair was tousled and matted together in clumps. She must have been drunk last night as she usually spent five minutes brushing her hair before bed. Slipping off her robe she winced as the soft fabric brushed her swollen breasts which also felt sore. The rest of her body seemed fine, it just ached in silly places like her wrists and ankles. Sinking into the warm water Felicity sighed and closed her eyes again. She needed to collect her thoughts before she went downstairs.

Trying really hard now she cast her mind back to the shoe shop and meeting her dad. He'd looked older than her mum, yet she knew they were both the same age, having been school sweethearts. How many times had she heard that story when she was younger, the fairytale gone wrong – when he'd left. Except now she knew why and she also knew her mother was not to be trusted. The name of the hotel popped into her mind and she decided she needed to go back and see him, hear the full story before she confronted her mum about the missing postcards. Sinking lower into the water she let her hands run down her skin and then she was fully under. Her hair started to loosen in the ripples of the water as the heat soothed her muscles.

Running her fingers through the strands it hit her violently, in waves of dark feelings…

She'd been wearing a blindfold…?

When?

How?

What happened?

She pushed to the surface, sucking on air as each new sensation of the night before hit her. But it hadn't been at the hands of Tony… it had been Malcolm… Daddy! She sat stunned in the cooling water, resisting the urge to throw up whatever was inside her. But this was replaced by rage as she remembered his words, "All part of the deal." Deal with who? Tony or her mother? She scrambled out of the tub and threw up into the toilet. Her blood boiled as her skin blazed crimson and she saw her bloodstained eyes in the mirror, bright against her pale, clammy skin.

Rushing back to her room she knew she had to get out, get out now. Get away from her mother's lies, away from him. She spat onto the floor of her room before she ripped the posters from the walls, littering the pink carpet with their remnants. She found her bag and after dressing, she crammed some spare clothes inside. On the landing she stopped to listen but everything was quiet. She crept down the stairs and paused again, hearing them both talking in the kitchen. Anger continued to blind her against them and she opened the front door before closing it and running down the driveway. She knew where the nearest bus stop was but he could easily find her in the time it might take between her means of escape. Rounding the corner she slowed to a walk, her breath shaking her body and making her lungs burn.

Sinking onto the bench by the bus stop she checked her watch, five minutes until her escape was complete. Staring down the street part of her was expecting his black car to appear round the corner. In the end the bus pulled up and she boarded. Shivering on the back seat she lay her head against the cold window. She watched the suburbs merge into the cityscape which, despite being a Sunday, was still bustling.

Getting off at the same bus stop she'd used the day before, she wandered down the street and paused before the grand frontage of the hotel. Felicity didn't feel her usual polished self and her head still felt muzzy and dark between the flashbacks she was experiencing. Each one seemed worse than the last as she held down the bile that kept filling the back of her throat. Despite her bath of the morning, her skin itched and she longed to scrub it again now she was remembering everything that had happened.

Stepping into the foyer of the hotel she approached the man on the check-in desk.

"Excuse me but can you contact Darren Jennings, I believe he's staying here."

"I'm sorry but I don't appear to have anyone booked in by that name," he replied, smoothly.

"Oh, he's with the band Steel Flowers." She racked her brain for his stage name but she'd never really followed the band, not knowing her father was the lead guitarist.

"Look, just wait outside if you're a groupie but they don't normally surface until midday," he sighed and turned away. Felicity looked around and saw a small group of chairs by the door.

"Well, if I wait there can I get a coffee?"

"Ok, but we don't want any scenes," he replied, looking again at the smartly dressed young woman and reassessing his evaluation of her.

Perhaps she was a reporter after an exclusive interview? She was certainly far better dressed than the crowd that normally hung around the doors. The waiter served her a coffee and she crossed her legs and pulled her latest novel out. An hour had passed before a commotion startled her from the lines of writing, not that she'd been concentrating much. As her mind had calmed it turned to revenge. Malcolm had not just Phillip to answer for... but her virginity too!

With much laughing and swearing three men stepped out of the elevator accompanied by three young girls. One of them was her dad so Felicity stood up and waited to catch his eye. When he did he quickly dropped his hand away from the young girl who seemed vaguely familiar.

"I'll catch you later Katie-Jane," he said, watching her follow the other girls and men heading through the revolving doors.

"Dad," Felicity stammered. "I needed to see you."

He watched as a tear snaked down her cheek and he quickly reached to pull her into his embrace. They walked past the astonished reception desk and back into the lift. Darren wished he'd cleaned the room up a little but it would have to do, his daughter obviously needed him. Pushing the door open to his suite he moved the litter of clothes from the small sofa and Felicity was able to sit down.

"I'll just tidy up a bit, I wasn't expecting visitors today," he mumbled, feeling the weight of her stare around the room.

"Was that the girl from the shoe shop?" she asked.

"Uh, yeah. It was nothing, just a one-night stand."

The thought of sex turned her stomach once more and she dashed through a door opposite into a small bathroom. Throwing up hardly anything except the small biscuit that had been served with her coffee, it seemed that all men only had one thing on their minds.

Back in the main room her dad had cleared up and was putting the kettle on but she walked straight past him and picked up the open vodka bottle. She took a long slug feeling it burn away some of the taste of last night.

"Sweetie, I don't think alcohol is the answer," he said, motioning for her to sit on the small sofa.

"Why not, perhaps it will make me forget."

"Forget what? When I saw you last you were excited about your date."

"Yup, but things change, in fact I don't want to go back home," she declared, reaching for the bottle that was just out of reach. He picked it up and took a swig before handing it over. "Can't I stay here with you?"

"Well I'm only around tonight for our gig and then we're moving on to Paris."

"Take me with you," she pleaded, turning her wide blue eyes on him. She lowered her lashes and squeezed out a couple of tears for effect.

"Look, you know I'd love to but we just don't have space for family on the tour bus. We're not big guns in the music business like many of the other bands around. You can come to tonight's gig if you like and I'll sort you out a room here for tonight and tomorrow night."

He turned away from her and picked up the phone, ringing reception and sending up a porter with a room key just down the corridor.

"Do you want to come to the gig, you can watch from the side of the stage?" he asked.

"Guess," Felicity replied, grasping the key in her hand.

"Look I've got to run to rehearsals now but I'll be back later. If you want food just order and book it to my room tab." He picked up his leather jacket and shrugged it on as she stood. She took the quarter bottle of vodka and the key.

"Thanks," she mumbled, feeling let down once more. But there was no way she could tell him everything that had happened last night. She was on her own, her plan fermenting in her subconscious. She watched him saunter down the corridor, resisting the urge to run after him like she'd done as a child. Inside the room she went straight for the bathroom and ran another bath. In the water she scrubbed hard at her skin, stripping a layer off in her attempts to erase the hands, tongues and touch that had been there. Then wrapped in the fluffy hotel dressing gown, she ordered some food and waited.

The flavours and taste of the roast beef dinner calmed her nerves and this time she held it all down. She got dressed again and with the spare key her dad had pressed into her palm, she went back into his room.

On the bedside cabinet she found his wallet. Opening it she removed most of the cash inside. It wasn't much but would do until she could get to the bank tomorrow morning. She'd have to be quick as knowing Malcolm, he'd be trying to close it once he knew she was missing. She hadn't even left a note for them. She looked around at his clothes littering the floor of the bedroom and the bathroom. The smell of stale body odour mingled with sweet, cheap perfume from last night. Felicity retreated back to her own fresh room and lay on the bed. Picking up the hotel paper and pen, she marked out her plan for the evening. With a backstage pass and her father distracted, she could carry out her simple revenge and still have an alibi of sorts. Her mother and Tony could wait for wrath.

CHAPTER 22

Malcolm stormed back downstairs.

"Martha, Martha she's gone," he yelled. "Did you see her leave?"

"No," was her quiet response as she quaked at his rage. "I'll ring the police, report her missing."

"Fucking hell, are you stupid, woman?" He raised his hand and aimed a slap that stung her cheek. "She's eighteen now, an adult and I don't need her going anywhere near the police after last night." He took to pacing up and down the kitchen tiles.

"I'll take a drive, she can't have gone far," he said, grabbing his keys. "Ring the club if she comes home but I will pop in here again before work."

"I'll ring her friend from back where we used to live in case she's gone back there, what about Tony?"

"I'll check in on him as I scour the city."

He drove straight to the club and called his security guards. Between the three of them they might see her somewhere. Then he parked in the car park complex for Tony's flat. He buzzed the intercom and after a moment, a voice answered.

"Tony, can I come in?" Malcolm asked.

Tony hesitated. "I'll meet you in the café on the corner in five minutes, just need to get dressed."

He didn't need his father to see the brochure spread out on the coffee table, the detailed plans he'd made and the appointment he had tomorrow. The cheque lay there in the centre, emblazoned with blood money.

Malcolm was waiting at the corner table, two mugs of coffee in the centre.

"Hi Dad, what's wrong?"

"Felicity's gone, ran out the house sometime this morning and I wanted to check she hadn't been in contact with you...?"

"Why would she Dad, she probably hates me just as much as you, maybe even more," he said, cradling the mug.

"Well, I need you to help me search for her."

"Ok, I'll get my car and then you let me know where I should try."

Over coffee Malcolm split the city into four parts and then they parted. Tony trudged back to his flat to get his car keys and then slipped onto the leather seat of his vehicle. He paused and hit his head slowly on the steering wheel, wanting the pain to block out the sick feeling deep inside his stomach. Every time he closed his eyes he saw images of Felicity there, on the beach, in the pool, her bright laughter and sarcastic wit. He'd fallen for her in a big way over the fortnight and wished that he hadn't been so driven by his own dreams to leave her there, with him.

He slowed as he passed every young woman with long black hair but none turned out to be Felicity. He watched the crowds gathering outside the theatre, clocking the sign for some band called Steel Flowers. There was no sign of her and after three hours of solid driving, he returned to his flat. He phoned and left a message for his father before he sunk down on the sofa. Opening a beer he slugged it back and once more retreated into his memories of the holiday.

Back at the club Malcolm and the security guys had also drawn a blank, short of calling into every hotel, guest house or hostel building – they had nothing.

"Get the club open and I'll be back once I've changed," Malcolm barked. His friend in the police had phoned saying they hadn't received any sexual assault claims. Malcolm knew the benefit of having friends in high places. Pulling into the drive he marched in to find Martha preparing food. Feeling sorry about the red mark that still graced her cheek, he reeled her into his body.

"Why don't we eat out and then you can come to the club with me for a change," he purred, stroking a finger lightly over her cheek.

"She's not home yet," she murmured, turning to press her lips to the skin of his palm.

"She'll return when she's cold and hungry, she didn't take much with her."

Martha let his lips touch hers, too afraid to say that she'd been up to Felicity's room. Yes she hadn't taken many clothes with her but the threadbare teddy was no longer on the shelf.

"Come on baby, let me decide what you're going to wear tonight," Malcolm said, taking her hand and leading her upstairs to their room.

Back from rehearsal, Darren knocked on the door of the room Felicity was in. "How are you sweetie?"

"I'm ok Dad, looking forward to watching you tonight."

"Here, I grabbed you one of our tour t-shirts to wear, I'm going to take a nap and freshen up and then it will be time to head back. The crowds are already queuing outside."

Two hours later she heard a knock on the door. She'd tried on the t-shirt which was way too big so she'd knotted it under her breasts and with her jeans and her hair tied into bunches, she looked younger than her eighteen years. The other members of the band were introduced to her and she tried to avoid their stares. In her bag she had her pack of cigs, lighter and fuel. Coupled with the plan in her head, she was ready to take revenge.

Getting out of the cars at the back of the theatre she could hear the chants from the girls gathered at the front echoing along the passageway. Her father grinned as the lead singer rushed around and waved to the crowds who surged forward for a closer look. Then they walked into the backstage area of the theatre and a maze of small corridors.

"Come on Flick, take a look at the stage before they start letting the crowds inside." He took her hand and pulled her along, again igniting childhood memories that had been dormant for too long. She giggled at his enthusiasm as they stood together on stage. He handed her a stage pass that she slipped over her head.

"I always hoped you'd come to a gig one day, and today is that day," he said, watching her stare out into a room of empty seats. He picked up his guitar and started to pick out a tune.

"You can hear all of this towards the end of the show," he said. "But I think you'll like it." He winked at her before placing his guitar back on the stand. Then he led her across to the far side of the stage.

"If you want to stand here for the show you can, or there are a few seats back there if you get tired," he said, looking at his watch. "I've got to go and get changed now but I'll be back here in a bit."

Felicity watched him leave again. He was good at that and wandered back out into the centre of the stage. Her heart was racing as she paced the floorboards, restless to get on with the plan, but knowing that she couldn't slip out until just before the interval. A stage hand gave her a look and she smiled at him.

"Are you with the band?" he asked

"Well, yes the guitarist is my dad, if that's what you mean?"

"Cool, I'm Keith. It's nice to meet you." He stuck out his hand and she shook it.

"I'm Felicity," she murmured.

"I work at the theatre while I'm at college, this is the biggest gig we've ever done here… it's kind of exciting."

"Yeah?"

"Oh, you've probably been to loads since you're with the band." He filled the silence between them with his chatter. Realising that she might need someone to let her out and back in, Felicity listened and nodded. This guy would be perfect if she could persuade him.

"Do you know where we can get a drink, that's if you can skive off a bit?" she suggested, flashing him her biggest smile. She watched his eyes glance from her lips down to her breasts and bare midriff.

He took her hand and she followed him through the maze of corridors to a small bar.

"This is for the VIPs but none are here yet," he said, scooting behind the bar and flipping the caps off two bottles of beer. He handed one to her and then watched as she pressed it to her lips. He was infatuated.

"Can I ask you a favour, Keith," she asked, letting her cold fingers stroke over his free hand.

"Yes, anything."

"I need to pop out for a little bit at around nine but I don't want my dad to know I've missed some of the performance."

"Ok, I'll sneak you out and I guess back in again. How long will you be?"

"Hopefully only half an hour." She beamed over at him and he returned it.

"I'll come and find you before then," he suggested. "But we'd better get back now before anyone finds us here."

With the band on stage and the crowds chanting, Felicity tried to let the excitement catch her rather than nerves. The plan tumbled over and over in her mind as she worried about every little chance that it could go wrong. At a quarter to nine Keith appeared in the shadows and beckoned her over.

"You can go out the dressing room door and I'll leave it wedged open for your return."

With a left and then a right along two corridors, he pushed open the door. Turning she leaned in and dropped a light kiss on his cheek.

"Thanks hun," she whispered and then slipped into the night.

It only took her ten minutes to reach the parking area outside the club. She saw his car there in the spot at the front next to a few others. She knew Sunday was not a very busy evening but it was one that Malcolm hardly ever missed. The doormen were still stood outside but as she checked her watch it turned nine and they stepped inside, locking it to prevent further entry. Felicity slipped silently along the hedge on the far side of the parking area and then found the bins and the fire escape.

Malcolm had once proudly said they'd never had to use it so that was why the bins were positioned there. Glancing around Felicity could feel her heart pounding throughout her body, increasing further as she lifted the lid from the first bin.

Inside were papers and urgh, she wrinkled her nose. It smelt like sewage and she stepped back a second, letting her nose fill with fresh air instead. Quietly she crept forward again and opened the second bin, giving it space to let out its fumes. She lit one of her fags and let it burn for a little bit before dropping it into the top of the first bin. She did the same with the second. A quick squirt of the lighter fuel set the smoulder to flames that started to eat up the rubbish. She trailed the lighter fluid over the door and then to the small window frame nearby and hoped at some point it would catch alight too. Quickly she kicked both of them at the base so that they fell against the old wooden door. She paused for a final second and then quickly ran back to the corner of the street. Trembling with fear and excitement she shut her eyes, imagining the smoke drifting along the corridor and into the bar area. Stifling the giggles that now bubbled to the surface, she turned and ran back to the theatre and crept in through the door. She could still hear the band hammering out one of their songs on the stage so she hurried back to her position in the wings.

At that moment her father looked over and gave her a grin. She hoped he hadn't noticed her absence for part of the set. As the curtain fell on the first half he crossed the stage and smiled.

"What did you think?"

"You were great, think I might have to buy some of your records for my collection."

"That's my girl." He patted her arm, leaving sweaty handprints on her skin. "You feel cold, come back to my dressing room for a bit to warm up."

Smiling she trailed after him and sat down on the chair as he pulled off his t-shirt and replaced it with a fresh one.

"The song at the end of the next set is one I wrote for your mum, you can't miss it." He rubbed his long hair on the towel and then drank from the bottle on the side.

"You'd better get back, I just need a moment or two before I go back on."

She returned to her position on the sidelines and discovered Keith waiting there for her.

"Everything go as planned?" he asked. "It's all kicking off outside... two fire engines just raced past."

"Yes, I'm good thanks. Any chance of another drink?"

"Stay here and I'll get one for you." He hurried off down the corridor and Felicity rubbed her hands together. If he wasn't dead she hoped he'd been disfigured by the fire. Keith took a while to return and when he did, he was full of more news.

"It's a massive fire at some private club just around the corner, the whole building is alight. Hey if you want to take a look, you can see it from the roof."

"Yes, might as well do something while I wait for the band to go back on."

Felicity followed Keith along some more corridors and then up a tiny flight of stairs, hidden behind a curtain. They pushed through a door and then out into the open. The city of London opened up on every horizon as she turned in a complete circle, only stopping at the sign of smoke plumes in the sky. She walked closer to the edge of the roof and watched the flames lick the sky. She covered her mouth with her hands, the shocking reality hitting her as she turned away and threw up the last of her lunch from earlier.

"Are you all right?" Keith asked, walking towards her as her hair hung over her face.

"It's such a scary sight," she mumbled, fishing out a small tissue from her back pocket. She wiped her mouth and stood up again. Keith held open his arms and she stepped into them.

"I'd love to see you again," he whispered into her ear. "Can I take you out sometime?"

"Uh, I don't know," she replied, catching his eager, lust-filled gaze.

"Here's my phone number, just give me a call."

More sirens screamed down the street and further blue lights mingled with the orange heat haze.

"Christ, there must be people inside," Keith said. "Perhaps we'd better get back inside."

Felicity nodded and took his hand as she followed him back down the staircase and into the corridor. The band had just launched into their second set so Keith returned to his post and Felicity to the small stool by the curtains. The crowd appreciated the music. Felicity decided it was ok but not a patch on her favourite bands. She looked at the piece of paper still in her hand, but she had no intention of going anywhere with Keith, after all his talk about his own flat and his ambitions of becoming a lawyer.

CHAPTER 23

The melody of the last song subdued the audience into silence. A few lit up their lighters and started to sway to the more melodic sound of a single, acoustic guitar. Her dad was centre stage now next to the singer. Something in the tune sounded familiar and Felicity shut her eyes. She'd heard this as a child echoing up the stairs of the small house as she fell asleep.

"This song is especially for my daughter, hiding in the wings," Darren said in the gap before Doug the singer started.

It truly was a tribute to her mother's looks and their youthful relationship. Felicity felt a tear slide down her cheek. She didn't want to admit it but she was missing her mum more than she thought. Perhaps she'd give it a few days and send her a letter. Perhaps she could forgive her for the lack of contact through the years from her real dad? But could she forgive her for leading her into the hands of Malcolm, or had his words been lies? The concert finished to rapturous applause and a couple more songs for an encore, before the audience filed out.

Her dad appeared in the wings and hugged her close.

"I remembered the song from when I was a child," she murmured.

"I thought you might, it was our biggest seller a couple of years ago, even made the top 20," he said, proudly. "Uh, why don't you head back to the hotel, I've got a few autographs to sign."

She nodded, realising she was unwanted yet again, understanding that female fans didn't want to see their idol with his grown-up daughter when they were barely older than her. She was about to sidle out through the back door when Keith spotted her and ran over.

"Are you going or do you fancy hanging around and coming out for a drink with me and the other guys and girls working here?"

Felicity shrugged. "Yeah, why not it beats sitting in a hotel room."

She followed the small crowd out onto the street. They could still hear sirens echoing from the fire and Keith took great pleasure in telling them all it was from the private club round the corner. He was holding her hand tightly but Felicity didn't mind, it felt good to have an even tighter alibi, should she need it.

After a few bars Felicity was yawning, the adrenaline wearing off after the excitement of earlier.

"I'm going to go," she said to Keith, swallowing the last of her drink.

"I'll walk you, unless you fancy coming back to mine." His hopeful expression was plastered in his puppy dog expression.

"Thanks Keith, but I'm going to crash and then spend a little time with my dad tomorrow morning before he leaves for Paris."

Luckily it was only a short walk to the hotel and Felicity endured the kiss that lingered on her lips. When he was gone she wiped it away. There would be no more love for her after Tony's betrayal. Crawling beneath the sheets she slept with no dreams or nightmares to plague her, just plans for the future.

The next morning she went down for breakfast alone, she'd knocked her dad's door but got no answer. In the dining room she listened to the buzz of the other guests and most of them were talking about the fire of last night. A couple discarded their newspaper so Felicity picked it up and took it back to her room. She knew she needed to get out to the bank as quickly as possible and withdraw all her money. But the headline on the local paper stopped her in her tracks:

Successful businessman suspected dead, killed in fire.

The room around her spun out of control, like a fast-paced fairground ride. Sinking to her knees Felicity felt tears prick her eyelids. She cried for a bit before the power and triumph took over. Her cries of horror turned to laughter; she'd accomplished more than she thought by her little act of vandalism. Oh and it had been so easy, so quick and so satisfying. She lay on the bed for a while, wondering what to do next. If she went back to the house today she could get some more of her things from it but equally, she could get collared by the police as it said in the article they were looking for a suspected arsonist.

A knock on the door interrupted her thoughts so she opened it to find Doug there.

"Have you seen your dad this morning?"

"Nope, I knocked but got no answer."

"Ok, I'll have to get the hotel staff to unlock his door, we're leaving in an hour," he grumbled, wandering off down the corridor.

Felicity waited in her doorway for the porter to arrive with Doug, opening the door to let him in. Following him in Felicity looked around at the room, littered again with further clothing and underwear. Doug rushed into the bedroom and then quickly backed out again, holding his mouth as his wide eyes stared at her. She stepped forward and he tried to stop her pushing past him. The stench of stale vomit filled the air. Two bodies lay prone on the bed, immobile, cold and dead. A needle was on the side along with the remains of white powder. Felicity turned and ran, her mind unable to cope with the full impact of the scene. Her legs refused to move any further than the hotel corridor and she staggered and fell against the wall. Tears stung her swollen eyes as she replayed the image from the hotel room and it morphed into her father on stage, singing the song for her mother. Her dead mother! She was now an orphan.

The police arrived to find her still slumped in the corridor as Doug tried to console her. A police woman sat down next to her.

"Who are you? Can you tell me your connection to the people in the room?"

"He was my dad," she squeezed out. "I only just met him again after thirteen years of no contact." Her sobs took control and she shook while arms stretched across to hug her.

"It's ok love, can we contact your mother for you?"

Felicity swallowed and then recited the phone number and address for her mum before she tried to stand up, her legs still wobbly beneath her.

Doug offered a hand and she took the few steps across to the room she was staying in. Not closing the door she crawled under the bed covers, shivers running through her body. The police woman followed her in and sat down on the edge.

"We've just tried to phone her but there's no answer. We'll keep trying and if necessary, we'll call to the house. Will you be staying here?"

"Yes."

"Well, if you need to call us here is the number for the station." She stood up and backed out of the room. The door clicked shut and rolling over, Felicity gave way to all the tears damned up inside her.

She must have slept because the next thing she heard was a knock at the door. She sat up and took a moment to compose her features. Her eyes felt sticky and as she crossed the room to the door, she glanced in the mirror. Her skin was pink and blotchy, her eyes red rimmed from the tears. The same police woman stood there, taking in the sight of Felicity in all her rawness.

"Can I come in?" she asked.

"Yeah." Felicity held the door fully open and let her inside. "Can I just pop to the bathroom?"

The PC nodded and watched the young girl move slowly out of sight. She looked around and found a kettle on the side so she flicked the switch and waited for it to boil. She heard water running and then Felicity returned, swathed in one of the hotel robes.

"Shall I make you a tea?"

Felicity nodded and sat back down on the bed, watching as the PC filled the cups and then passed her one. She perched on the edge of the bed and took a sip, clearing her throat of the bad news she had to impart.

"I'm afraid I have some more bad news for you. I tried to contact your mother and received no answer so I called to the address and there was no one home. I guess your mum remarried as the house was registered to the owner of the club that burnt down last night." She gulped, watching Felicity's pale skin turn even whiter.

"Yes, my stepfather Malcolm," Felicity stammered out, looking down at the cover on the bed beneath her.

"The police are still searching for bodies this morning but everyone in the club perished. His car was outside so we assume he was inside and your mother may have been with him since we can't find her."

A solitary tear ran down and dropped over the ledge of her cheekbone, making no sounds as it landed on the bed cover. Felicity covered her face with her hands, partly from the shock and partly to hide the grin that threatened to spill out onto her features. He was dead.

"Have you got any other family you can stay with while this is all sorted out?"

"My nanna and granddad, they live in the Midlands somewhere."

Felicity gave as much detail as she had but since they'd moved recently, she had no idea of their new address.

"We'll find them for you, but in the meantime do you have a friend who can stay with you?"

Felicity shook her head. "I'll be fine here."

The PC nodded and stood up, finishing her cooling cup of tea. She reached out and placed a hand on Felicity's shoulder. "Pretty rough day," she whispered. Felicity just nodded and kept her head down.

Once the door closed and the footsteps had disappeared, Felicity let out a howl of laughter. Her plan had worked and by the sound of it, she was not at all implicated at the moment. Jumping off the bed she danced round the room until her thoughts took her back to her real mum and dad, now both gone. A fresh start in the Midlands with her grandparents might be just what she needed to escape the horrors she'd endured whilst also giving her time to plan her revenge on Tony. He still needed to pay for leading her to Malcolm, even if he had been ordered to.

A little later in the day she got dressed and walked out into the fading light. She wandered up the street and turned the corner to see the smouldering ruins of the club. It was cordoned off and the firemen and police had left. She turned and walked quickly away. Finding an open chip shop she bought some and scurried back to the safety of the hotel room. Outside her door stood a guitar and tapped to it, a short note. She ripped it open and discovered it was from the rest of the band, a condolence card for her loss. She held the neck of the guitar and carried it into the room. She would never play it but it could sit with her teddy bear as a reminder that one man had truly loved her, a long time ago.

CHAPTER 24

Felicity settled into life with her grandparents. They had been devastated at the death of their daughter but surprisingly, not so about her new husband. Felicity had wavered between wanting to comfort and cry with them or tell them what he had done to her that apparently her mother had known about. The three of them had made a small party at the funeral, while Tony was noted for his absence. The police closed their investigations after finding the remains of a cigarette in one of the bins and deciding that it was just an unlucky accident that it had caught fire. Felicity guessed that there were a few people who'd had grudges against Malcolm and his door policy in the past and she also knew that a police commissioner was one of his regulars and didn't want too much investigating to take place. He had secrets to hide. Felicity did too but she was a good actress and just applied her sorrowful face whenever strangers asked about her parents. Her real dad's death had also made the headlines a couple of days later, after the coroner reported accidental death and drugs as the cause. Her mother never got a mention in that report.

Life near Birmingham was much quieter than she was used to. She soon got a part-time job in a nearby estate agents with her secretarial skills and twice a week she went swimming at the local pool. She'd noticed a sign saying they were holding training courses to become lifeguards so with some trepidation she applied. Being in the water was a bittersweet experience for her. It would forever remind her of Tony and she still felt the pain in her heart at his betrayal. But he'd been a brilliant teacher and six weeks later she was a fully qualified lifeguard.

With nervous excitement she arrived for her first day and discovered that she was the only female amongst the men.

"Hi Felicity," Mr Crane, the leisure centre manager greeted her.

"Hello," she replied, watching his eyes slide over the curves she couldn't hope to hide in her uniform of shorts and t-shirt.

"Let me introduce you to everyone before I hand you over to Richard who will talk you though the various jobs we do. Don't think for one moment that you'll be just swanning around the poolside all day." His eyes were now fixed to her chest and Felicity tried not to move and jiggle.

"This is Anna the receptionist," he gestured over to the plump, blonde woman behind the counter.

"Hi Anna," Felicity smiled, but again felt the grimace of a woman less than friendly towards a nubile eighteen year old.

"Here's Richard, Derek and Sam." The three other lifeguards stepped forward. Richard was in his late twenties but the other two were around her age, possibly a little older. Felicity noted their cocky smiles and hungry gaze as they appraised their new workmate.

"Hi," she replied, licking her lips slightly to put the sheen back on the gloss she was wearing.

With Derek and Sam taking the first shift poolside, Felicity followed Richard through the men's changing area before the centre opened.

"So the women's is the same layout as this, just on the other side of the staff area behind reception. Now we have you on the team, Anna and Cass the other receptionist won't be called upon to check the cleanliness of this area. That will be your sole responsibility with the guys doing the gents' area." They walked through a door and found the staff area. Shelves loomed from floor to ceiling, tagged with numbers and coloured boxes.

"Have you ever worked in this environment before?" he asked.

She was pleased to note that he actually looked her in the face and was treating her like a person, not an object.

"Nope, just at my stepfather's club as a cloakroom attendant."

"Well, it's probably a similar system then. Each bay has a box and a corresponding ankle tag. As a customer comes in you give them a box, they then change and place their clothes and bags into it and hand it back to you. You then give them the ankle tag from the board. Pretty simple eh?"

"Yes, no problem."

"So part of your shift will be doing this, part will be checking and keeping the showers and toilets clean and up to standard, with a rinse over the tiles on the floor twice a day. Then the rest will be on poolside. We always double up unless we're really short staffed."

They walked into the staff room area which was tiny and held two chairs, a kettle and some mugs.

"Let me make you a brew and you can take a look at your shifts. I'll have to wait to introduce you to Rob and Gareth who will be in later in the week and Cass who's the other receptionist."

Felicity could hear the excited hubbub of parents and children arriving for the first session of the day. She peeped through the crack in the door and saw the pool starting to fill up. She saw Sam perched on the highchair at the deep end whilst Derek lingered near the shallow end. She finished her tea and Richard stood up.

"Here, I'll show you the rest of the centre, gym and the small refreshments area upstairs and then we will take over on the poolside."

"Lead on," she replied, although she already knew the upstairs layout, having been using the place ever since she'd moved in with her grandparents. It had sort of become her refuge from the slow pace of life she inhabited once she stepped through the door of their house. Felicity was saving all her spare money so that she could buy her own place. Malcolm's will had failed to acknowledge his second marriage and step-daughter. Her father's legacy had been pumped into him through drugs and alcohol dependence and she guessed that his guitar would not be worth much.

Shaking free of her memories she smiled and nodded her way around and onto the poolside. She enjoyed the feeling of stepping along the tiles, glancing over the various ages in the pool. Shouting or blowing her whistle if anyone stepped out of line or failed to adhere to the rules of the posters. Her first day went fast and once she finished her shift she changed and did her lengths in the pool. Leaving the centre she heard Sam shout her name.

"Hey, Felicity do you want a lift home?"

"No thanks," she muttered, turning and taking the normal path. She enjoyed the walk and took an interest in the building work taking place on a large mansion. The local newspaper had reported it was to become a hotel but had failed to reveal the mysterious owner. Felicity hadn't spotted him yet but she admired his ambitions. Having tasted the luxury life with her stepfather, she longed for it again.

Work the next day included meeting Rob, Gareth and then Cass. The bubbly blonde on reception was a year older than Felicity and in that moment a friendship was formed as Cass spotted a kindred spirit.

"Hey, can I call you Flick?" she asked, chewing on her gum and smiling broadly.

"Sure Cass."

"Yeah it's short for Cassandra, what a crap name to get stuck with," she chuckled.

Felicity basked in the warmth of her newfound friendship as they shared a cup of coffee later in the morning.

"So, are you doing anything Saturday night?" Cass asked. "Cos I fancy checking out the new nightclub in Birmingham and could do with a new accomplice."

"Yeah, sounds ok," Felicity replied, caught in her infectious chatter and deciding that she couldn't sit at home alone for the rest of her life.

"Great, we can have a gossip away from the guys here, who believe it or not are the biggest blabbermouths I know."

"Oh, they've been pretty quiet around me so far," Felicity confessed.

"That's cos they've all got bets on who snogs you first, well except Richard who's a sweetie and married."

With this information to hand Felicity nodded, realising the requests to go out for drinks, walking or driving her home were fuelled by more than just being friendly. Men were all the same, only after one thing, but they'd be waiting a long time for her. Or maybe she could have a little fun here? As she sauntered round the pool with Sam she kept glimpsing over at him, letting her eyes appraise the body beneath his uniform. It wasn't bad but nowhere close to Tony, who appeared to be her benchmark. His blondish ginger hair was kind of cute as it flopped over his eyes. Passing along the side she let her hand glance across his arm, brushing it softly. He looked at her in surprise and then grinned before they lost contact. Over the rest of the week she did similar things with Gareth, Rob and Derek. All it took was a tiny touch, a flutter of her eyelashes, a brush of her body if they passed in the corridor. By the end of the week they were all panting for her, each believing they stood the best chance of a date and the pool of money for the winner of the bet.

"So Flick, what are you up to this weekend?" Sam asked, as they cleaned up after the final swimmers on Friday evening.

"Out with Cass tomorrow night."

"Where you going, perhaps I can join you?"

"Ok, but keep this secret. I'll be in The King's Gate pub from seven."

Sam grinned, blushed and then hurried away. The next to approach her was Derek, who she fed the same information but changed the time to 7.15pm. She'd let Cass in on the joke so she had informed both Gareth and Rob about their fictional night out. Each of them had a slightly different time for the same pub, with her and Cass planning to pop in for a quick drink at eight to see them all looking bemused. Cass had also entered the sweepstake at the last minute and although the guys had been surprised, she knew that she would win it. The plan was foolproof.

The next evening Felicity scanned her wardrobe and found her favourite mini skirt, boots and fringed, low-cut top. With her hair flicked out in the latest Farrah Fawcett type style, she slicked her red lipstick on. She looked in the mirror and smiled. *Look what you're missing Tony.* She always spoke to his picture that was taken on holiday. Her emotions for him swung to and fro like a pendulum. One minute she was yearning for his touch, remembering his words and the way he obeyed Malcolm. The other she hated him for being a coward and not standing up to his own father. With her coat on she slipped out of the door.

"Bye Nan, I'll be home tomorrow," she shouted.

"Yes, dear," her Nan replied.

Felicity trotted off down the drive and took the short walk into town. It was almost eight and she met Cass on the corner of the main street.

"You ready?" she said, linking her arm through Flick's.

"Yeah, you bet," Felicity replied as they marched up the street and into the warmth of the pub. The guys were all stood together, each having looked sheepish, as each had arrived earlier in the evening to find no sign of Felicity. They knew they'd been played.

"Oh look, everyone from work is here," Cass said, pushing against Sam so she could get to the bar.

"Well, that's a surprise," Felicity laughed, looking at each of them in turn. "I'm sorry that none of you are going to win your sweepstake." She flicked her hair over her shoulder and turned to Cass.

"I think I might," Cass said, hearing her cue. Stepping forward she snaked her arm around Felicity's waist, pulling her tight and then reaching to plant a kiss on the lips of her friend. The guys gasped at the overtly sexual display of two girls kissing. They broke apart and Cass squared up to them all.

"Where's my money, I believe I'm the lucky winner."

Each of the guys produced their five pound notes and passed them to Cass who bestowed a kiss on each of their cheeks as a consolation prize.

They downed their drinks and then walked back to the door.

"Oh aren't you at least going to buy us a drink?" Sam whined.

"Nope," Cass replied, as they stepped outside and walked to the bus stop. They giggled their way to Birmingham and shared stories of their past. Well Cass did, Felicity shared very little, not wanting anyone to know what she'd endured. Her mind had locked it away where it festered and grew into a bitter ball of hatred and distrust against everyone.

The club was crowded and both girls enjoyed the loud mix of rock and pop music that flowed through the hot atmosphere.

Upstairs in the private bar, Tony was startled to see Felicity in his new haunt. *What is she doing here?* He'd tried to forget her and had deliberately resisted attending the joint funeral. His mother had received the full estate, including the house and had decided to sell it. She'd split the money between the two of them, so he'd put his with the early inheritance money and was now renovating his first ever hotel and health spa on the outskirts of Warwick. Meanwhile he enjoyed the social scene in Birmingham in his penthouse flat. Life was good and he kind of got the feeling that Felicity would not be too happy to see him again.

Felicity gazed around at the opulent surroundings whilst Cass tried to get her to talk to the friend of the guy she'd pulled on the dance floor. With a sigh Felicity smiled and nodded in all the right places but when the time came to leave, she backed away from any contact.

"Mick gave me his number," Cass said, as they settled back down on the back seat of the last bus.

"He seems nice."

"Gorgeous more like, guess you weren't interested in his friend then

124

as we could have arranged a double date?"

"Well, if you want to I will but he's not really my type."

"And what is your type then?" Cass asked, curious about her friend's mysterious past.

"Someone I just couldn't have," she sighed and turned away, the image of Tony uppermost in her mind as Cass draped an arm around her shoulders.

"Let's go again next week, perhaps we'll try another club?"

Felicity giggled and rested her head against her friend's, tired and just a little bit drunk.

CHAPTER 25

1985

By 1985 Felicity had become the leisure centre manager, Cass had left to get married and have babies and most of the other lads had long since been replaced by a new team of young, handsome lifeguards. A few tried it on with their attractive boss and sometimes she enjoyed a little playtime in her office. One of her previous lovers had introduced her to bondage and domination. Sitting in her office which overlooked the pool she closed her eyes and remembered Vince. They had only split up the previous year after he had tried to be her master, but had failed miserably when he realised that she preferred to be in control. Giggling softly she sipped the hot coffee that Brad had brought in for her a few minutes ago. He was her newest lifeguard and he was creating a stir amongst the women who used the pool. Going back to her daydream she substituted Vince for Brad and thought about how he'd look chained up in her spare room that doubled as her playroom.

He was only nineteen to her twenty-six years but she knew she could pass for younger most of the time. She still kept her hair long but preferred to wear it tied up in a high ponytail, which drew attention to her sharp blue eyes and the bright red lipstick she always wore. Licking her tongue over them she watched Brad walk around the perimeter of the pool, his firm ass filling the tight red shorts to perfection. How she'd love to pull them down and turn his ass the same shade…

Grinning, she finished her coffee and paperwork before wandering down to the pool.

"Hi Brad, how are you finding things?" she asked, relishing the looks a few of the female swimmers were shooting at her.

"Good thanks, Miss Jennings."

"Oh just call me Felicity, we're all on the same team here," she replied, letting her hand reach out to touch his shoulder.

"Felicity, um. I do need to ask about annual leave when you have a moment?"

"Sure, pop up to my office when you finish your time here and we'll take a look at the planner, together." She dropped her voice, leaning in so that her breath tickled his ear. She felt him flinch slightly at her close proximity, enjoying the sharp scent of his aftershave even though he probably didn't need to shave that much.

"Thanks, Felicity," he finished, staring down at the swimmers in the water.

"See you later," she breathed, letting her hand run down the firm muscles of his back before giving him a tiny tap on the butt. She flicked her ponytail and then sauntered casually past Martin who she smiled brightly at, making him blush. She loved being the queen of all she surveyed.

Brad knocked on the door and waited for her reply.

"Come in," she answered. "Lock it behind you, we don't want to be disturbed."

She watched him look flustered at her request but he did as asked and then she motioned for him to sit down on the chair. Sauntering around, she perched on the desk in front of him, crossing her legs and kicking off her trainers. Brad couldn't help but admire her thighs.

"So which dates did you want?" Felicity continued with the business in hand, leaning over to the side to grab a pen and her diary.

"That seems in order but only if you pass your three-month trial period."

"Well do you have any issues with my work this month?" he asked, his eyes straying up to hers, but taking a while as he took in the cleavage of her low-cut white t-shirt. It wasn't strictly uniform but as she was the boss it didn't matter.

"I might need to take a look at your final clean of the changing facilities this evening."

"Ok." He nodded and waited for her to say anything more. Instead she uncrossed her legs and stood up before him, wandering around the desk and giving him a good view of her ass, tight in the shorts. Brad stood up and walked towards the door.

"Just a minute," she called, watching him turn. "Any chance you can give my shoulders a quick rub, they're feeling a bit tight."

She licked her lips, putting the shine back on the red gloss. He nodded and walked around to stand behind her chair. His hands touched her shoulders and started to press and squeeze as Felicity let out a long sigh

"Oh that feels like magic, you have a lovely touch," she purred.

She also knew that he would be enjoying the view of her ample assets as they jiggled in their tight confines.

"Thanks Brad, I'll see you later."

Her day dragged as she ploughed through the paperwork, a list of new applicants for the receptionist job which she sorted into a pile for interview. Perhaps she'd ask Brad to help her, see if the applicants could keep their mind on the job and not the men. Then as she heard the front door lock she sprayed her perfume and went down to the changing rooms. Becky, one of only two female lifeguards, was cleaning the ladies' changing room. She doubled her efforts when she saw Felicity stalk in.

"Looking good Becky, just go when you're finished."

Then she turned away and walked through the staff area to find Brad unfurling the hose pipe.

"Just forget I'm here, I'll just observe," she said, walking past him. She held her hand on the tap. "Just tell me when."

He turned and nodded, his eyes so focused on her that as the water shot out of the hose it splashed across her t-shirt.

"Oh god, I'm so sorry," he stuttered, blushing as her lacy bra came into view. Shocked by the cold water, Felicity stepped closer to him and turned the tap back off.

"I have a spare t-shirt in the staff room, pop and get me that and a towel." He rushed away and she followed him so that when he turned around she was there in the room. The door behind her pulled shut. Slowly she slipped off her t-shirt to reveal her wet skin.

"Oh, I'll just let you change," he mumbled, trying to step past her but she caught his arm.

"I think you'd better help me dry off and apologise for your lack of concentration."

She could feel the tension in his body at her request and she smiled as he clumsily patted the skin of her stomach with the towel he held.

"Bit higher," she said. "Don't worry, I don't bite unless you want me to." Her voice was low and seductive. Brad swallowed and allowed his hands to touch gently across her bra, the towel the barrier.

"Why don't you take it off," she murmured, letting her head nestle into the crook of his neck, breathing in his youthful scent. He dropped the towel and reached around to the catch that held her supported. She shrugged it from her shoulders and let it slide down her arms. Before he could back away she caught the hem of his t-shirt, pulling it over his head in a swift move. Stepping back slightly so she could take him all in, she let her nail run casually from his shoulder blade down to the waist-band on his shorts. He was about to say something as his mouth opened and then shut again as she slipped his shorts down, letting them fall and hit the tiles.

Brad was blushing and trying hard not to feel aroused by the sight of his boss, topless and just in her shorts. His cock stirred and rose to attention for her. She smirked and looked at the clock on the wall.

"Oops, I have a date," she said, grabbing her spare t-shirt and covering up. She deliberately turned and bent down in front of him to retrieve her bra. She let her ass rub over his cock briefly before she stalked out of the room. Brad stood there, confused and aroused in equal measure. Did she want him to follow her? Force himself upon her? Or was she just playing games?

"Brad, can you lock up when you finish," she shouted.

She didn't wait for his reply as she walked out through the door, still chuckling over his shocked face. Fair play, he had a great body and maybe next week she'd sample him!

Feeling violated he tried to sweep the images of her beautiful breasts and the feel of her firm ass from his mind. In the end it was no good as he reached down and with a firm hand, dealt with his erection.

For the next week Felicity played the game, flirting madly with Brad when they were alone, brushing past him in the tight staff corridor and generally toying with him. On Friday evening they were the last two in the building as Steve had gone home sick earlier in the day. Cleaning the changing rooms always made Felicity feel grubby so once she'd finished, she stood naked in the showers and let the water swill over her body.

"I'm finished now, can I head home?" She heard Brad shout.

"How about I take you for a drink first," she replied, turning the shower off and wandering into the staff room where she'd left her towel. He was pulling his bag from the locker but turned and dropped it to find her naked.

"I'm supposed to be meeting my girlfriend."

"Oh, we'll be quick. I'd hate for you to have to pull all the weekend shifts the rest of the month."

Brad checked his watch, he wasn't meeting Jess until eight so he had a couple of hours until he had to pick her up. He nodded and looked away as she dried off and dressed.

Felicity had chosen her favourite tight fitting dress for this seduction. Her skyscraper heels made her the same height as him. She pulled on her coat and they stepped out of the building together. They stopped outside the wine bar at the corner of the street.

"Here will do just fine," she murmured, waiting as Brad opened the door for her and they entered. It was quiet at this time of the evening so they picked a table in the corner and ordered. Two martinis on the rocks made their conversation lively and free flowing. Felicity endured Brad enthusing about his girlfriend Jess whilst beneath the table, she rested her hand on his thigh, feeling the firm defined lines of his muscles.

"Look I'm going to have to get going," Brad apologised as the time ticked on.

"Well at least walk me back to my place, it's not far."

"Sure."

At the door of her house, Felicity pulled him close.

"Do you really have to leave?" Her voice tickled the tiny hairs on his neck as she kissed his ear. Pushing her body in closer so that he could inhale her perfume, she said, "You can call your girlfriend from here, say you've been held up at work."

Her lips were working their way around his chiselled jaw line, catching on the beginnings of stubble.

"I... I guess I could, but just half an hour," Brad relented before their lips met in a kiss that left Felicity in no doubt that he was open to more.

She turned the key in the lock and they stumbled through the doorway before Brad pinned her against the wall. In the pause she took his hand and led him towards her bedroom.

"I'm just going to freshen up," she said, "but make yourself comfy."

Her eyes gestured towards the large bed that dominated the room.

She wandered into the spare room where she kept her clothes. She chose her favourite basque, bright red with black lace trim. It accented her slim waist and pushed her breasts to a point where they looked ready to topple out. Shaking her hair loose she pulled on her stockings and heels and picked up her favourite toy from the top of the chest of drawers. Grinning, she slicked on more red lipstick and sauntered back.

Brad was lying naked on the bed, obviously happy in his skin and physique. His hand was idly stroking his cock as he checked her out. He'd always wanted an older woman, so perhaps he'd learn a thing or two to show Jess.

"Mmmh, I see you're ready and waiting..." She stepped closer. "...but I think I'll restrain you."

A brief glint of apprehension coloured his expression but was overruled by lust as she bent across him, allowing him the full view of her cleavage.

"But I want to touch you," he breathed.

"All in good time, if I only teach you one thing this evening it will be patience."

"Yes, Felicity," he replied.

"No, it's yes Mistress," she intoned, her hand running up his arm to lock his wrist in place. She did the same with his other before standing back, pondering if she needed to do his ankles.

Grinning down at him she did his ankles too before standing back to admire him stretched and spread-eagle before her. A brief moment of utter power bloomed inside her and radiated through to stain her cheeks pink.

"So you're going to do exactly what I ask of you, understand?"

"Yes."

"Yes, what?" She picked up her riding crop from the side table and tapped him lightly on his thigh, liking the sound of the thwack it made.

"Yes, Mistress," Brad said, still smiling as she let the leather end run higher up to skim the underside of his balls.

Then she laid it back down on the covers of the bed and stalked around to stand at the head of the bed. She loosened the first two catches on her corset and freed her breasts, cupping them in her hands and watching the breath catch in his throat. Bending over him she dangled one just out of reach of his mouth, watching him strain against his bindings to reach. She dipped lower and felt the soft skin of his lips graze hers. The stubble on his chin was just a brief roughness as his mouth opened and she felt the first tentative touch of his tongue. Then, feeling braver he nibbled lightly, waiting for a sign that she was enjoying this. Felicity kept her eyes open, she was always in control and it was the power trip that was feeding her desire. She moved so his tongue trailed between the valley and back up to do the same to her other breast.

Straightening again she looked down at Brad.

"Not bad," she murmured.

Hooking her fingers into the elastic of her knickers she slid them down her thighs and stepped out of them. Picking them up between her fingers she dangled them over his face. Brad's nostrils quivered as he took a deep breath, relishing in the scent of her sex that clung to the lace.

Straddling his face she lowered down so that he could let his tongue do the work. His touch was too eager, flickering here and there with no real movement or understanding of the female anatomy.

"Slowly," she whispered. "Do it like you're savouring your favourite food and I'll do the moving."

Her orgasm began to build as she swung her hips so that his tongue caught her clit with every lick. Closing her eyes she saw him, his blond hair slick against his head, his dark dangerous eyes and the way he'd moved her body in a way she still didn't understand. The desire faded and she pulled away, watching Brad lick his lips of her juice.

Would she ever be free of the ghost of Tony?

"Not bad, there's still room for improvement though," she said, granting him a swift kiss of her lips. She picked up her crop again and trailed it down his sternum and then flicked it lightly over his erection. Bending down again she let her mouth open to swallow him, flitting over the head with her tongue. Because he was so tightly bound he was unable to buck against her and she kept her touch light, knowing it must be torturing him to hell.

"More Mistress, more," he groaned.

Knowing he was close she pulled back and curled her hand around his girth.

"Let me love you," he pleaded, but she was silent to his whims.

He spurted his arc over the covers and the top of his thighs. Felicity dropped her hand away and wiped her palm quickly, feeling dirty and ashamed as well as jubilant. Another helpless male had got off on her power trip!

She stepped out of the room and immediately into her bathroom, letting water spill into her bath. Wrapped in her dressing gown she returned to unbind him. He moved to wrap her in his arms but she stepped away.

"I'm your boss remember," she scolded. "Now, you'd better get dressed or you'll be very late for your date."

Brad was stunned by her reaction but still reeling from his orgasm, he did as she asked, slipping into his clothes and shoes. By the door he paused.

"Can we do that again sometime?"

"We'll see." She let her finger run up his arm and she leaned in to kiss his cheek. "If you're a good boy and keep this our little secret."

CHAPTER 26

1988

The scent of gardenia filled the house as Felicity poured her glass of wine and then slipped under the surface of the bathwater. Its heat scalded her as she scrubbed furiously for the first few moments, ensuring no trace of Brad was left. No matter how much she was attracted to them, none of the men she'd had could measure up to Tony and she wondered if any would. In the silence of the house she sank back and relived her favourite memories but they were always tainted at the end. Malcolm would appear, his face puce, his eyes dark and filled with forbidden desire. It was strange but those memories always had her floating above the scene, watching her body at the mercy of him and his friends. There had to be more to life than this? When was it her turn to find love or was she forever scarred? To remind her of this thought, the towel she rubbed over her body caught the brand on her back.

To all those around her, Felicity led a charmed life. She moved to a larger house and began to manage two leisure centres in 1988, driving between the two in her company car. She demanded this from the owner and after a few mutual sessions of intense discussion, she'd gotten her way. She had a busy day ahead, more interviews for more lifeguards. Staff turnover was relatively high, partly due to her she guessed. The men who remained discreet stayed, the others were found breaking the rules and summarily dismissed. With her first cup of coffee and the sounds of staff cleaning, ready for opening, she pulled out the interview questions and the list of candidates. By midday she was bored, two of the candidates were just out of high school and still needed to take their lifeguard exams, so she had little use for them as she needed someone to start immediately if not sooner.

Stepping out of her office she stopped in her tracks. A guy stood there and he reminded her of Tony, except for his blue eyes as he looked up and then stood.

"Hi, I'm James Cooke," he said.

"Hello, I'm Ms Jennings but you can call me Felicity." She let a light girly giggle lift her voice. "Follow me."

Turning, she made sure her ass swayed as she walked down the corridor and they entered the office. Unusually, she felt flustered as she shuffled his CV and application form to the top. At the same time she allowed her eyes to peep over the top edge of the paper, taking in his short blond hair and the long lashes that framed the blue of his eyes. Something about him drew her back to the sun of Spain and the swimming pool where she'd begun this journey.

Rattling through her questions Felicity tried to contain her breathing, but it felt like she was eighteen again as she realised that James was on the verge of turning twenty-one.

"Well, I believe that you're just the person I've been looking for," she concluded, standing up and reaching her hand out to him. "Welcome aboard, the job's yours if you want it."

"Thank you," James said, feeling relief flood through him. He now had a job that would keep him going until he could apply to the Fire Service. Not bad for the first week in a new place. His day would be made up if Stephanie had sent him a letter. He kind of hoped she had. Blinking back the image of her standing in the rain, he shook Felicity's hand.

"So I'll pop you a letter in the post to confirm the appointment and I'll see you here bright and early next Monday morning."

"Thank you Ms Jennings, oh I mean Felicity," he replied before leaving the office. Felicity watched the trousers of his suit cling to his ass as he walked away. She couldn't wait to see him in the uniform for his first day. She dismissed the rest of the candidates waiting and then sat back in her office chair. She let it swing around so she could stare out over the pool area. Her battered and bloodstained heart was beating ever so slightly faster than she was used to. Perhaps she was capable of love and could move away from her destructive past?

Picking up the phone she dialled Cass and waited for her to answer, at the same time kicking off her shoes and regarding her painted toenails. She desperately needed a girly chat and a pampering.

"Hi Cass," Felicity said, when the phone clicked in.

"Ooh Felicity, now to what do I owe a phone call in the middle of a working day?"

"I thought we should have a catch up, perhaps at the new health spa hotel."

"Sounds serious."

"It might just be Cass, it might just be. Oh and I'll treat you," she finished.

"Thanks hun, I need a break from the kids," she said, as the sound of a scream rent through the air from her side of the conversation.

"Excellent, I'll pick you up on Saturday morning." She didn't wait for Cass to answer, knowing that her attention was already on her offspring.

The drive to the spa on Saturday morning was a good one; the mood between them was just like it had been for those few years when they'd been out and about on the town together. Felicity cast a critical glance at her friend, now suffering from a deluge of baby fat that she was struggling to shift. With two kids under five, Felicity wondered how she'd cope if she ever had a child of her own. Shrugging the dark thoughts away of her own mother and father, she smiled brightly.

"I've booked us in for a manicure and pedicure before a massage and a swim," Felicity said, as she parked the car in front of the imposing building. Felicity couldn't believe how long it had taken to build and finally open, mystery still surrounding the reclusive owner. News had spread that this was just the first in a chain and work had now started on one in Manchester and London.

Smart-suited men and women milled around the foyer and although Felicity fitted in nicely in her bright red mini suit, she tried to avoid the looks her friend was getting. The scent of money was in the air and Felicity breathed it in, knowing that she would inhabit this world again one day.

Feeling the luxury of the padded, plush dressing gowns they followed the women to the treatment room. With an accompanying glass of champagne Felicity took a sip and smiled. This was the life, as she imagined swanning around this palatial place, clicking her fingers for a member of staff to fulfil her every whim.

"So, what's the pool gossip then?" Cass asked, as she let the beautician go to work on her toes.

"What gossip do you want? Mr Crane has given me a company car which we've just driven here in, all expenses paid and I might even claim this back off him." Felicity grinned, loving the way she had that old man wrapped around her finger.

"Any new lifeguards, it was a shame Brad didn't last longer, he was a real hit with the ladies."

"Bit too much of a hit, couldn't keep it in his pants most of the time," Felicity said, thinking of their many brief soirees. He'd kept her amused but in the end was driving her for more commitment and that was a place she hadn't been willing to go until this week.

As they chose their varnish, pale pink for Cass and a deep burgundy red for Felicity, she let a smile play over her features.

"Hey, what's the joke?" Cass asked, chuckling as the bubbles of the champagne tickled her nose.

"I just recruited a new lifeguard called James and he's rather stunning."

"Hey, he must be if you're mentioning him. You normally only tell me the details when you've sacked them!"

"Come on, I'm not that bad am I?"

"Yup, in all the years I've known you, you've never admitted to a guy turning your head. Just hinted at someone from your past that you've never said much about."

Felicity felt a blush move over her cheeks as they waited for their varnish to dry.

"See you're blushing now, this guy must be a serious hottie for you, the self-proclaimed ice queen."

"Look, it's probably nothing, perhaps I'm getting hormonal now I'm nearly thirty," Felicity said, scared to admit that she might just have feelings for this new member of staff, purely based on his looks. She stood up and waited for Cass.

"Come on I need some hot bubbly water to go with the cold one." She tapped her glass and one of the staff hurried off to get them both refills.

Soaking in the Jacuzzi, Cass pressed on.

"So, why this guy?"

"Well, if you must know he reminds me of my first boyfriend." She stumbled over the last word, not sure whether they were even that. "We were only together for a short time but…" She trailed off, struggling against the lump that still formed when she thought about Tony and what could have been before his betrayal.

"Well I'll be in on Tuesday morning for splash time so I hope he's around so I can check him out."

Felicity laughed and they sank back, letting the stress float away. Felicity was looking forward to her new employee starting work. It had been a while since she'd flirted with any of her staff. In fact rather than let any of the others show him around, she'd do it personally. Her plan was in place and later at home she plotted her moves. This time she'd go slowly, not be too overt and maybe, just maybe he'd be the one.

CHAPTER 27

She was waiting in the staff room for James to arrive so that she could introduce him to the team before the doors opened and the day began. She watched him stride inside, dressed in ripped jeans and a sweater against the cold of the February day. She had his uniform ready for him to collect in her office.

"Morning everyone," she began, commanding attention as the room went silent. "I'd like to introduce you to James Cooke, he's moved here from Herefordshire where he was a lifeguard at the council pool there. I'm sure you'll make him welcome and I'll be showing him around today."

"Thanks Ms Jennings," James said, shaking hands with the other guys in the room as he was introduced to Ian, Michael, Shaun and Kayleigh the receptionist. All the while Felicity silently studied him, the way his jaw line blended with his neck and down to the broad shoulders that then narrowed into a typical swimmer's slim waist and tight ass.

"Kayleigh, I'll patch my phone through to yours while I show James around and Ian, can you make sure that the men's changing area is spotless?" she barked, the happy atmosphere evaporating quickly as Felicity gave orders and the others scurried off.

"So James, if you follow me I can give you your uniform to change into. Then I'll meet back here," she said, letting him follow her again, hoping his gaze was appreciating the view of her long legs in the mini skirt she wore. But glancing over her shoulder she saw he was looking out over the pool area instead.

She passed him the white t-shirt and red shorts, obligatory uniform with his name already embroidered onto the small pocket by his chest. She threw him a whistle and then explained where the changing facilities were. Closing the door behind him, she leaned again it, all this professionalism a strain. With the blinds closed she shrugged off her suit and shirt before pulling on her own uniform. The material of the t-shirt just that tiny bit too small, so that depending on the light a small glimpse of her white bra could be seen. She'd had the shorts taken up and they hugged her behind to perfection whilst barely glancing the top of her thighs. Felicity was in perfect condition. She used the gym and pool every day to maintain her shape and tone. She quickly slicked on her bright red lipstick and pouted in the mirror on the back of the door. She was ready, but was James? With the blinds back up she could see him wandering around, taking in the various health and safety posters on the wall.

Stepping into the room he turned around and put his hands behind his back, like he was standing to attention.

"Put the kettle on first and we'll have a quick chat before we take in the centre," she said, watching him turn to flick the switch on the kettle.

"How do you take yours?" he asked.

"Strong with just a splash of milk." Her heart seemed to be hammering in her chest as he passed her the mug and their fingertips touched. She sat down to stop the tremble that was running down her legs and stared across at him while he stirred his cup and sat down opposite.

"So why the move here?" she asked.

"Mum and Dad made the decision as it will mean they're closer to my grandparents," he said. "This place is much bigger than I'm used to, how many pools do you have?"

"The main pool, a children's one and then the diving pool."

"Oh excellent, I'd love to improve my diving skills. We only had a small board at my last pool."

Felicity briefed him on the health and safety file, the log book for accidents and where the first aid kit was kept in the staff room. Then she stood up and they walked the building. James gasped at the large gym, filled with all the machines he would need and some he'd never seen before. Then they wandered out through the changing rooms and walked along the length of the Olympic-sized pool. He walked alongside her and

Felicity resisted the urge to rub her hand against his bare thigh.

"Wow, this is excellent," James breathed, taking in the high board of the separate pool. He saw Ian sitting in the chair at the one end whilst Michael wandered between the two smaller pools.

"Swimming is permitted after working hours and so is the use of the gym, not that you look like you need to work out that much," she flirted, letting her eyes linger over his body.

"Well, do I get started?" James asked, feeling on edge being so close to his female boss. There was something predatory about her and the way she was with him. But perhaps he was overacting on his first day. Felicity glanced at her watch to discover that the morning was about to end.

"Yes, take your lunch break and then I'll team you up with Ian for the afternoon shift poolside. I'll pop and let him know." She sauntered away from him and beckoned the other lifeguard down from his perch. Walking back through to the staff room James grabbed his lunch and the letter from Steph that he'd picked up off the mat on his way out. Her words would brighten his day like no others; perhaps there was a chance that they could be more than just friends?

Back in her office Felicity took her messages and then sat back in her chair, visibly shaking from this morning. James seemed to be everything that she could wish for, in his looks and his demeanour. She just needed to find out if he was single. Hopefully Ian would be able to answer that as she'd sent him off to the staff room for lunch and to glean this information from James. She picked at her salad but with her stomach doing somersaults she hardly touched it.

"Hi James." Ian strolled into the staff room and filled a glass with water.

"Oh hi, I think I'm working with you this afternoon."

"Yes, it will be good to get to know you and fill you in on some things you really need to know," Ian said, sitting down and opening his lunch box. James folded his letter away into his bag, hardly having read past, *Dear James...*

"So what's with Felicity?"

"You noticed then, I could see it a mile off mate, she's got the hots for you."

"Well, I guess she's kind of attractive for an older woman but..."

141

James trailed off, watching Ian furtively glancing around. Then leaning closer he kept his voice low.

"Best thing to do is just your job, don't aggravate her or you'll end up pulling all the shit shifts. She's got a temper on her but she's also a bit of a man-eater."

James breathed a sigh of relief at the last comment. "At least I wasn't just imagining the looks she was giving me."

"So are you single then?" Ian enquired, leaning back with a small smile on his face.

"Well, sort of. I left a friend behind in Ross-on-Wye and we were close but I didn't want to start anything as we were moving away but I'm really missing her."

Over lunch Ian heard all about Stephanie, and James heard all the gossip from the pool and the fact that all the staff thought Felicity was shagging the owner of the two leisure centres. James was also pleased that Felicity had already approved his leave for Valentine's Day weekend as the more he missed Stephanie, the more he knew he might just have to take the chance on a long-distance relationship.

With James on poolside Felicity was able to enjoy the uninterrupted view of him either striding around the perimeter, or sat on the chair at the far end. Before the shift finished, she wandered down and intercepted him as he walked.

"Settling in?"

"Yes, it's such a great facility. I'm looking forward to trying out the pool later."

"Perhaps I'll join you," she murmured before continuing round to speak to Ian.

James watched as she ran her hand up his thigh, leaning on it whilst he bent down to catch her words. So this was what Ian had meant in the staff room. On finishing her conversation she sashayed on round the edge and James noticed the many men staring at her as she passed them. He could tell she was drinking in the adoration. With the pool closed to the public and the changing rooms and other areas cleaned, James headed for a cubicle, determined to test out the diving boards.

"Either of you guys joining me?" James asked, as he heard Ian and Michael opening their lockers.

"Nah, got to get home," Michael said.

Ian nodded. "Me too, sorry mate, looks like you're on your own but I'll join you tomorrow after shift."

Stepping into the deserted pool area James looked around to check he was alone before diving into the main pool. Twenty lengths later and he was ready to try out the diving boards. He climbed out and walked across to the diving pool. He'd start on the small springboard first before moving up. It felt strange not to have any swimmers to avoid and he couldn't help but think of all the times he'd shown off in front of Steph and her friend Sarah. Happy memories followed him as he took three steps and bounced on the end before being catapulted into the air and over the water. He used his hands to part the surface on entry as he skimmed down to the depths before surfacing. Shaking his head he climbed out and moved to the set of three boards, low, medium and high.

Unbeknown to him, Felicity was watching him from her office, his sleek form gliding through the calm surface of the pool, spinning her back to daydreams of Tony. It was too soon for her to try anything as she watched him climb the steps to the first platform.

CHAPTER 28

The week slipped past and on Friday, Felicity called James into her office for an appraisal of his first week.

"Come in, sit down," she said, leaving him a small gap so that he had to brush past her to take a seat. She perched on the edge of her desk, kicking off her one heel and then the other.

"I'd rather be comfortable as we talk," she said, taking in his glance across at her abandoned stilettos. Her skirt rested high on her thighs and she grinned as like any red-blooded male, his eyes wandered up her legs. A pink blush touched his cheeks in an endearingly sweet way and made her smile even wider. She'd been careful not to push things, just a friendly pat on his arm when they passed in the corridor or on his shoulder when they chatted on the poolside.

"It's been a good week, but I have a slight problem with your leave request." James' face fell but he hid his disappointment.

"I need you to work on Saturday the thirteenth of February and possibly the Sunday too."

"Well, I can do the Saturday but I'm afraid I have a family engagement to attend on Sunday, back in my hometown."

"Oh." Her face fell as she slipped off the desk and placed her hand on his shoulder.

"Well that's reasonable I suppose, perhaps we can go for a drink after work on the Saturday then as I'll be covering the shift with you."

"Sure," James agreed, after all he'd heard from both Ian and Michael he'd just have to resist her advances to get the Sunday.

A tap on the door startled them from anything further.

"Hi Ian," Felicity said, opening the door.

"Here's the money from the till for today and I'm off for a quick half at the pub, are you coming Jim?"

"I'll meet you there," James replied, looking at Felicity. "Is there anything else we need to discuss?"

"Nope, off you go." She looked away as he left her office. Her best opportunity was next Saturday and she was going to take full advantage. Feeling surprisingly happy for a change she grabbed her bag and locked up. She watched James and Ian disappear into the pub on the corner but she just got in her car and drove home. Pizza and a plan of action were required for next weekend.

On Saturday morning a parcel arrived for James. Beneath the brown paper and the familiar handwriting was a Valentine's card, a brightly wrapped present and a letter. Like a child at Christmas he unwrapped the parcel and found a model kit to make a fire engine. Steph really did know him. The card was typically girly and covered in a message created with Love Heart sweets. It would make a great addition to his shelf next to the elephant toy from their last day together. Smiling, James took the letter and his coffee and retreated to the privacy of his room. His mum and dad were great but didn't half rib him sometimes. He had an hour before he needed to be at the pool so plenty of time to indulge in her words...

Dear James,

I am writing this letter to tell you how I really feel about you. I am hoping that you will read it and perhaps, you might decide that what you have read is what you might want. If not then I am sorry if this will spoil our friendship and hope that perhaps it won't.

Ever since I first saw you at the swimming pool, I knew I fancied you. When we started to become friends, I started to feel it was even more than just a crush. Then when you kissed me for the first time under the water, I didn't know what to feel. I could only hope you felt more than just friendship for me.

Now that you have gone, I just seem to miss you more and more. Your letters are great but I want more than friendship. I want love. I want to be your girlfriend. I know that I am only sixteen but don't let that be the barrier between us trying to have a relationship that is more than just friendship. I also know that it will be harder due to the distance between us but I hope that we can work it out somehow.

Well, that's all I can say and I am just wishing and praying that you might feel the same way too.

I hope you like the present?

Love Stephanie x

Reading it a second time, James felt a grin stretch across his face. The fortnight they had been apart had made him realise that his feelings were deeper than friendship. Now sat staring at her words that echoed his feelings, he knew that tomorrow was going to be the perfect day. He had planned it in his mind and had been nervous about just turning up on her doorstep, but now he knew that he had to go.

"James, are you going to work today?" his mum shouted from the bottom of the stairs. He picked up his bag and folded the letter into the front pocket. He wanted to read it again later over lunch.

"Coming now," he replied. She was in the hallway leafing through the rest of the post but she looked up and smiled.

"Nothing for you," she asked, arching her eyebrows but with a glint in her eyes.

"Yes, a card, letter and model fire engine kit from Steph."

She tiptoed to drop a soft kiss on her son's cheek. She'd never seen him this happy before.

"Well, I just hope your father has got me something nice for tomorrow," she exclaimed loudly, returned with a muffled reply from the kitchen, "Hey, are you dropping hints?"

James laughed and stepped outside, still admiring his new car that sat in the driveway. The pool wasn't far away so he walked instead, enjoying the crisp bite of the breeze on his skin.

Kayleigh greeted him as he walked through the doors and stepped into the staff room. Peeping through the small window onto the pool he could see Michael and Dave on duty. He had cleaning and changing room duties first before he took over with Felicity. On the turn of the hour he stepped onto poolside and wandered past to say a quick hello to Michael and Dave.

"See you've drawn the short straw, new boy," Dave ribbed as he walked past.

"Just keep your guard up and no flirting with the girls in the pool," Michael said, tipping a wink to a gaggle of teenagers who were giggling in the shallow end. "Oh and no doubt she will disregard the rules and be checking out any eligible men."

"Don't you mean prey," Michael managed to squeeze in, although his voice dropped as he uttered the last word.

They all fell silent as Felicity stepped out from the staff room. Radiating glamour, if that was possible, she wore the uniform teamed with her obligatory red lipstick. Her hair swished against her back, tied in her usual high ponytail. The other guys slipped quickly away, leaving James and Felicity alone.

"I'll take the chair," she said, and sliding past him, he felt her hand brush his ass. Shaking the touch off as nothing, he stepped forward and started to walk his favoured circuit between the main pool, toddler's pool and the diving boards.

With it being a Saturday the place was packed with both families and youngsters. Swimming was kept to an hour for each customer to retain a limit on the people in the pool. Over by the board a group of lads who looked a little younger than him were fooling around. Felicity pointed them out so he stepped over. Being almost the same age James was able to calm them down from their antics on the steps and edge of the board. He even went on to give them a few tips on their technique. The girls from the other pool were eagerly swimming over to lean on the side of the main pool and watch the handsome lifeguard. One even startled him with a wolf whistle. James was about to turn and smile when he heard the whistle and saw Felicity advancing on them.

"Out now," she shouted. "We'll have none of that lewd behaviour towards my staff."

Silence reigned over the pool; even the water seemed to have stopped lapping against the side. James walked over and tapped Felicity on the shoulder.

"Don't you think that was a bit harsh," he whispered.

"Nope, my pool, my rules." She glared at James and then transferred the same look to the four girls now silent and pale as they clung to the edge. They swam to the shallow end and climbed out, aware that the whole pool had stopped to watch their disgrace. The lads from the diving pool sheepishly followed, the place no fun without their audience.

Felicity stalked back past James, her blue eyes sending icy shivers through him. The other guys had warned him but he thought she had stepped out of line with that call. The noise level rose around the vast area and normal service resumed as Felicity climbed slowly back onto the highchair. Walking into the staff room at lunchtime he found Michael waiting to take over.

"You're either brave or stupid," he said, clapping him on the back.

James was tense as he ate his lunch, nervous that Felicity would walk in and bawl him out for questioning her. But he remained alone, except for his letter. The afternoon flew by and this time James took the chair whilst Felicity sauntered around the pool. Every time he looked across at her she seemed to be staring at him, her mouth trying to restrain a smile. They closed an hour earlier on the weekend as the pool always started to empty at around four. The final few swimmers finished up their lengths and climbed out just as Felicity blew her whistle. James did the final walk around all three pools, fishing out a lone armband floating forgotten in the kid's pool. His body itched to dive in but he attended to his cleaning, knowing that Felicity was sure to check. With the last soapy water swirling down the grid in the showers, he turned to find her standing in the doorway, clad in a bikini.

"Are you joining me?" she asked, turning and walking through to the pool. James guessed he had no choice. He'd got off lightly after earlier so perhaps he should just do his mile and then go home. He stepped into the cubicle and stripped off, pulling on his trunks and finding his mind drifting to his favourite image of Stephanie. It was the look on her face as he'd pulled her in for that very first kiss beneath the water, innocent shock and delighted surprise when his lips had brushed hers.

Felicity was poised on the low board and seeing James emerge through the staff-room door, she lifted her arms, took a tiny step and let her body fly and fall into the deep water beneath. James couldn't help but watch before he slid into the water of the main pool and took off in a fast crawl. He didn't stop until he finished the tenth lap and saw her legs dangling in the water in front of him. He swerved to the side and held on. Running his hand through his short hair to wipe the droplets away, he looked up at her.

"You remind me of someone," she breathed, slipping from the edge to hold on next to him.

"Oh?" James turned to look down the length, nervous at this personal statement. She seemed to be in a trance as he slowly swam away, this time breaststroke. After a few moments he could hear her behind him as they both cut through the empty water. Another ten lengths passed in silence, James already ahead. Behind him Felicity tried to control her breathing at their close proximity, her eyes betraying her feelings as he morphed into Tony and then back again.

Stopping again it was James' turn to speak. "Look I'm sorry about earlier, I was out of order to question you."

She swept the hair from her shoulder which had slipped from its band and undulated in the swell of the surface.

"Apology accepted," she said, letting her hand rest on his forearm.

She felt a bolt of sheer delight run through her skin. James was about to move away when she swooped in, plastering her body against his and gripping the side beyond to hold him in place.

She nibbled gently on her lip, moisturising it despite the water droplets on her skin. He had nowhere to go unless he physically pushed past her. Closing his eyes he prayed that this was just a brief moment of misplaced memories making her behave like this. Felicity felt his hesitation and broke away, shaking her head of the reverie she was in.

She was a mess. Despite all her pre-laid plans, she couldn't go any further. She let him free and swam quickly away down the pool, climbing out and disappearing into the changing rooms. James watched her go and then finished off the rest of his lengths. He guessed he'd had a lucky escape. By the time he reached the staff room she was gone, just a waft of her perfume left lingering in the air. Once dressed he paused in the main entrance and shouted, "I'm off home now."

He got no reply but he knew she was still in the building as the light shone out from the crack at the bottom of her office door.

Felicity heard the key turn in the door and then let go, tears spilling down her cheeks in a waterfall she felt would never stop. Crawling into a ball in the corner she rocked and howled, lamenting her memories of a love that for her had been perfect.

CHAPTER 29

Two hours passed before Felicity could unfold her body from the foetal position. Hiccupping the final sobs from her throat, she straightened up and caught her face in the mirror. She was a mess, her hair hanging in damp strands on her cheeks and her eyes bloodshot. She knew she was alone in the building so she shrugged on her coat, set the alarm and left. Sitting in the car she paused, wondering what to do with her evening ahead, now she had failed to carry out her plan. Driving through the streets she just kept seeing happy couples, walking together or sitting in the warmth of pubs and restaurants. Valentine's Day had started early for them but for her there was nothing, no one to keep her warm at night. With the music playing loud in the car she drove, not home but down the motorway to the leafy suburbs of London.

She didn't know what had brought her back here after so many years as she sat at the bottom of the gated driveway of Malcolm's old house. Memories assaulted her as she drove on into the heart of London and found the hotel car park where she had last seen her dad. She only had her handbag with her but she straightened up and with some well applied make-up and lipstick, she covered her pale tearstained face. The whole place had gone upmarket as she stepped inside and crossed to the reception desk.

"Do you have a room for tonight?"

"Why certainly Ma'am." He slid the registration form across the counter and she quickly filled it in, with a false name and address.

"Do you have any bags I can arrange to have taken to your room?"

"No, I travel light." She turned on her heels and with the key in her fingers, she stepped into the lift. She walked down the corridor past the room her dad had been in and the one opposite. She missed him but she still couldn't forgive his lack of interest in her life.

She freshened up in the room and then went back out onto the street. Her body was still pulsing from the feelings that James and her memories of Tony had awakened. London was never dark beneath the bright streetlights and the never-ending traffic queues. Walking down the pavement she turned the corner and found that the pile of rubble she remembered had been replaced by the start of a new building. She was drifting in the sea of glee that the flames had produced as she'd seen them burst into life.

"Felicity… FELICITY… is that really you?" a voice shouted, getting louder as the footsteps got closer. She turned, afraid to see who could possibly know her after so long. Standing beneath the glow of the street lamp she saw a man in a suit, dark hair cut short, but something stirred. He was the lad from the concert.

"Wow, it is you," he breathed, stopping in front of her. "You look just the same as I remember."

Frowning she let him shake her hand. "It's Keith, Keith Madison… I know it's been a long time."

"Yes, Keith." She smiled, glad to have found a friend in this lonely place. She looked back across the building site.

"It's going to be another club, although whether it will be exactly the same I just don't know. I try and keep up to date with things around here. I have a house not far away."

Felicity still held his hand, and feeling a band on his ring finger, she relaxed.

"Hey, how about a drink for old times, I'm only here for the night and I'm on my own."

Keith checked his watch and then folded her arm into his. "Can't see why not, her indoors will just have to wait."

They turned and walked back into the heart of the city, finding a discreet wine bar on a slightly quieter corner. With drinks, Felicity was able to study him further.

"So did you become a lawyer then?"

"Well, I qualified yes but I now work slightly undercover, it pays better."

"Undercover? Are you a spy or something?"

"Nah, not that glamorous, I'm a private detective."

Felicity let him talk away, filling the silence as she gazed around at all the people. The bartender tipped her a wink and she fluttered her eyelashes and received a free drink accompanied by a note. She slid it beneath her napkin and continued to nod in all the right places of his story. Finishing his drink Keith stood up, again checking the time.

"Look it's been great catching up but I've really got to go. Can I walk you anywhere?"

"No it's ok. I might order some food before I go back to the hotel."

Keith passed her his business card. "Here, you never know when you might need my services, or just a friend in the city," he said, leaning down to press a soft kiss on her upturned lips.

"Thanks Keith." She watched him leave and then motioned to the waitress hovering. Placing her order she sat back and enjoyed the ambience. In her heart Felicity missed the hustle of the city and being able to be anonymous and do whatever she wanted, and tonight it was the bartender. She watched the place empty until it was just the two of them left.

"Can I call you a cab?" he asked.

"Yes but only if you'll share it with me."

They went back to the hotel and fucked. For Felicity it was merely an itch reliever as he pushed, grunted and groaned before slumping down beside her. She rolled away from him and in the morning he was gone. After breakfast Felicity drove home with a slightly clearer head.

She knew now that she wanted James more than anything in the world and she was going to get him.

CHAPTER 30

After a couple of days off, enjoying time with his new girlfriend Steph, James returned to work with a spring in his step. It lasted about an hour and then he glanced at the rota. It had been amended and pinned up on the staff notice board, his name highlighted in red. Fucking bitch had earmarked him for the rest of the weekends in February and he still wasn't sure what he'd done exactly. Ian walked in and saw James' face.

"Christ you really must have upset her on Saturday."

"Well, I only questioned her decision to throw some teenagers out. But I apologised later," James said.

"I guess it depends how you apologised," Ian smirked. "I've been there, if you know what I mean." He gave James a nudge and a wink before the kettle boiled. Letting his mate's words sink in, James cradled his mug.

In her office Felicity grinned like a Cheshire cat, she was delighted with her decision to keep James busy with her for the next few weekends. She knew she could only impose three straight weekends on the trot before she had to offer him one off. This would give her plenty of opportunity to deploy all her various strategies. Gazing out over her empire she watched him on the poolside, dreaming about her missed opportunity in the pool. Just before lunch the emergency buzzer sounded through the building. She looked up from her paperwork and saw James swimming frantically to the deep end. Quickly she made the short journey from her office to the poolside, finding Michael poised and waiting with the first aid kit.

"What happened?" she asked, blowing her whistle and motioning for everyone else to clear the pool.

"A chap dived in and went a bit deep, think he might have hit his head on the floor of the pool."

A thin line of blood was drifting in the water as James returned to the surface with the disorientated man and started to swim to the side. Graham was waiting to help lift the man out as they quickly laid him flat. Felicity phoned for an ambulance as Ian herded the rest of the swimmers away from the scene.

"I don't think it's too bad," James said, kneeling beside the man as Graham applied a bandage to the cut. Looking up Felicity was beside them both.

"I've called for an ambulance and cancelled the rest of the morning sessions as we'll have to filter the pool and add more chemicals."

"They're here," Kayleigh called as she escorted two paramedics onto the poolside. "Oh and I'm offering all the swimmers a token for a free session."

"Good work. Well done, now let's stand back and give the professionals room to operate."

James was the last to leave the scene as the guy stood with help and then reached out to shake his hand.

"Thanks mate," his voice stuttered as shock took hold and they wrapped him in a blanket. Graham followed them with a bag containing the man's clothes whilst Felicity held out a towel to James.

"Take an hour, get dried and then pop up to my office as I keep the spare uniforms in there."

James nodded and turned away but not before he caught her smile. This was the first time he'd ever actually deployed his lifesaving skills and he was glad to slip into the showers and feel the heat before he pulled his jeans and jumper on. He knocked the door and waited.

"Come in," Felicity called, remaining behind the desk, so he shut the door and sat down quickly. The spare uniform was on the desk between them.

"That was quick thinking out there, well done," she praised.

"Well, I saw the angle of his dive and knew he'd gone in a little sharp for the depth. It was nothing, just part of the job."

"Look, I'm sorry about the other night, I was kind of feeling a little lonely with Valentine's Day on Sunday and you reminded me of someone from the past. Let me make it up to you and say thank you for today with a drink after work."

James hesitated, wondering if he should just ask about the change in shifts, but in the end he stayed quiet. He was learning to read the body language. Perhaps over a quiet drink might be a better time to broach the subject. He nodded and reached for the clean, dry t-shirt and shorts.

"Ok, that sounds good," he replied.

"Great, meet me in *Maison D'Heures*, it's just down the high street on the left."

"Thanks, I was just about to ask you for directions, I'm still finding me feet around the area."

Lounging back in her chair she watched him walk away, wondering if she couldn't have asked him to change in her office before he went back on duty. Ah well, tonight was her chance and she was going to grasp it with both hands.

James wandered around the pool thinking about Steph, his girlfriend. Why did Friday always seem such an age away until he could speak to her on the phone and then it was only for an hour. He loitered at the end of the shift and let the other guys head out before him and wondered if he should wait for Felicity. He wasn't exactly dressed for wine bars in his jeans and jumper.

Loitering outside the place James felt wary; he was more used to noisy bars with the lads than wine bars with older women who happened to be his boss. He stepped inside to find it relatively quiet so he ordered a beer and sat at the table in the far corner. He almost didn't recognise Felicity as she stepped inside, swathed in a long velvet coat of jet black. The only splash of colour was the red trim around the collar and cuffs. She stopped and ordered a bottle of wine and then walked over, leaving the waitress to follow with the tray.

"James," she purred, her voice soft and lilting. "I'm so glad we have this chance to talk away from work." She shrugged off her coat and the waitress carried it away. James nodded and took a sip of the beer, hoping to calm the nerves shooting through him.

"So, tell me a bit about Herefordshire, it's somewhere I've never been."

"Uh, well it's a bit more rural than this and kind of slower but in a nice way."

"And your family event went all right?"

"Yeah, in fact I was kind of hoping that as I'm down to work the next few weekends, I will have a free one for Friday 11th March through to the Sunday?"

"Mmmh, I guess so." She poured the rich merlot into her glass and then filled the spare one for him.

She enjoyed swirling the liquid over her tongue, its rich plum and oak flavours relieving her stress in a couple of mouthfuls. James finished his beer and wondered if now was a good time to leave.

"Try the wine, it's delicious. Surely you don't have to rush off yet?"

"I'm cool for an hour but then Mum will be expecting me home for tea."

"I forgot you're so young." She giggled and raised the glass to her lips. She could see him staring but she lowered her lashes, letting the liquid slide down her throat.

"So do you have a girlfriend then?"

James paused mid mouthful, his mind in turmoil. If he said yes would she take back her promise of the requested weekend? He swallowed and looked away, shaking his head.

"Plenty of time to find the right woman," she said, watching the blush rise on his neck.

James swallowed the rest of his wine and then stood up, uncomfortable with the direction of the conversation.

"I'm sorry, I have to get going. But thanks for the drink."

"Sure, of course you do." Her voice was smooth but didn't quite hide the edge of desperation. "See you tomorrow."

Felicity turned to watch him walk away, pleased with the information he'd provided. He was single, he could be hers. She poured the second glass of wine and clicked her fingers for the menu, now she was here she might as well eat.

Over the next few weeks James worked hard and Felicity continued her flirtation, but in a subtle way so that none of the other staff would guess her intentions. It was only ever a brief touch as they passed, whispering in his ear when they were on poolside and sharing the odd shift together.

James tried to ignore it but out of politeness he never said anything, just did his job. His mind was on Steph's birthday on the 11th March, she would be seventeen and he was determined to spoil her. By Thursday night everything was ready and he whistled as he cleaned the changing rooms at the end of the shift.

"Someone sounds happy," Felicity said, as she wandered through.

"Yeah, good weekend ahead. I'll see you Monday," James said, finishing off and curling up the hose. Felicity stopped to watch him, admiring the flex of his forearms and his ass as he bent down. But she resisted the urge to run her hand over it and just smiled as he turned around.

"Hope yours is good too," he said, gathering up his bag. "Going to get a quick session in at the gym first before I leave."

With her check on the pool complete, Felicity changed into her leotard and footless tights. She preferred to swim but as James was in the gym that's where she was going to be. Perhaps she could tempt him into another drink or even, walking her home. The music on the stereo system was up loud and James was pushing weights at the far corner so he didn't hear her arrival.

She jumped onto the bike and started to pedal, slowly increasing her speed. Looking over she noticed that James had moved to the running machine so she did the same. Taking the treadmill next to him she smiled across.

"Hope you don't mind the company?"

"Nope," he said, sweat running down his shoulders and into the fabric of his vest top.

As they slowed down to walking pace she reached for his towel and passed it to him. "Here, you might need this"

"Thanks, so how is it that women never seem to sweat as much," he mused

"Oh we do, but it makes us glow instead." She giggled lightly and then stepped over to the weights. Knowing that he had just been on there she sat down and was about to reach for the bar. She knew it would be too heavy to lift but she hoped it would tempt him over. He saw her reflection in the mirror and rushed over as she started to stretch her arms.

"Hey, wait you'll never manage that." He straddled her and grabbed the bar, taking it from her grip to slide it back into the hooks. Felicity looked up at him above her and let her hands lightly smooth up his thighs before he stepped off and to the side.

"What weight do you want?" he asked. "Sorry, I left mine on there, I'm training to apply for the Fire Service."

"Oh, don't worry. I think I'm done for today."

He held out his hand and helped her up before she ran her hand further up his arm to rest on his shoulder, revelling in the trail her finger left through the sweat. James stood stock-still, afraid to move but even more afraid of what she was doing.

"Thanks," she breathed, and on tiptoes she planted a feather light kiss on his cheek and then let go, grabbed her towel and sauntered away.

James let out a breath, perhaps he'd bring Steph swimming on Saturday, let Felicity see he was taken. Grabbing a glass of water he headed for the showers and to change, more than ready to go home and check his mum had bought the right set. As he made for the door Felicity appeared and locked up.

"Which way are you going?" she asked.

"Left at the end."

"I'll walk with you, my house is not far in that direction and with the evenings still being dark, I always feel a little tense alone."

Being a gent he reached and took her sports bag, carrying it with his. The silence stretched between them, James not wanting to say anything more to his boss and Felicity mulling over her next move.

"This is my place," she said, reaching the end terrace on the corner. "Would you like to come in for a drink?"

"Nah, thanks but I need to get home." He passed her the bag and walked away, leaving her fuming. Felicity was not used to being so politely rebuffed of her offers, and she didn't like it. Here she was trying to turn over a new leaf, be a normal person and James was ignoring all her subtle signals. She watched him jog to the corner before he disappeared, a grin spread over her face. Perhaps he'd have to work on Sunday after all.

CHAPTER 31

Stepping in, his mum peeped around the kitchen door.

"Hi, you've got time to shower before tea."

"Thanks Mum, did you manage to get it?"

"It's on your bed but next time it's up to you!" She smirked and then laughed. "But I know what you mean. Lingerie shops can be daunting."

Peter appeared in the corridor and joined in. "But your mum and me had a good time looking around." Pam reached and tapped him on the arm and then blushed. Peter winked at his son, they loved winding him up but secretly couldn't wait to meet this girl who had turned their son's head.

The next afternoon in the car, James drove to Ross. He'd left the present and her birthday card wrapped and on the spare bed for later. He was still feeling nervous about the weekend but as he pulled up outside the school gates, he spotted her. The look of shocked surprise was delightful as without a thought, he picked her up and whirled her around in his arms before planting a kiss on her lips.

"Aren't you a sight for sore eyes," he whispered in her ear.

"So how did you manage this?" Steph asked as they drove back to her house.

"I got here early and called in to ask your mum if I could come and pick you up," he said, grinning. "I just couldn't wait any longer to see you."

With the mix tape playing in the car James made short work of the journey home, relishing in the feel of his hand resting on her leg or vice versa. Pulling up in the driveway he knew his mum would be waiting to pounce as he walked around and opened the door for Steph. He could see she was nervous so he quickly pulled her in for a hug and kiss before entering. His mum was waiting and engulfed Steph in a hug.

"Hi, I'm Pam and this is Peter," she said, motioning to an older version of James. "It's lovely to meet you, James is always talking about you."

James showed Steph up to the spare room after they'd had coffee with his parents. He couldn't wait for her reaction to his present. The meal was perfect and later in his room, he realised that she was wearing her present. He longed to slowly undress her and he struggled to keep his cock from rising to the occasion. But in the middle of the night his lust pulled him to the spare room.

"I was cold and missing you," he murmured, but Steph held open the covers and he slipped in, letting her curl up in his arms and press her body into his. They fitted together perfectly and he knew he'd made the right decision. James took her breakfast in bed and after some more exploration on both their parts, they decided to get up.

"Shall we go to the pool, I can show you the diving boards," James suggested, feeling he needed the cold water to cool him down. There was just something so alluring about his Steph. She was sweet, kind and innocent but he knew a sexy siren was hiding beneath all that, just for him to let loose when she was ready. Steph agreed and they went out to the pool where he was able to introduce her to both Ian and Michael. Showing off his skill as he dived from the high board, they swam and frolicked together, recreating old times in a new pool.

As they were about to leave James heard a female voice shout his name. He stiffened and turned to see her walking towards them. He was about to introduce them when Felicity stepped in the way.

"I'm Felicity, you must be Stephanie," she said.

James was shocked, how did she know about Steph? Someone had been talking…

Felicity looked down on the auburn haired girl clinging to James' arm. So this was her competition? This young slip of a thing barely out of a training bra! She tried to hide her disdain as she hid it behind her false smile. Then in a moment she turned away, gazing at James directly.

"We're a bit short-staffed on Sunday, is there any chance you can fill in?" she asked.

"I can only do the evening as I have to take Stephanie home that day."

"Great, see you tomorrow at six then," she responded and promptly turned, clicking her way back to her office. "Oh and don't be late, no excuses."

In her office she slumped in the chair. She'd heard the whispers in the staff room about this friend of James' but now she knew she was real. She had competition to win his affection away from that school girl. At least she was in the right place to win this battle and win it she would, tomorrow evening.

"Hi, is that Graham?" she asked, as she waited on the other end of the phone.

"Yes, speaking."

"Can I swap shifts with you tomorrow evening; you can do Monday morning instead."

"Yes Felicity," he replied and was about to ask why the sudden change but the line was dead. She knew that this was the push she needed, she thrived on a challenge.

James tried not to let the sudden shift change spoil the rest of his weekend with Steph. They had fun roller skating in the park before he drove her home and after a quick coffee, he was straight back to work. In the staff room he glanced at the rota and saw he was on with Graham but as he stepped onto poolside, it was Felicity that he saw there, regally perched on the highchair at the end. James gave her a nod and a tight smile but she beckoned him over.

"Graham had to change shifts so you're stuck with me," she said, letting her legs change position and draw his eyes to them. "Oh and it was so lovely to meet your friend Stephanie."

"Yes, girlfriend." He turned to gaze across the pool, it was quiet for a Sunday evening and she probably could have managed without him there.

"Looks a bit young," Felicity said, struggling to contain her need to add to the comment.

"It's really none of your business who I share my private life with," James said, feeling angry at her inquisition. He strode off round the pool

161

and took up station at the farthest point. He could have been with Steph for a few more hours instead of here. He really needed to get on with his application to the Fire Service and escape from his boss, one he was really growing to hate for all her manipulation of staff.

With the end of shift nearing Felicity jumped down from the chair and walked over to James.

"We need to clean the filters out this evening so I'll meet you in the pool."

James nodded, though this was the last thing he needed – another encounter with both of them semi-naked. Pulling on his shorts he took the deep end and started work, waiting for her to join him. But by the time she appeared he'd finished them all and was about to start on the diving pool.

"Are you helping or just watching," he demanded. "It's a job for two people you know."

She flicked her foot into the pool and then out again. "I'm the boss, you'll do what I say."

"Yeah, but within the confines of the job."

"Well your contract says you work for me." He looked up to find her ice-cold eyes blazing into his, her lips pursed together. He leaned his hands on the side and pushed his body out of the water, but she was too quick and planted her foot on his chest.

"I think you missed one." She pushed him back into the water and watched as he swam to the last. She liked being in control.

Stepping away she jumped into the diving pool and started on the filters. She hated this job but she was waiting to make her next move. It was like a game of chess but she was the grandmaster. James slid into the water on the far side and worked his way around until she was next to him by the last trap.

"I've done this one already," she murmured, waiting for him to relax against the side and that was when she made her move. With her arms either side of him she pressed against his cool body, letting her hot skin touch his. James realised that her bikini top was missing as her ample breasts pressed tightly against his chest. Shit, what was he supposed to do, protest or accept this as the other guys had hinted they had done in the past. Ian's words echoed in his mind but he didn't want to be here, with her. He was a straight down the middle guy and the only girl for him was Stephanie.

"Touch me, hold me." Her voice low and demanding in his ear, it shot icy arrows through his body. Then her lips captured his, not allowing him the chance to speak. Felicity plundered his mouth with hers, crushing him against the hard tiles of the side. He didn't want this, he'd never wanted this, and he pushed her away and swam frantically to the side.

"Look, I'll forget this, but I can't go there," he said, hastily grabbing the towel and running into the changing room. He heard her laughter fill the room, echoing over the silence and crashing against the tiles. He was dressed when she appeared, naked except for her bikini knickers.

"I won't forget it either. You'll change your mind."

He opened his mouth but she laid her finger there in a silence motion before turning away and leaving him gaping.

"See you tomorrow," she called, before she clicked the shower on.

Felicity waited for him to follow her into the enclosure but instead, she heard the door slam shut. She listened as his footsteps echoed in the corridor.

"Fuck," she sighed, as she thought she'd had him, pinioned between her body and the side. His body so perfectly like Tony's, she had reeled back to that time. She let the water run over her sensitive skin and let her fingers release the tension inside.

CHAPTER 32

Felicity lulled James into a false sense of security and made no mention of the incident in the pool. She approved all his forthcoming leave and was civil to him like all the other staff. She knew there would be another moment for her to strike. She didn't have long to wait before she bumped into James and his little girlfriend again during the annual May funfair in the park. Her trusty snitch Ian had said they were all planning to go and watch the band and that he would be sure to invite James along. Dressed in her favourite tight jeans and a slinky t-shirt that showed off her assets, she wandered over, remaining a short distance away from her staff. She soon spotted James with Steph, wandering around the fairground rides and eating hot dogs together. With her plastic glass of awful warm white wine she lingered near the other refreshment tents, despising their sickly sweet show of affection.

"Hi Ian, Shaun, glad you invited us along it's heaving here," James said, his fingers still sticky from the hot dogs. Stephanie noticed this and before the guys got engrossed in a conversation she butted in.

"Do you want any popcorn?" she asked, craving some sweetness.

"Yes, sounds good… want me to come with you?"

"No it's fine."

Felicity watched her walk to the popcorn cart and she followed, positioning herself so that she was sure to be seen. It was even better when Steph bumped into the back of her, toppling popcorn from the overfilled box.

"Hi Felicity."

"Hi… um, what's your name again?" Felicity loved playing the innocent, her eyes wide and surprised.

"Steph, I'm James' girlfriend."

"Oh yes, how could I forget? Can't understand what James sees in a girl like you... he really needs a woman in his life."

Felicity watched as Steph stared at her open-mouthed. "I see James every day and when he's not poolside, he's in the gym working out like a maniac, which is normally a sign of sexual frustration. Oh but you wouldn't know anything about that I guess, at your age." She arched her eyebrows at her last comment, staring daggers into the eyes of her enemy. Felicity was enjoying the hurt look on Stephanie's face at her comments.

"James loves me, he told me," Steph retorted, her face red with rage and upset at her remarks.

"Well, we'll see about that. I should keep a close eye on him if I were you. He's a good-looking guy and there are a lot of distractions at the pool." With a flick of her hair and a final disdaining look, Felicity sauntered away to the exit. She didn't need to stay, her work was done and the seeds of doubt were planted in Stephanie's head.

She watched from afar the desolate figure of Stephanie slumped on the bench. She couldn't stop the grin spreading over her lips. By the railings she saw Keith waiting, her new secret weapon.

"She's the girl. I need her college schedule and anything else you can find out about her. She lives in some dismal small town called Ross-on-Wye."

"Anything else you need from me?" Keith asked, taking a good long look at his target.

"Everything, her friends and what she does outside of school. An update once a week will be fine."

"I'll phone you on Friday and if I have photographs, then I'll arrange to meet you somewhere."

They separated before anyone saw them together and Felicity took a final look at Stephanie, back beside James. His arm was draped over her shoulders and it made Felicity feel sick with longing. That was all she wanted – to just be loved.

In the wine bar later she met Jason, another young man who had blond hair. Perhaps he would do, perhaps she should try making James jealous with her own love life...well, she could pretend at least! A few weeks later and her friend Ian filled her in on the weekend's plans. A group of them were off to the local nightclub and with luck, James was off so there was a chance that he might be there and with him, Stephanie.

Rifling through her wardrobe that afternoon she found just the dress. It was blood red and so tight fitting she struggled to breathe in it. But fashion was sacrifice or so the beauty magazines told her. Her nails were painted to match as was her lipstick and instead of following the trend with big, bold hair she kept hers slick and long.

"Wow, you look gorgeous," Jason breathed when he called to pick her up. She was the same height as him with her heels on, black patent leather to match her handbag.

"Thank you." She smiled and allowed him to peck her on the cheek, she didn't want her lipstick smudged this early. A taxi dropped them into the centre of town and they shared a meal at her favourite wine bar. Felicity hated nightclubs, the loud music, youngsters throwing themselves madly around the dance floor or getting drunk and disorderly. At least she didn't look her age and could still pass for younger than her years.

She could feel the nervous tension in the pit of her stomach as she sipped her chardonnay and tried to stay connected to her date's conversation. Quite frankly he bored her, he was an electrician and she really didn't need to know all the detail of how to wire a plug. Stepping into the dark atmosphere of the club she could hardly hear over the beat of the base, but at least the same could be said for her companion's conversation. While he bought drinks she swept her gaze around the seating booths. Ian saw her and raised his hand; he was sitting with his girlfriend April. Graham was also on the opposite side of the table with his partner Lizzie, so with drinks in hand Felicity and Jason joined them. There was no sign of James yet but from her vantage point Felicity had the perfect view of the entrance.

"Is anyone else coming from work?" she asked.

"Oh we saw James in town earlier and asked if he was. He's got his girlfriend staying so I think we persuaded them," Ian said.

April stayed quiet. She despised his boss and the way she treated her staff. She'd heard the stories about her dominance at the pool, but her cold blue eyes were enough to wither any thought of questioning her.

*

In the queue James squeezed Steph's hand. Her new dress was stunning and far too figure-hugging for James to even want to stop staring at her. He was captivated by their love. Her hair was loose and hung in soft curls that bounced on her shoulders and in doing so, wafted the sweet scent of her perfume to his nose.

"Hey, perhaps we should just go home," he suggested, wanting nothing more than to peel the dress off and worship her.

"I don't think we have a choice now," Steph replied as they reached the counter and paid. It took a moment for their eyes to acclimatise to the darkness before James pulled her towards the bar so he could get some drinks. Then he scanned the tables and saw her... Felicity. He was in two minds to just walk the other way but Ian was waving at them now so they walked over. James could feel Steph's hand trembling in his so he squeezed it and she returned it.

After all the introductions Felicity turned away from the group. She slid her hand up Jason's arm, curling her fingers into the hair at the nape of his neck. She knew that James would be watching, and as she let her lips part his, she wanted him to see what he was missing.

"Shall we hit the dance floor?" James asked, trying to ignore Felicity's blatant show of her sexuality.

"Sure," Steph replied, feeling the beat of the music invading her body like a drug.

They found a spot and James held her close as they moved together in time to the rhythms. After a while they headed for the table and James reluctantly left Steph there while he bought a round of drinks at the bar.

Felicity had disappeared so Steph turned to include Jason in the conversation and they were soon chatting away about music. She didn't notice Felicity's return until she was stood there, her eyes blazing.

"What do you think you're doing?" she snarled, enjoying the scared look that crossed Stephanie's perfect features.

"Just chatting about music," Steph answered. She looked to and fro, obviously for her hero to save her, but James was nowhere in sight.

"You leave Jason alone," she growled. "He's mine."

Ian suddenly piped up, his heart in his stomach, but he couldn't ignore it after April gave him a sharp poke in the ribs. "You should leave Stephanie alone, they were only talking."

"And you should remember who your boss is before you speak."

Graham had started to move away as had Jason, an embarrassed look on his face. At that moment James returned and the mood turned cold like her icy gaze. He slammed the drinks down and squared up to Felicity but she never gave him the chance to say anything as his mouth gaped open.

"I think I'll need you to work tomorrow afternoon," she said. "And in future, could you tell your schoolgirl here to leave my man alone otherwise there will be trouble." Felicity loved calling her that, it was so condescending as she let her eyes move down over her slim frame. She was almost the exact opposite to her in looks. She had pale skin, slim with no apparent breasts, compared to her own magnificent curves and ample assets. What the fuck did James see in her? A mere child when he could experience a real woman. Her!

Seeing her full glass of wine on the table she promptly picked it up and slowly poured it over the front of Stephanie's dress, smiling all the while. Then she grabbed Jason by the arm and propelled him to the door. She left the occupants of the table shell-shocked by her childish display.

"Sorry," everyone said at once as they turned to Steph, April being the first to find some tissues from her bag.

"It's ok," Steph stammered, still in shock, what with cold wine against her skin, trapped in the fabric of her dress.

"She's a fucking bitch," Graham said. "You're so lucky to be leaving," he asserted, looking at James who was standing there.

James knew he'd brought this on Steph with his continued refusal to go out with Felicity or play to her desires at work.

"Can we go home?" Steph pleaded, her voice breaking through his reverie.

"Sure," he replied, as he took Steph's hand, helping her up and then saying goodbye to his workmates.

Outside the club Felicity hailed the next taxi and when it arrived, she got in.

"Bye Jason, thanks for everything."

"Oh, I thought we could continue what we started in the club..."

"No chance, you're just not my type after all." She slammed the door in his face and left him standing on the pavement.

Safe in her own home, she replayed the events of the evening...

The drink had been a genius idea, putting Stephanie in her place.

A letter was lying on the mat so she picked it up, the writing familiar. Slipping into her dressing gown she poured a neat whiskey and silently toasted herself as she sank into the cushions of the sofa. She picked up her paper knife and slit open the envelope, her thoughts straying to a much darker place and the burgundy stain blood would leave on a pretty pale dress like Stephanie's.

Her collection of information was growing as she leafed through the latest arrival from Keith. She didn't really know why she needed all this, but perhaps something would surface that she could use to poison James against his sweet, innocent girlfriend. With the second glass of whiskey slipping down she closed her eyes and wondered what she could do next. The scent of the drink stirred up memories of Malcolm and her abuse.

She wondered what had made her so sleepy and pliable…?

CHAPTER 33

He'd done it. Reading the letter again, he slowly walked into the kitchen.

"Mum, Dad I've got in. I'm going to be a fire-fighter," James said.

It was the icing on the cake after his perfect birthday celebrations with Steph and then his family. Drifting slightly he remembered the moonlight on her skin in the garden. Making love with Stephanie was the most perfect thing in his whole world but this kind of came a close second.

"Hey, you can get away from that dreadful boss of yours who keeps phoning you and making your work rota a mockery with all her changes," Pam said, having been on the end of one of these sarcastic calls when James had not been home.

"Yes, Mum. In fact I think I might just have time to write my resignation letter now before I go to work."

"Well done, son," his dad congratulated from behind his newspaper.

Taking the stairs two at a time James sat at his small desk and pulled out a sheet of paper. Apart from all his letters to Stephanie which were always a joy to write, this one was short and straight to the point. He sealed the envelope and pushed it into the front pocket of his rucksack. The sunshine made his walk to work a joy and he went straight to Felicity's office.

"Come in," she answered his knock, and he stepped inside. Over recent months she'd seemed less interested in him. But he didn't care now as he passed her the envelope.

"It's my resignation," he said, watching her read the few words on the page.

"I see." She folded the letter back up and put it in her tray for filing. "Just don't think it means you can slack off for the month."

"No, of course not," he replied, turning to leave.

"Wait, I think we'll have a little leaving party for you, keep the last weekend in August free."

"Thanks," he mumbled, confused by her change of tack and her good mood. She dismissed him and then stood up and paced the small confines of her office.

Felicity picked up the phone and called Keith's office. Over the months she'd been doing some research and now she just needed someone who could get hold of some strong sedatives for her, ones that would dull the memory at the same time. Ones she now believed her stepfather had used on her. Her conversation with Keith was short and successful. He could get hold of something that was easy to slip into a drink, no strong smell or taste and would hopefully do the trick. Now to bully the rest of the staff into attending, although she was sure they would as James was popular with most of them and she'd provide a tab at the bar.

James wandered into the staff room, relieved at her reasonable reaction.

"Hey Ian, put the kettle on," he said.

"What's with the grin?" his mate asked, doing the honours.

"My letter came through this morning officially offering me the job at Warwickshire Fire Station. I start in September so I've just handed my notice in."

"Congratulations, but why are you looking so chipper? I'd been expecting to see the visible scars of Felicity ripping you to shreds…"

"Ah, perhaps her friend Jason has mellowed her," James replied, enjoying the scent of freedom carried on his morning coffee.

He spent the rest of his last month at the pool expecting retribution from Felicity but none came. Finishing his last shift on the Friday night, they all wandered to the wine bar which Felicity had booked exclusively for all of the staff to enjoy a buffet and free drinks from the bar.

"James, it's been a pleasure having you at work," Felicity trilled, and many of the guys groaned loudly at her pun. Then cheering and laughing ensued as James blushed and Felicity handed him a glass of champagne.

171

"Thanks everyone for making work fun and giving me some friends in what was a new place for me. You've made me feel right at home and don't worry I won't be a stranger... I still need to swim and use the gym to keep fit."

"Cheers," Felicity chimed in, taking the space next to James and clinking her glass against his. She leaned in and whispered, "You'll still get staff rates for the facilities or Felicities." She giggled before following it up with a kiss on his cheek. Her red lipstick marked him. Kayleigh carried in a cake shaped like a fire engine as Ian shouted.

"Guess you've just swapped your small hose for a bigger one."

"Well, I kept telling him it was too small." Graham joined in the ribbing as Felicity ordered more beers and slipped the liquid in the one for James. As the guys downed their pints Felicity kept them topped up, at the same time keeping sober so that she could carry out the rest of the plan.

With midnight chiming many of the staff had left for home.

"Come on Grey," Lizzie said, grabbing his arm as a taxi pulled up outside.

"Is there enough room for us?" April asked, pulling Ian up from his slumped position on the small sofa in the corner.

"Hey, what about James?" Ian looked across at his mate, also the worse for wear.

"I'll drive him home," Felicity said. "He's more my direction than yours."

"Thanks Boss," Ian said on his way through the door.

"Yes and don't be late tomorrow, hangovers are no excuse," she called back, but she didn't think they heard her.

James stared up at Felicity, no longer his boss, and then realised that the room around her was spinning.

"Thanks for the offer but I think I can walk home," he said, pushing against the arm of the chair and feeling the room spinning even more.

"Nope, I may not be your boss anymore but I think as a friend I should make sure you get home safely." She hooked her arm into his and tipped a wink at the owner. She'd settled the bill and arranged for the leftover buffet food to be transported to the pool for staff to pick over at lunch the following day.

172

Her car was parked just behind the bar and with James in the passenger seat, she pulled onto the road. His eyes were closed so he had no idea that they were heading out of town. Felicity knew a secluded parking spot, one she'd shared with Keith who would be hidden and waiting. When the car stopped James opened his eyes. He felt sluggish and thick headed.

"Where are we?" he mumbled. "Think you might have taken a wrong turn."

"Oh no wrong turn at all, I think you've been waiting for this moment as long as I have," she whispered, lifting her top over her head. Before James could try the door handle she had straddled him.

"I'm not your boss anymore so whatever happens here tonight, no one will ever know. Call it my goodbye gift to you." Her tongue licked around her lips, moistening them to reignite the shine in her lipstick. She pressed them against his, letting the tip of her tongue gently probe his mouth open. Closing his eyes James wondered if this wasn't just an intense dream. Beneath his eyelids Stephanie lurked with her beautiful blue eyes and soft touch.

"Miss you baby," he breathed, her soft kisses on his skin as he reached to run his hands down her back.

Felicity could feel him responding beneath her. She quickly wriggled her hands down to unbutton his jeans and slid them down enough to find his cock, straining against the fabric of his boxer shorts. She moulded her hand around its width, enjoying the feel of it growing from just that single touch. His eyes were closed and he was thinking about *her*, but that didn't matter. Hitching her skirt further up her thighs she moved into position. Knowing the plan she'd removed her knickers in the bar so that she wouldn't need to worry about them. She knew she was wet, every look at his face reminded her of Tony as she nuzzled into his neck before lowering down onto his cock. Slowly she started to ride, letting his hands grip her waist whilst her every stroke seemed to be matched by his. Out of the corner of her eye she could just make out a shape – Keith with his camera. She hoped she wouldn't have to use the photographic evidence but having it was her insurance policy.

"I love you James, I've always loved you," she whispered in his ear, raking her fingers through the fine strands of his crew cut.

"I love you Steph," he moaned and with a final thrust he was spilling into her. Reaching down Felicity rubbed her clit until she found release and sagged onto his chest, both of them caught up in their own dreams.

Easing off him Felicity reached for the tissue she kept in the glove box and wiped the excess away. She hoped enough of it would have reached its destination. James had started to snore lightly so she reached across and tucked him back in.

Looking into the darkness she saw the rear lights of another car leaving the parking area and she smiled. Keith had done his job and would get well paid for the photographs when he sent them. She started the car and the radio came on, playing from her favourite Marc Bolan album, the song 'Hot Love', which seemed to fit the occasion. Singing along she giggled at the word witch. Oh… and she'd certainly twitched. By the time they arrived at James' house, he was awake but still slurry.

"I can help you to the door," she offered, watching him pull the handle and get out.

"It's ok, not used to drinking that much anymore. Oh and thanks for the lift home, I can't remember much of it, guess I fell asleep."

She watched him wander to the door and fumble with his key until it fitted the lock. Then she drove away, eager to get home and relive the first moment he was hers. She leafed through her file at home, staring at the phone number she had for Stephanie's home. The vindictive part of her itched to dial it, tell that stupid innocent schoolgirl what her beloved had done this evening. Tell her that she had just lost the competition.

Lying in bed she let her hand rub over the smooth flat skin of her stomach, her lips breaking into a smile.

CHAPTER 34

James woke up with a fierce headache and a mouth that tasted like cotton wool. But despite this he was now free of Felicity and the pool, ready to embark upon his career as a fire-fighter. He'd have to try and sneak in and out of the leisure centre to use it, although the station had its own small gym. He hoped that he would never have to see Felicity again, well except maybe in passing.

A week later, Felicity held the grainy photographs of the two of them in the car, enough to break them up if the main plan failed. By the end of September there was no sign of her next period and a test confirmed her thoughts – she was pregnant and the father was James. Now she just had to find the best time to tell him.

Keith was her eyes and ears as he was now tailing both Stephanie and James and had provided Felicity with details of his 'watch' schedule at the Fire Station. To everyone at the pool, she was still dating Jason and she arranged for him to accompany her to any of the work events, but this was just her cover.

"Felicity," Keith called her on the phone.

"Yes, do you have news? I need to bump into James, but somewhere that Stephanie is going to be around," she asked.

"She's staying with him this weekend and I think they will be at the new club on the Saturday night. Most of his fire station colleagues have been talking about it in the pub this week."

"Give me a ring on Saturday night then, if you definitely see them going out."

"Ok," he replied, but the phone was already dead.

She didn't need to wait for his answer, he loved his job and Felicity paid him well for all the information and his discretion. She snuggled up on the sofa as October had blown in with a cold blast to the air, but she wondered whether the pregnancy was making her more susceptible to the changing season.

James was overjoyed, his first month with the Fire Service had been filled with training, training and more training, but the buzz of the job was amazing and kept him going. He was also excited to have Steph with him for the weekend and they were going out to the new nightclub in town with most of his watch colleagues. They were getting ready to go out when he noticed the scared look on Steph's face, trying to hide it beneath her make-up. He held her close, wrapping her slender frame in his arms.

"You're quiet, what's wrong?" he asked.

"Nothing, just remembering the last time we went out. I hope we don't see Felicity."

"Well, you'll be well protected this time with all of us strong fireman to look after you," James replied, kissing her lightly on the tip of her nose. "Anyway, we may not be there long as you look so sexy tonight," he said, letting his eyes and hands wander over her curves.

James stepped back and let Steph straighten his tie. This new club had a strict dress code policy and he walked over to grab his jacket. A sexy smile played on the lips of his girlfriend as he held open her coat and slipped it over her shoulders, letting his fingers run though her loose curls. Stepping inside out of the pelting rain they didn't notice the car that had followed their taxi move off from the kerb. Keith drove round to Felicity's house, making sure that he parked at the corner of the street and walked quickly to give her a knock.

"Hi Felicity," he said, as she opened the door swathed in a thick fluffy dressing gown. Her face was pale and she let him in before rushing past him to the downstairs cloakroom. He listened to her retching into the bowl before the running of water.

"Oh, you're sick… I could come back another time. But you said you wanted to know if Stephanie and James were out this evening and I've just watched them enter the club."

"Thanks Keith, I'll go and get ready. Would you mind waiting and giving me a lift into town?"

"Do you think it's wise if you're not feeling well?"

"This is the best time, I need to speak to James." And with that she hurried upstairs. Pulling on one of her dresses she eyed the mirror. Was she starting to show already? It was doubtful at only two months in, but she checked all the angles and she definitely felt pregnant and the sickness was hideous. It didn't seem to be just the morning and instead, she was randomly throwing up at different times through the day.

With her long fur coat on she slicked her lips with her deep red lipstick and kept her eye make-up to a minimum as she knew she needed to cry to be plausible, but she still didn't fancy her mascara running in dark rivers down her cheeks. She'd hate to look like Alice Cooper! Back downstairs and she found Keith looking at the guitar that hung on her wall.

"Was this your dad's?"

"Yeah."

"I can't believe that was his last concert, just goes to show that life can be too short."

The scent of Chanel nestled in his senses and he turned to look at Felicity, standing in the doorway. He still had a huge crush on her and he saw a glimpse of something in her cold, steel eyes. It looked like sorrow or despair. She blinked and a teardrop glistened on her lashes but dropped and disappeared – and she was back to her usual self.

"Let's go, I need to get this done and then get back home," she said, opening the door. Keith nodded and hurried past her to open the door of his car. The drive was silent and Felicity sucked on a mint, finding it soothing on her stomach, the last thing she needed was to throw up in the club toilets.

Entering the club she found a space by the end of the bar and ordered a glass of red wine. She'd been craving vinegar on all her food for the last week. Ignoring some of the unwanted male attention she scanned the club, immediately finding the crowd of rowdy firemen, some with girlfriends and some without.

James left Stephanie and walked towards the bar with the long order of different drinks in his head. The evening had been great fun and he felt happy to leave Steph with all of them... until he saw her.

"Oh James, what a nice surprise."

"Uh, Felicity," James stuttered, and fumbled to find another word to say but she filled the gap between words and them. Pushing up against him at the bar she finished the last dregs of her wine.

"We need to talk, but away from here."

"Talk... about what? We have nothing to discuss." James turned to the barman and started to reel off the list of drinks.

Felicity knew it was time to pull out all her acting abilities. She stifled a small sob and it was enough to make the barman look over.

"Ju... Ju... James, please we need to talk." Her next sob was louder and feeling under pressure, James turned away from the bar and propelled her into the lobby.

"What the fuck are you crying about?" he hissed into her ear.

"Us."

"There is no us."

"I think there will be when you hear my news." She slipped into his arms so that she could whisper in his ear. "I'm pregnant, it's yours."

James tried to push her away but she held tight, tears still streaming in a torrent down her cheeks.

"But when? How?"

James heard another sob behind him and he quickly withdrew his arms from around Felicity as he tried to step into her way. He watched Stephanie rush from the building and he paused. How much had she seen, or heard?

"I'm sorry," James said, backing away from her, the words echoing in his head. She must be lying, but why? Out on the street he just saw Steph disappear round the corner and followed, Felicity's words still ringing in his ear. He found Stephanie hunched over on a bench in the park, the rain matting her curls onto her wet skin. He carefully draped the coat over her shoulders.

"It's not what you think," he mumbled.

"What am I supposed to think when I see my boyfriend with his arms around another woman?" Steph spat back. James took a second, Felicity's vile words still echoed around him, but he pushed them away and lied.

"Felicity has just broken up with Jason and needed a friendly shoulder to cry on," James replied. "And I just happened to be there to provide that."

"So when did the two of you become good friends?" Steph retorted.

"Well, she was a lot better once I handed in my notice at work," he replied, slowly reaching out to take her hand in his. He rubbed it between the two of his as it was numb from the cold and to disguise the shake in his.

"Please believe me Steph, I would never lie to you or hurt you. I love you… till the end of time…" His words trailed off, as his voice caught on a sob.

Even though his mind was still lost in confusion, Steph leaned into his arms. They sat silently on the bench in the rain but when James began to shiver he took her hand and they walked back to the house. There were no stars in the sky that night; the way was lit only by the artificial streetlights along the path. James never took his arms from around her and although they didn't talk, the silence was safe. In his sleep James clung to his girl, his Stephanie, refusing to let his mind replay her words.

CHAPTER 35

A week passed before she heard a knock at her door one evening. Peeping out of the curtains she saw James highlighted in the glow of the street lamp. Her sickness had been getting worse and sometimes she barely managed to get through the day at work.

"Hi James," she said, opening the door to him.

"We need to talk. Well you do and explain that stupid accusation."

She stood aside to let him in. She was wearing a long silk slip beneath her dressing gown which she loosened slightly. Just having him step past her left her senses reeling.

"Coffee?" she enquired.

"Yes."

She gestured for him to enter the lounge as she stepped into the kitchen. Rapidly she returned with drinks for them both. She resisted the urge to sit next to him on the sofa and instead took the armchair.

"So what's with this talk of being pregnant?"

"It's simply the truth James, it happened the night of your leaving party."

She watched confusion spread across his features, searching his memories. She let the silence stretch between them, feeling supremely confident and feeding from the terror in his eyes. Before he could speak again she stepped out of the room, returning with the wand from the pregnancy test. She dropped it into his lap and smirked.

"But I still don't understand, what does this prove?"

"It was you. Surely you remember our time together in the car. You couldn't keep your hands off me even though I tried to stop you. I knew you were taken, but you even called my name." She moved to kneel before him. "It was the best moment of my life, knowing that my feelings for you were being returned in such a passionate way."

Felicity turned her wide eyes upon him as he looked down at her, feeling her hands softly caressing his thighs. James just found darkness. He remembered being drunk in the wine bar and then nothing until she had stopped the engine in the drive.

Standing up, he shook off her grip. "No, you're lying, there can be nothing between us. I'm in love with Stephanie."

His words sounded hollow because there was a big blank space of time in his mind, planted there by her. He knocked the table lamp in the hallway as he pushed past it towards the door. It crashed to the floor, breaking the bulb and leaving it littered in her carpet.

"You can run now James but you can't escape your responsibilities. I know where you live and I'll tell your parents, your friends at the pool and your girlfriend the truth."

He slammed the door upon her goading words, but they clung to him. Breaking from his walking pace into a jog he tried to empty his mind and remember that night, now so long ago. As he reached home he grasped a short image of a wooded lay-by and the feel of hair on his skin.

Throughout October Felicity kept up her side of the threat and told her work colleagues about her pregnancy, as she was now three months in and starting to show a little. Ian and Graham had looked incredulous at the news but when she'd slipped little mentions into conversations about the drive home from James' leaving party, they saw no reason not to believe her. Felicity kept phoning his house and if she got James' parents, she remained silent and just hung up.

Then she hit gold one morning when Stephanie answered her call. Stifling her laugh, she held on long enough to hear the worry in her voice. Then when she rang back the next morning it was James that answered.

"Was it you yesterday afternoon?" he asked.

"No idea what you're talking about," she replied.

"Just stop phoning me, I have nothing more to talk to you about."

"Oh, but I think you have because next time your adorably cute schoolgirl answers the phone, I'll tell her about our affair."

"What?" James felt the skin on his forearms prickle from distaste.

Stephanie padded down the stairs and he hoped she'd not heard the earlier part of the conversation. He tried to plaster on a grin as she mouthed "coffee?" at him before disappearing into the kitchen. His t-shirt hardly hid her pert, naked bum from view.

"Are you still there?"

"Yes."

"Meet me next week, call round at your convenience and we'll talk. I have a proposition for you."

"No."

"You will, or you'll be sorry." She hung up, leaving her veiled threat ringing in his ears. James gulped back his apprehension at what she would consider to be a proposition. A blood test would reveal who the father was and he was willing to take one if it got her off his back.

Stepping into the kitchen he found Steph pulling cups from the cupboard so when she turned he hid his worry behind a smile.

"Hey sexy," he said, but his voice didn't quite sound light enough.

She held her arms open to him as he quickly lifted her up and placed her on the worktop so that she could wrap her long legs around him. Her eyes widened with the shock of the cold work surface on her ass before his lips captured hers in a kiss so long and sensual, she surrendered completely to him as he fucked her in the kitchen. It was short, sweet and satisfying.

As they ate breakfast together Steph turned to James. "Who was on the phone?"

"Just Aunt Sue wanting Mum but having a general catch up," he replied. "It's ok, it hasn't ruined our morning. Sex in the kitchen is just as much fun as sex in the bedroom," he insisted, grinning at her. He hoped that she hadn't noticed the veiled shadow in his eyes at the lies he was telling.

Felicity had to wait until Saturday evening before James once more rang the doorbell at her house. She was wearing her new soft wool dress which highlighted her dark hair against its smoky grey colour. She was over the worst of the sickness but her cravings ran from the sublime to the ridiculous. At the moment it was salted crisps laced with vinegar and then dipped in toothpaste. It looked hideous but tasted sublime. She poured him a glass of wine and itched to have one herself but she knew that it was wrong to indulge. Instead she sipped peppermint tea and watched as he stared at the bump. She rested her hand over it and rubbed it as she looked into his eyes.

"It's yours," she said again, reaching to grasp his hand and place it beneath hers. James yanked it away and sat in the far chair.

"Look, when the baby is born they can check who the father is. I believe it's just a simple blood test. Then if it's mine I will support you financially and play a part in the child's life," he declared, crossing his arms across his chest.

"Sorry that's not enough."

"Not enough, I think that's perfectly reasonable."

"James you have two choices and here they are. Firstly, you can sever all links with that little slapper in Ross, marry me before the child is born and this will never be spoken about again. Or secondly you will never see your child again and I will tell Stephanie the truth about our sordid and passionate affair."

James sat there is silence before swallowing the wine. It tasted sour on his tongue as he saw Felicity pull out an envelope.

"I don't want to do either."

"I think you will when you see these photographs."

She emptied the contents onto the coffee table and watched as they slid towards him. They were grainy but he could tell it was him and Felicity, locked in a passionate embrace. A second showed her skirt hitched well up her thighs and his jeans scrunched upon his knees as she straddled him. "Now do you remember?"

James felt his mind clearing, the images showing a wooded lay-by, well known by courting couples as a secluded spot. He hid his face in his hands, trying to stop the bitter taste of the wine from recoiling in his stomach. She had him and all he could think about was the look on Steph's face if she ever found out. He'd been stitched up and it seemed that the first option was his only one. He knew that he'd never live with his guilt if Felicity told Stephanie the lies he knew she was capable of.

"Have a week to think it over but I know you'll do the right thing. If not these photos might make it in an envelope to your innocent girl's home address."

She moved aside as he stumbled out of the house again. He was out of sight round the corner when he bent over and threw up the remains of his lunch and the red wine. It dripped from the corner of his mouth before he wiped it away on his sleeve. He was a fucking idiot; she'd left him no choice, no way out.

In his room that night he wrote the letter that would seal his fate. He knew it would break Stephanie's heart but she was better off without him and the terror that Felicity could unleash if she chose too. Stephanie was worth far better than him and although he longed to tell her the truth to appease his own guilt, he just wouldn't. The pen trembled in his grip but he knew he had no choice.

Dear Stephanie,

In the past few weeks I have been thinking very deeply about our relationship and have come to the conclusion that it would be best if we split up. I was trying to work up the courage to tell you the last time we were together so it could be face to face as I feel I owe you that, but there hasn't been the right moment or if there was I was too much of a coward.

The tears that fell when I left you standing in the driveway were genuine tears of anger that I had failed to do this and have had to resort to words in a letter and tears of regret that we can no longer be together.

You have been the best girlfriend a man could ever hope to find in a lifetime but I feel that I have made you grow up too quickly and therefore have not given you the chance to date a few more boys of your own age as I was your first. I am also aware that you have hopes and dreams of our relationship becoming more permanent in the next year as you talk of learning to drive, colleges in Warwickshire and of a daughter called Charlotte. This scared me to death as there are so many more things that can be accomplished before talk of marriage and children should ever be considered, even between two adults who love each other.

Finally the distance between us is proving to be a big problem especially now you are studying media and enjoying your shifts on Hospital Radio. My job in the Fire Service is extremely demanding and working around your study and my shifts means we are seeing each other less and less. Keeping our relationship growing under these difficult circumstances would take a lot of hard work and effort on both our parts. I also know how much our parting each time we are together makes you crumble, I have seen your tears and I want to stop them so much but I know I can't.

I hope that you are mature enough to understand my reasons for breaking things off between us and that perhaps we can remain friends?

Fondest regards

James

He read it back through, agonising over the choice of his words but he hoped they would leave her with hope and not despair. Quickly he folded it and addressed the envelope before going back out of the house to post it at the corner. He couldn't wait in case he changed his mind.

Over dinner Pam and Peter exchanged worried glances at their son's lack of appetite but when they asked him if he was ok, he stood up and left the table. On Tuesday evening the phone rang and Pam answered.

"Hi Pam... can I... can I speak to James?"

"Yes I'll just shout him for you... are you ok?" Pam said, worry in her voice. It sounded to her like Stephanie was crying or had been.

"Yes, I just need to speak to James," Steph stammered, holding back tears. She waited a few seconds and then she heard his voice.

"Hi Stephanie, I guess you got my letter?" he answered, a hint of nervousness tingeing his voice.

"Yes," she whispered. James could hear her sobbing over the phone line. He cradled the receiver and let his own tears fall silently.

"Steph... Steph, please don't cry... I'm really sorry that I had to tell you like that."

"But why?" was her muffled response. James took a deep breath. He had to lie, her future happiness depended on it.

"I've told you why in the letter."

"I know... but I love you... I will always love you... till the end of time, remember?" James heard her voice trail off, listening to the jagged desperation of her cries.

"You'll find someone else, you're very attractive, intelligent and sexy," his voice trailed off into the distance.

"But I don't want anyone else, I WANT YOU!" she shouted. He knew she was trying to change his mind, luckily she couldn't hear his own heart breaking. He was shaking in the silence between them, the shock at what his words had done was tearing his resolve apart. His future without her was a hopeless tunnel of blackness. Yet he couldn't step back from it.

"Are you still coming down this weekend?" Steph stuttered.

"Well, I don't really know."

"Please come... I need to talk to you in person, face to face, you at least owe me that." He caught the change in tone, it was hope he heard in her soft plea. Closing his eyes he knew he had to say yes, just to see her one last time. Just to try and make things right for her when his whole life was falling apart.

"Well," he paused. "Ok then, I'll come and see you and we can sort everything out. Bye."

CHAPTER 36

The next morning, on his way to work James called on Felicity. He refused to enter when she opened the door for him.

"I choose the first option," he replied in a monotone voice. He was afraid his voice would break with despair over his decision. "I'll be seeing Steph for the last time this weekend and then after that, it's up to you."

"Just move in whenever you're ready. Oh and I guess I should pop round for dinner with my soon to be in-laws," she quipped.

The glow of the red sunrise reflected in her eyes, making her the devil incarnate. James was about to walk away when she lunged for him, letting her dressing gown fall open so he would feel her body naked against him. He let her kiss him but he didn't respond and instead untangled her arms from around his body.

"I've got to go, or I'll be late for work." He turned his back and hunched over, he walked away.

"Later, honey," she trilled, her voice grating on his nerves.

On the Friday when he was due to drive down to see Stephanie, James received a call from Felicity at his work. At home he grabbed his bag and left a note for his parents that he'd be back tomorrow. He phoned Stephanie's home and left a message with her dad regarding the delay. He knew she'd be questioning that, wondering if he was going to show up. He parked on Felicity's driveway and rang the doorbell.

"Darling, do come in."

"What do you want? I changed my plans to be here."

She passed him a door key. "I thought you might like this, I want us to start getting comfortable together before the baby is born. Oh and we need to plan a wedding, honeymoon and possibly look at moving house because I just don't think mine will be big enough."

He still felt uncomfortable as he stepped past her and dropped his bag in the hallway.

"Are you staying already?" she remarked.

"My mum and dad think I'm going down to Steph's tonight, I don't want to alarm them. It's going to be hard enough breaking the news tomorrow."

"Well, grab a beer from the fridge. I'm just on tea at the moment and we can have a chat."

"Thanks but I'm a bit knackered, if you let me know where the spare room is I'd just like to shower and crash."

Felicity kept the smile plastered on her face. There was plenty of time in the future for her to get her way once he was truly free of his ties in Ross. Keith was on his way there to keep her abreast of the situation. He followed her up the stairs and she pointed out the bathroom and then opened the door to the spare room.

"I'll just pop some of my things away," she said, rushing in to sweep her favourite whip into the top of the drawer.

She didn't need him to see all of that just yet, in fact she was contemplating giving up domination and seeing if being with James would make her happy without the power trip. Time was all they needed.

"I was just going to order a takeaway, so if you're hungry later just come down." She backed out of the room, letting him look at the vibrant shade of red that dominated the one wall.

"Thanks," he muttered.

He felt so uncomfortable here but he had nowhere else to go. Once everything was in place and he'd told Stephanie, then he could work on trying to make his life with Felicity bearable. The only thing that kept him going was the possibility that the child would still turn out not to be his. Then he'd just have to get divorced, even though it would be too late for him and Stephanie. As if to echo this thought he heard a clock chime from the hallway.

James crashed completely for the evening, waking at midnight, the house around him felt strange in the quiet, yet it would soon be his home.

He crept downstairs and found a half-eaten pizza on the table so he picked up a slice and forced it down with a glass of water. Sitting at the table he turned the radio on and found a late night station as he tucked into the next slice. Then he heard their song, 'Take My Breath Away', its lilting melody lifting him into his happy memories before crashing him on the rocks below. He sobbed at the table before he went back to the spare room and a sleepless night.

Felicity popped her head in the next morning.

"I'd bring you a cup of coffee but at the moment the smell of milk is turning my stomach." And with that she lurched off to the bathroom and James tried not to listen to the sound of her retching. Then as the shower turned on he quickly dressed and left the house, the key tucked deep in the side pocket of his rucksack. He took the drive slowly, the mix tape playing endlessly over the memories that kept flashing up in his head, like an unwanted film reel.

Stephanie was waiting for him in the doorway as he pulled up on the driveway. He hesitated, part of him not wanting to leave the safety. Her face was pale and wan, her eyes red and sore beneath make-up. He stood looking out of her bedroom window into the dark sky beyond, too afraid to start talking. James heard her pad across the carpet, so close he could smell the candy perfume she favoured as she wrapped her arms around his waist. He remained motionless, a lump caught in his throat as she went up on tiptoes and he felt her breath on his neck.

"I don't think I should be here," he said softly.

"But you are and I need you," she replied, as he turned to face her. Stephanie saw the sorrow and regret in his blue eyes, turning them from vibrant and bright to dull and clouded, like the sky outside. Tears had started to form in her eyes and James watched the first one slide over the skin of her cheek.

He reached out and wiped it away with his finger.

"Please don't cry, this is hard enough as it is," he whispered, his voice breaking as more tears stained his fingertips. Her lips found his and she kissed him until he gave in and kissed her back. His lips were hard and urgent as they pressed into her softness and he pinned her against the bedroom wall, his breath ragged with desire.

Steph looked up at him from her kneeling position and saw the tears falling from his eyes. Did this mean he was sorry? Would this mean they were back together? She didn't stop as her hands ran up his firm thighs. There, his hands grabbed hers and he pulled Steph's all the way up before he let go and grabbed the hem of her dress, pulling it off in a single move. He remembered the underwear, it was his favourite set from their first night as lovers. However it didn't stay on for long as he picked her up and carried her the short distance to the bed. Stephanie lay naked before him and he knelt down, his tongue capturing her sweet wetness. She shuddered and came quickly before he lay on top of her, suddenly pushing his raging desire into her. He was out of control as he pounded her deeper into the covers of the bed, until she gasped out his name as they came. Tears still fell down her face and he let her hold him close, hearing her whisper, "I love you, till the end of time."

James remained silent in that moment. He hated himself and what he had just done. So he gently untangled her and sat slumped on the edge of the bed.

"I'm so sorry, I shouldn't have done that."

"Don't apologise, I'm not sorry. I know you still love me and you still desire me, so why can't we still be together?" Stephanie implored, reaching out her hands to him but then she stopped and withdrew.

"I've told you why, it's just not working for me." James almost choked on the words. He hated lying but he saw no other way.

"But we just made love together?"

"No Steph, we just had sex."

"Is there someone else?" Steph asked.

"No," he replied, but he looked away so that she couldn't see the emotion on his face. And the dark lies in his eyes. He knew if she did he might just break his resolve.

"I can move to be closer to you, we don't have to live together or anything, we can take things slow, I just want to be with you... together forever." She sobbed. It masked the sound of his heart breaking.

"Stephanie, I do love you but things are too complicated to explain. I will always hold a place in my heart for you but we can't be together any longer."

He stood up and quickly pulled his clothes back on. He needed to get out before he gave in, before he begged her forgiveness and put her at risk from the wrath of Felicity.

"I'm sorry I shouldn't have come," he said, walking towards the door.

He paused and looked back at her, naked and cold on the bed. "You take my breath away," he said, sadness haunting his features before he was gone forever.

CHAPTER 37

The drive home tortured him with the last image of Stephanie, looking so bewildered and confused. Then he still had to break the news to his parents. He trudged into the house and saw his mum in the kitchen.

"Mum, can I talk to you?"

"Yes." Pam was surprised at her son's sudden return from what she thought was a weekend in Ross.

"I've just split up with Steph." He struggled over her name as sobs threatened to spill out. "It just wasn't working out for us anymore and I've got feelings for an ex-work colleague."

James hated lying to his mum and he kept his head bowed. "I wanted to speak to Steph face to face but it was hard."

"So which work colleague? Do I know her?" Pam felt distraught at the news but tried to remain calm, it was never any good trying to run your child's life for them.

"You'll be meeting her soon Mum, she's pregnant and it's mine."

He quickly got up from the chair, letting it fall and clatter on the floor to fill the silence. He rushed up the stairs and locked his door to her and her multitude of questions.

Pam went into shock and boiled the kettle for some tea so she had an excuse to talk to Peter who was in the garage tinkering with the lawn-mower. James sat on his bed and let the tears cascade down his cheeks, especially as he saw the elephant and the fire engine on his shelf. Finding one of his spare rucksacks he put their memories inside it, all the letters he'd received, cards and the presents from Stephanie. Then as all was quiet on the landing he pulled the loft ladder down and hid them in the attic. Over the next week he quietly moved all his clothes to Felicity's house and finally invited her to dinner at his parents'. Felicity appeared at the front door in good time and he ushered her inside.

"Mum, Dad this is Felicity."

Pam plastered a smile on her face but instead of a hug she extended her hand, staring Felicity up and down. She was older than her son and she already hated her for the hand she kept on his arm. It looked like a claw with its scarlet talons. Peter smiled and offered her a drink and then stopped.

"Just a glass of iced water," Felicity simpered, trying to fit into this family who obviously despised her. The dinner was silent and stilted as Pam asked questions about Felicity's past and she dodged them.

"So has James told you? We're planning to get married before the baby arrives. It'll be at the end of January."

"What?" Pam exclaimed, shocked by this sudden revelation.

Things were moving too fast.

"Yes Mum, I think it will be best if we make sure everything is legal," James replied, almost like he was reading from a rehearsed script.

"It's all booked at the registry office and then a reception at the health spa hotel. I do hope you'll both be able to come as I have no parents on my side." She cast a sorrowful look straight at Pam.

"We'll see," Pam muttered, pouring tea and offering everyone slices of cake.

At the door Felicity pulled James in close and whispered, "I don't think they like me."

"Give them time," James replied, but he wasn't too sure that they would ever come around. He knew his mum had seen though his lies about the whole thing. He didn't have the guts to tell her the truth.

"Are you moving in tomorrow?"

"Yeah, I'll be round at ten." He kissed her once on the lips and they said goodbye. He turned to find his mum staring from the kitchen doorway.

"I don't like her, I should feel sorry for her with no parents but there's just something…" She tapped her finger on the doorframe. "She's so cold! But it's your bed and you'll have to lie in it."

Never had his mum's words cut him to the core so James wandered back for his last night alone in his room. He picked up the Christmas card he'd bought for Steph, wrote inside it and tucked it into his bag, planning to post it a couple of days before Christmas.

Felicity opened her door as his car pulled onto the driveway. Once they were married, then she could breathe and know that she had claimed her prize. Ok, so he was no Tony, but perhaps he might be moulded to fit her desires and wants.

James walked inside and deposited the last box of items inside, dreading tonight as he assumed they would be sleeping in the same bed. The thought of Felicity repulsed him but he was a good guy and he didn't run away from his mistakes.

"So I've got a wedding dress fitting later today so can you organise some food for later. Oh and the estate agent is calling round to take photographs of the house so it can go on the market tomorrow morning. I have my eye on our new home and I'm sure with your salary and mine we can afford something so much better and larger."

James stared silently as she grabbed her handbag and left him alone. He wandered around his temporary new home and then took a look in the kitchen cupboards. He put together a stew and then watched television until she returned.

"Mmmh, that smells nice." She sniffed the air and passed him her coat.

"I'm going to run a bath, fancy rubbing my back?"

She didn't give him a chance to say no as he trailed after her. Thank goodness he was on the overnight shift for much of next week and he knew Felicity was still working so he wouldn't need to see her much.

Like a dutiful boyfriend James knelt by the bath and ran the sponge over Felicity's back and neck. Then she took his hand and placed it on her belly. "This little one is our future. Let's be happy together and forget all that happened in the past."

James helped her out of the bath and she clung to him, dripping onto his jumper and jeans as her lips sought his. Shutting his eyes James responded and tried not to think of Stephanie but she was there. She lingered at the periphery of his vision, her curly hair, pert breasts and long, lean legs. Felicity felt him respond and she steered him into the bedroom, helping him to peel off his wet clothes.

"Let's start now," she breathed, nibbling his neck before she stepped away and lay down on the bed. James gulped but at least the part of him that needed to respond seemed to have no qualms about who the recipient was! He suckled her breasts, struggling to cup them all in his palms before he rained kisses in a trail for his first taste. He kept looking up to gauge her response but her eyes were tightly closed. Felicity writhed beneath his touch, but he was still missing the spot that somehow Tony had found. Feeling irritated by his soft caress she reached down with her hand.

"Be hard, be rough with me," she demanded.

Then to demonstrate she started to rub her clit, feeling his stare before he took over.

"Inside me now," she barked and James realised that their lovemaking would never quite be that if she was going to order him around! Within a few pushes he felt her hands grab his shoulders, urging him on as her hips bucked to meet him.

"Faster babe, harder, fucking hurt me." Her cries were guttural as she finally started to feel the pressure building towards the pinnacle. Her groans echoed around the room as she let go and then James followed suit.

Pushing him off, she turned to a box of tissues on the side and wiped his seed away. She hated the feeling of the sticky mess men left. Then as James lay spent on the covers she got up and he heard the shower start.

He was still there when she returned.

"Aren't you going to have a shower, you're all sweaty," she said, pulling her nightdress and dressing gown on.

James nodded and did as he was told, meeting up with her again in the kitchen.

CHAPTER 38

While James was working nights, Felicity took the time to rifle through the things he'd brought and she found the Christmas card, tucked away in his gym bag. Carefully she found a piece of paper and managed to trace through the address written on the front of the envelope. Then settling down at her desk she started to write out the few wedding invitations they were planning to send. Trying to control her giggles she managed a passable copy onto one of the thick cream envelopes as she sent an extra invitation. One she knew she'd never get a reply from. Then gathering them all together she waited for the postman to arrive the next morning and cheekily asked if he would take them for her. Sitting down for her first cup of tea she let the laughter out before phoning Keith.

"Hi Keith."

"Oh hi Felicity, what can I do for you? All is kind of quiet in Ross unless you want lots of photographs of Stephanie moping around."

"Just do a bit of surveillance around New Year's Eve and day. I know it's a holiday so I'll pay you double."

"Will do and merry Christmas." Keith finished the conversation. He knew his wife would not be happy at the change of plans but she'd be made up with the extra money.

James and Felicity spent a quiet Christmas together amid packed boxes as they prepared to move into their new house the week before the wedding. James had fielded a number of surprised calls from his colleagues at the pool. They had all replied, "Yes," to the invite. On his side James had only asked his parents, refusing to involve the rest of his relatives, and some of the guys from the fire station. He had tried to keep in touch with Stephanie but since the Christmas card, he'd heard nothing. Perhaps she'd moved on? Made a fresh start without him. He was working New Year so that was a relief as Felicity had decided to have a quiet one with her friend Cass and her husband and kids.

It was nearly four in the morning when Felicity woke to the sound of her telephone. She stumbled downstairs to answer it, ready to give the receiver a piece of her mind.

"Hi Felicity."

"Oh, for fuck's sake Keith, why the call at this stupid time?"

"Thought you might like to know that Stephanie has been rushed into hospital. I don't know the full facts but she was in a night club with her friends and then some guy from the hospital staff, think his name is Mark, kissed her and she fled. I followed at a distance and waited in the car just down the road. Her friends followed her home and then an ambulance turned up not long after."

"And?" Felicity barked.

"From what I could glean it was a suicide attempt, but she's still alive."

"Thanks, and I'm back to bed now," Felicity replied, dropping the receiver and grinning into the hallway mirror.

Stephanie had crumbled and that was good, such a shame she'd never died Felicity thought. Storing the happiness away and patting her bump, she went back to bed.

After a fairly stress-free house move their wedding day loomed. Felicity had refused a hen party (being pregnant and unable to drink) and instead treated herself and Cass to a weekend away at the new health spa hotel in London. It was owned by the same mystery man at the helm of the Warwickshire and Birmingham ones so they knew it was going to be good.

"Have you got everything?" James asked, carrying her cases to the taxi.

"Yes dear, have a good time on your stag night."

"Yes the guys at the station have organised it."

"Well, just behave. I have eyes and ears in this area." She pecked him

197

on the cheek, leaving her words hanging in the frosty cold air. He stood and watched the taxi leave, wishing he could relax and have a laugh, but his impending marriage was nothing to celebrate.

Cass had farmed her children out with relatives so that her husband Robert could attend the stag night. He was the obvious mole in the party. Checking his watch James realised he had hours before he needed to meet the lads. He jumped into his car and pulled off down the road. He only had one destination in mind as the car covered the miles between him and his old hometown.

He drove to his house first, stopping on the opposite side of the road and letting the memories overwhelm him with their power. The sight of Stephanie as she'd tried to walk away from him on what had seemed to be their final meeting. Her forlorn face in the rear-view mirror when his dad had driven them away. Next he drove slowly past her parent's house but he didn't stop, he couldn't risk that his heart would make him get out and knock on the door. Then he went down to the car park by the swimming pool. He looked up at the large windows where he had waved to her before he crossed the tarmac and took the small path that led to the river. It was deserted on this cold, colourless morning. Even the river water looked washed out and grey as he found their bench and sat down to remember. For a brief moment he thought about ending it, jumping into the icy depths and hoping the strong currents would take him away. Then he remembered the child growing inside of Felicity. If it was his, he couldn't contemplate leaving it fatherless.

James heard voices in the distance and quickly got up, jogging back to his car. He had to go back, back to her demands and desires, back to his bed of thorns. Driving through Ross he wished that Chris was around to talk to but he'd started his army training and wasn't the best letter writer in the world. On the drive back, the rain started to fall and a thunderstorm shattered the silence of his thoughts. Slotting the tape into the player he turned the music up and tried to get the melodies to take him away.

Felicity and Cass arrived at the spa hotel and allowed the bell boys to carry their bags inside. Cass had lost some of her weight in line with Felicity's request for her to be both bridesmaid and witness at the ceremony. Stepping inside Felicity gasped at the vivid colours that scooted across the opulent foyer as her heels tapped against the granite tiled floor. She'd booked them adjourning rooms at the top end of her budget and as she signed in, she felt at home. In fact the chandeliers reminded her of ones from Malcolm's club. In fact as they wandered to their room, she took in the maroon paisley wallpaper that graced the walls.

"So what are we booked in for first?" Cass asked, clearly soaking up the luxury.

"Afternoon tea and then a massage," Felicity said. "I'll just freshen up and meet you out here in ten minutes."

Dropping her coat onto the bed, she looked around at her room and picked up the brochure. Flicking though it she tried to decide what other treatments she needed before her marriage the following weekend.

"Are you ready Flick?" a voice sounded through the door after a small knock.

"Just coming," she replied, leaving the brochure on her bedside table for later.

As Anthony let the doors of the elevator close he saw a glimpse of two women walking past in the corridor. One of them had long dark hair that reminded him of Felicity. In his office he phoned down to his receptionist.

"Can you tell me who's booked in today?"

"Why certainly sir, Mr and Mrs Benjamin, Mrs Stiller, Ms Jennings, Mr Barton," Victoria replied.

"And what is Ms Jennings' forename?"

"Felicity, sir," she replied. "She came in with Mrs Stiller and they are staying in rooms 68 and 69."

"Thank you Victoria."

Sitting back in his chair he knew it was her, and she was staying in his hotel. He needed to be careful that he wasn't spotted as he didn't need a showdown. But equally his curiosity was aroused as to what she now looked like. Much as he'd disliked his father, there was a part of him that was still his son. He enjoyed the feeling of power that his money and looks could and did wield. He turned around to check the hidden cameras that he had all over the hotel. Of course there were none in the bedrooms but from here he could keep his eye on the residents in the restaurant and bar areas, the foyer and the swimming pool and spa area. Looking at the dining room he just saw the back of her head as she chatted with her female companion. The phone interrupted him and he turned away to answer it but when he returned to the camera screens, she had gone.

Relaxing in the Jacuzzi after being pummelled lightly, Felicity sighed and enjoyed the small flute of champagne they had both been offered.

"You really shouldn't drink," Cass said.

"Just the one to toast my forthcoming marriage," she replied, holding aloft her glass to her best friend.

"Guess you've got over the morning sickness now."

"More or less, occasionally a smell will set me off or certain foods. I'm still addicted to vinegar though."

"So how's James?"

"Let's just say I have some teaching to do once this pops out."

Felicity stroked her bump but at the same time, knew she wasn't feeling an ounce of maternal instinct towards the baby. On the way back to their rooms Felicity felt the lurch of the alcohol in her stomach and hurried the final few yards, covering her mouth.

"I'll knock you later for dinner," Cass called, as her friend disappeared into her room.

After heaving up the remains of lunch Felicity slept for a while before a tap on the hotel room door woke her.

"Cass, is that you?"

"No, Mam I have a delivery for you."

Opening the door Felicity saw the bouquet first before the polite staff member.

"These are for you, can you please sign to say you have received them?"

Felicity signed the slip and then let the scent of roses, lilies and gardenias fill her senses. *Oh they must be from James trying to be romantic.* But as she turned the card over she gasped, staggering backwards to land on the mattress in shock.

"Ms Jennings, I request the pleasure of your company in the main bar at midnight."

Felicity read and re-read the card, searching for clues as to the identity of her apparent secret admirer. She had just finished putting the flowers into one of the tall glasses when she heard a second knock.

"Flick, are you awake? Our dinner booking is in an hour," Cass said, turning the doorknob and wandering in.

"Thanks hun, look I've just received these." She watched Cass read the note.

"Oooh, perhaps it's James come to surprise you."

"Doubtful, but a secret rendezvous sounds delicious."

"Sure it's not your hormones?" Cass giggled. "But it's up to you. You're not married yet!"

"I'll think about it whilst we dine, now shoo I need to get glamorous."

Felicity luxuriated in the shower and then slowly brushed her long hair so that it hung in a slick waterfall, with just a small cascade over her shoulders. Her new dress flattered her fuller breasts whilst partly concealing her bump beneath the flowing material in her favoured shade of vermillion. In the end she was ready before Cass and waited impatiently outside her door. They strolled down to the dining room and revelled in the splendid candelabras that graced each table. Felicity spent the evening between courses and gossip, scanning the other residents, trying to pick out the mystery man.

"What about him?" Cass said, as a dark Italian looking man nodded to the two of them as he passed their table.

"Mmmh, maybe," Flick replied, feeling more optimistic about her sort of blind date.

"Why don't things like this happen to me?" Cass sighed, her spoon delving into the creamy chocolate dessert.

CHAPTER 39

With Cass off to bed, promising that she wouldn't spy on Felicity, she sat in the lounge bar and sipped her Earl Grey nervously. She watched the hands on the clock tick by the last fifteen minutes before midnight. The bar staff were cleaning glasses and shooting her looks that said, "If you leave then we can." At five past, Felicity had decided it was all a big hoax and stood up slowly. A soft breeze made her skin prickle and she picked up a scent she hadn't smelt in ten years. It brought both pleasurable and painful images to the back of her eyelids as she blinked. A hand touched her shoulder as a voice whispered, "I wasn't sure you'd come."

Leaning on the table for support she still hadn't seen him but she knew that voice, had dreamt about it for years, hearing it echo in her dreams and nightmares. She slowly turned around and stared up into his steely olive eyes. Her heart punched against the confines of her chest and the air around her disappeared.

"Hello," she muttered, before her legs gave way and she started to fall. He caught her before she hit the ground and managed to rest her back in the chair. He placed his cool hand on her forehead before clicking a finger to his nearest member of staff

"Water please, then leave us alone."

The waitress placed it on the table and then left the room with the other two, all curious at the scene they had witnessed. But they knew their boss' short temper so they obeyed.

"Felicity... Flick," he murmured, watching as she slowly regained consciousness and flickered open her eyelids.

"Tony, is that really you?"

"Yes, now take a sip of this, you just fainted."

Feeling the coolness touch her mouth she obeyed and swallowed the liquid.

"How nice it is to find you staying here," he said, maintaining eye contact. Feeling more awake, anger flamed inside her.

"Just wish I could say the same, after what you did." She narrowed her eyes and glared back. Then standing up, she turned to walk away. Tony caught her arm and stood up to reel her into his embrace.

"Not so fast Flick, I had my reasons for doing what I did. If I could change my actions then I would."

"Fuck off, I'm pregnant and getting married next weekend so just leave me alone."

Like a hot potato, his arms dropped their hold upon her and he stood just inches away, surveying her. He pulled out a business card and passed it to her, seeing the tremble in her fingers as she grasped it.

"Well if you ever change your mind... I can see and feel how affected you are by my presence, just don't forget what I can do to you."

And with that he strolled out of the bar, leaving her breathless and staring after him. For a brief second she debated dropping the card on the table but her happy memories stopped her and she placed it in the inside pocket of her clutch bag.

Back in her room she peeled off her clothes and lay seething beneath the covers. His touch had awakened the desire in her and a red hot longing between her thighs. If she gave into him, what would it achieve? Would he still cast her aside after the encounter? Pulling a pillow between her thighs she rubbed herself to a small orgasm, thinking only of his intense stare and feeling like an eighteen year old again.

"So what happened last night?" Cass asked over breakfast.

"Oh, he wasn't really my type so I went to bed."

"Alone?"

"Yep, now let's hurry up as we're booked in for a manicure, pedicure and a full facial ready for next Saturday. Oh, have you heard from Rob about last night yet?"

"No, he probably won't be up yet if he had a skin-full, I'll ask him when I get home and let you know."

"Good." Felicity crunched down her toast and tried not to drift off into memories from last night and her encounter with Tony. She was turning over a new leaf with her marriage, going straight in her own little way. She pushed the image of Keith away, not ready to get rid of her favourite spy.

They spent the rest of the day talking about the forthcoming wedding at the registry office. Then their taxi arrived and finally Felicity was driving away from him. She glanced back at the vast expanse of the hotel and thought she saw a shadow in one of the upper windows. *Could it be Tony, watching me?* The thought brought a sharp tingle to her twisted heart.

James had made them dinner and helped carry her bags back upstairs.

"You're looking good," he said.

"Thanks, honey, you too. How was your stag night?"

"Nothing special, just drinks and a curry with the lads, I was in bed at midnight." He didn't add that he was so miserable that he had tortured his ears with the mix tape and cried. But he was moving on so he'd put the tape into a small shoe box and hidden it in one of the boxes still packed from the move but destined for the attic.

On Friday evening James kissed her goodbye. In the tradition of not seeing the bride before the wedding, he was staying back at his parent's house. They had just about forgiven him for finishing with Stephanie and although they still didn't know the full facts about how Felicity had got her own way, he thought it best they didn't. Instead he hoped they'd be excited to welcome their first grandchild.

"Hi son," Peter greeted him at the door and he walked into the smell of his mum's leek and potato soup. She peeped out of the kitchen and smiled.

"Hey, it's nearly ready."

"Smells delicious, you'll have to teach me how to cook it."

"No chance. I need something to keep luring you home for." She tried to giggle lightly but he could tell it was an act. He'd seen the way she looked at Felicity when they were together and knew that she disliked her but was trying her best for her son.

The evening felt like old times with a film in front of the fire.

"We might get a dog," Peter said, breaking the companionable silence.

"Sounds like a great idea," James agreed, dipping his hand into the popcorn bowl before passing it on. He tried not to look at the gap next to him or feel the torn edges of the aching hole in his heart.

"It's a shame we didn't have enough time to invite the rest of the family, what about your best mate from Ross?" Pam said.

"He's still in basic training at the moment, so he's not allowed out," James lied.

He had tried to contact Chris but had yet to receive a reply. In a small way he was glad as he was sure Chris would see right through his lies and tell him to snap out of it. But he had no idea what Felicity was capable of, he had an inkling her work persona was only the tip of the iceberg.

The end of January was dark, overcast and held the promise of a storm later. The drive to the registry office felt more like a funeral cortege. It was a small party of guests and James had persuaded his mate Ian from the pool to be best man. His throat was dry as he adjusted his tie and waited for Felicity to arrive. She stepped through the door with Cass beside her as chief bridesmaid. Apart from their mutual friends Felicity had no parents in attendance, just her grandparents. They seemed rather bemused by the whole affair and James realised that he'd never met them until this point.

Felicity smiled broadly while she swayed down the small aisle in her long gown. It accentuated her breasts and although it was not a huge ball gown affair, it hid her bump nicely. She'd filled her bouquet with bright red roses against the lilies and green of the ivy. Her dark hair was fastened up but she had decided against a veil, instead a small tiara sparkled in the lights. Feeling regal she stopped beside James and took his hand, her possessiveness showing.

They had picked the shortest possible service and apart from the tense minutes waiting to see if anyone had any objections, the deed was done. Felicity had officially become Mrs Cooke.

James kissed his new wife with little passion and then smiled for a few photographs before they departed for the reception. Again it was only a small affair with no formal speeches, just a nice meal before they left for a week's honeymoon down on the Devon coast.

Watching them depart, Pam walked over to Felicity's grandparents.

"I don't think we've been introduced, we're James' parents."

"Nice to meet you, this was a bit of a surprise to us too but they seem happy."

"Yes, we're looking forward to meeting our new grandchild later in the year." Pam watched the shock rise in her face before a mask of composure fell again. "Yes, now I'm afraid we're about to head home."

Pam glanced at her husband. "Oops I don't think they knew about the baby."

"Strange couple, I was hoping you could ask them about Felicity's parents…"

"Me too, oh well what's done is done now."

CHAPTER 40

The rain and wind lashed the hotel frontage and keep them confined to the bedroom and the amenities of the hotel. Felicity felt satisfied and decided that she could officially give in to her growing appetite and belly. James worked out his frustrations in the gym and the hotel pool and then put up with her demands in the bedroom. After one session she seemed more amenable and James had a few questions he wanted answers to. Cutched under the covers, James wondered if knowing more of his wife's past, then maybe he could grow to love her.

"It was nice to meet your grandparents on Saturday, you've never told me much about your past. I'd like to know before we become parents."

He felt her stiffen in his arms at his question and it took a while before she reached and turned out the lights.

"I'll tell you what I can, but it's painful for me and I prefer to look forwards rather than back." Her voice was quiet and faltering.

"Take your time," James murmured, touching his lips to her temple in a tiny kiss.

"I grew up without my dad from the age of five, he just left my mum to pursue his dream of being in a rock band. I watched as she entertained numerous men over the years until she met and married my stepfather Malcolm when I was seventeen. We moved to this big house in the suburbs of London."

"So are your mum and stepfather still in London?"

"No, they died in a fire and then my real dad died of a drugs overdose so I moved to live with my grandparents. That's it really, not much to tell."

"Well, I hope I'll get chance to get to know your grandparents then."

Felicity sighed and turned away from him. That was all she was willing to disclose, she didn't need James raking up the past, especially after her encounter with Tony. Feeling baffled by such a short and emotionless speech, James turned the other way and wondered whether something else lay behind Felicity's closed-off attitude.

The months flew by and James settled into the routine of work and obeying Felicity at home. The larger she grew, the crankier she got and the more he had to bend and scrape to her every whim and desire. He loved escaping to his parents' for an evening meal when he could. Sometimes Felicity joined him but more often than not, she chose to stay home.

Felicity had been thrilled that Stephanie had stopped her letters and in doing so, James his. But she knew that he still thought about her and even more irritating, dreamed about her. She listened to him whisper her name and hatred kept growing inside her. As the first pangs of contractions started, Felicity rang Cass.

"Can you drive me to the hospital, it's nearly time."

"Yeah, but where's James?"

"Out on a shout, they will release him once the fire's under control."

"I'll be right there." Cass left a message for her husband and raced to the assistance of her best friend. Cass knew that first babies took time but she wasn't looking forward to seeing how Felicity coped with the pain.

As the women drove to the hospital they never noticed the dark car that followed at a distance.

Cass left Felicity in the doctor's capable hands and wandered down the corridor to find a coffee machine. Being nosey her ears pricked up when she overheard Felicity's name in the next corridor. Sneaking towards the corner she stayed silent.

"I can't really tell you much at the moment, she's just gone into labour. But as you're a friend please feel free to stay."

"Thank you, I might call back later," a male voice replied.

Cass knew it wasn't James so she edged closer and watched as a tall blond man in a suit turned and walked towards the exit. He looked vaguely familiar but she couldn't place him. Walking quickly back to the room she found Felicity red faced and panting.

"Have you asked for pain relief? Gas and air? Epidural?"

"Nope, but where the fuck is James. Can you get them to call the station again?"

Cass did as she was told and then returned to find Felicity pacing as the midwife monitored everything.

"It's going to be a while yet, ladies."

She left them to it and Cass let Felicity lie back down before asking the question.

"There was a man asking about you in the corridor, tall, blond... but he left."

Fuck, it had to be Tony, but what was he doing there? How did he know?

"No idea," Felicity replied, "maybe there's another Felicity in labour," she managed, before the next contraction made her scream. Luckily Cass missed the brief look of terror on her face, garnered by the conversation. James arrived and took over from Cass, the contractions were close now and while the midwife did her job, James grasped Felicity's hand.

"Push now and hard."

"Arrgh, fucking hell," Felicity screamed, "get it out NOW!"

A few minutes later a wail filled the air as the midwife wrapped the tiny bundle up and passed him to Felicity.

"It's a boy," she said.

Felicity was shattered but looked down to see bright blue eyes staring back at her, then a tiny mop of black hair.

"He's beautiful," she said, even though she wished he'd inherited James' blond hair. James peeped over and lost his heart to his newborn son. The eyes were like a mirror image of his own. Stroking Felicity's hair he made up his mind to try harder to love her for his son's sake.

"Here, you hold him," Felicity said, grinning at the look of love on her husband's face. She had him now, the pain of the birth had been worth it.

"Do you have a name?" the midwife asked, surveying the new family in front of her.

"Darren, after my dad," Felicity said, looking up at James who was still transfixed by the baby in his arms. He just nodded and smiled at her suggestion. A small whimper sounded.

"I think he might be hungry," he said.

Felicity took him back and opened her gown to let him suckle.

"I'll go and let Cass know and then ring my parents," James said.

Cass jumped at the chance to take his place, after two kids of her own she was always broody for more and loved sharing other people's.

"Oh what a sweetie." she cooed, taking him from Felicity who looked distant and shattered. "What's his name?"

"Darren," Felicity sighed, just wishing everyone would leave her alone so she could go to sleep.

"Great name, he looks just like the two of you."

James poked his head around the door. "I'm going to pop home and then be back later with Mum and Dad, you kind of look like you need a rest."

"Thanks," Felicity breathed, snuggling back into the pillows and watching as Cass took the hint and placed the sleepy child into the cradle beside the bed. Before they'd even left the room, both were asleep.

Wailing cries woke Felicity and for a minute she forgot where she was. It was only the stark white room and medicinal smell that jolted her into reality. She staggered over to the crib and picked up the furiously red faced bundle.

"Ok," she said, carrying him to the bed and then helping him to latch on again. She felt no immediate connection or rush of love for the baby, he was just a product that had got her James and a new life. Closing her eyes she drifted again, dredging up memories of Tony. A small knock roused her as James appeared with his parents.

"Here he is Mum, Dad," James said, proudly. He watched their hearts melt like his had at the tiny life he plucked from Felicity's arms.

"Beautiful," Pam breathed, letting James hand over her first grandchild. Peter looked over her shoulder and started making funny faces at the baby's inquisitive gaze.

"He's smashing," he said, chucking a finger under the tiny chin.

Felicity tried to hide her scowl. Why did Darren not make her features soften and glaze over with love?

"I have to stay in tonight but then if everything is ok, we can come home tomorrow," Felicity said, turning all eyes to her.

"That's great Flick, I've booked a week of leave to give you a hand," James said, but he turned back to his son, now being held by his dad.

Once back at home, Felicity realised that she was not cut out for motherhood and soon found she was competing for James' attention against her own son. Her plan had failed and she felt it more and more over the years. She watched the close bond that James shared with Darren, like it was the two of them against her and with it, her resentment grew like poison ivy.

CHAPTER 41

1991

"I think we should have a weekend away for our anniversary," Felicity mentioned over breakfast. The physical side of her relationship with James had dwindled to nothing and Felicity had a plan. Over the years her mind had lingered more and more on Tony, realising she could only be free of her despair and loathing when she took her revenge for what he had done.

"Mmh," James replied, watching as Darren crammed toasted soldiers into the top of his egg.

"Here, looks nice. Your parents can look after Darren for a long weekend?" She pushed a brochure for the latest Carmichael-Astaire health spa resort across the table.

"Yes, book it if you like," James replied, wiping up the egg that had fallen onto the table. He knew Felicity liked things clean and tidy to the point of obsession. He still had no idea what plagued her from the past but he'd given up asking now.

His mum and dad happily took Darren from his arms for the weekend before they set off to Manchester. The spa was on the outskirts of the city and James soon discovered that she had booked them into one of the penthouse suites. The room held a four-poster bed and for a brief moment, James remembered a more modest room that he'd shared once. He still missed Stephanie but he had moved on completely. He'd been hurt to discover that since the split, Chris wanted nothing more to do with their friendship. He'd given no reasons except that it was hard for him to maintain the bond whilst in the Army.

Felicity had paid Keith to do his snooping in another direction and knew that Tony was in residence at this hotel. He moved around between the five he now owned and was still considered to be an extremely eligible bachelor in certain social circles. But no one knew him the way she did.

"I've booked in for a massage before dinner, sweetie," Felicity purred, stripping off and then pulling on one of the luxurious robes that came with the room. "Our dinner is booked for eight I'll see you later."

She stepped out of the room and left James at a loose end. Afraid to let the surroundings overwhelm him with the guilt he still carried, he grabbed his training bag and went in search of the gym and pool.

On her way to the beauty rooms she stopped by at reception.

"Can you give this to Mr Carmichael-Astaire, I'm a close friend of his," she asked the young girl, slipping her a dazzling smile.

"Yes ma'am," she replied, watching the woman walk away before she entered the nearby office.

"Sir, for you." She handed him the envelope and withdrew. He lounged back in his chair and opened the letter.

Dear Tony,

Ever since we met again I've been struggling to forget my feelings for you and we need to meet up. I at least owe you the chance to explain.

I am here with my husband so you will need to be discreet, but I'm currently enjoying some pampering and a massage. I'm sure if you still feel the same you can find a way for us to meet.

Love Flick xx

Well this was a change of tack after she had brushed him off last time. He'd enjoyed many women over the years but none had matched her response or the feeling she had ignited in him.

He pulled out a sheet of paper and replied, sealing inside the envelope the spare key to his private coach house for her. He just hoped she'd be able to escape at one of the times he'd suggested. He buzzed Miriam on reception and she stepped back into the room.

"Can you give this to the friend who dropped me off the letter. I believe she's enjoying a massage at the moment."

"Yes sir." She dipped her head and hurried off. She'd not seen her boss look so animated before, his expression was usually hard to read. She stepped through into the beauty salon and found Astrid at the desk.

"Is a Mrs Cooke still here?"

"Yes, she's just in with Fabrice at the moment."

"Can you give her this, apparently she's a friend of Mr Carmichael's," Miriam lowered her voice, "but be discreet."

As her hour came to an end, Felicity felt anxious, wondering how her letter had been received. She didn't need to as she was presented with a thick cream envelope. She tucked it into the gown pocket and returned to the room. She knew James would be in the gym but to make sure, she ran the bath and then locked the en suite door for complete privacy. Pulling out the letter she almost dropped the small silver key enclosed.

I'm so pleased that you have changed your mind. To remain discreet, book a massage with Vincent at any of the following times through my chief receptionist Miriam. This will give you the perfect alibi to come and visit me. The coach house is directly to the rear of the therapy rooms. I'll be waiting. Tony x

Settling into the water Felicity smiled. Little did he know that this weekend was purely the tip of her plan, the entree to the main course. Giggling she splashed water on her skin, revelling in the way it tingled and brought pinpricks of joy. She was just towelling off when she heard the door of the room open.

"I'll just be a few minutes," she trilled, quietly unlatching the door and hiding the letter at the base of her vanity case.

"No rush, but I could do with a shower before dinner."

As he opened the door she slid past him, batting her eyes in what she considered a coquettish manner. She let the towel drop and pressed against James, all the while her mind elsewhere.

"Later," he muttered, knowing how she generally preferred him fresh from the shower.

Over dinner Felicity floored him again.

"I think we should try for another baby, you know a brother or sister for Darren."

James looked up from his soup, eyes wide with shock. "Really?"

"Yes, I know I haven't quite been the best mum in the world with Darren but they say the second is easier. I want us to be a family. I was an only child and I'd have loved a brother or sister to share things with."

Chewing his bread roll meant James didn't have to reply straight away. He felt her foot on his leg beneath the table and for a change, her smile seemed genuine.

"I guess we can try," he replied, knowing that was what she wanted to hear.

"Good, excellent," she replied, leaning over the table to pop a kiss on his cheek. "We'll start tonight."

James lingered over his meal for as long as he could. He found Felicity to be too bossy and overbearing in the bedroom. She'd even tied him up on a couple of occasions which he hadn't enjoyed but had indulged, for a quiet life.

Returning to their room she stepped out of her dress.

"Make love to me," she whispered. "I'm all yours, I want to change and be the only woman for you." Her voice was light, hypnotic and not at all like her usual demanding barks. Her skin glowed and she was wearing a lovely white bra and French knickers that ruffled as she stepped towards him, hinting of an innocence and purity that softened him to her. He closed the gap and took her in his arms, letting his lips glide up the pale, light skin of her neck. He breathed in and smelt a different scent, not her usual Chanel.

He led her to the bed and stripped off the filmy garments. He couldn't deny that she was an attractive woman and many of his work colleagues affirmed this. She would never be his Stephanie but perhaps finally, he could learn to like her for the sake of his son Darren. With her eyes tightly shut, Felicity thought only of Tony and resisted calling the shots as she felt him inside her. James needed to believe that the baby would be his, should the first part of her plan with Tony fail. The thought of it bubbled and churned inside her as she gasped, moaned and perfected the art of the fake orgasm.

"Shall we do something together today?" James asked, watching her in the mirror as he shaved.

"Oh, I've got some more beauty treatments booked for a couple of hours between eleven and two. I'll meet you in the pool at four."

"Ok." He saw the day ahead stretching in front of him and knew that he could indulge in his passion for cycling.

Kissing him goodbye, Felicity rang down to reception and made the arrangements with Miriam before spending the time preparing. She wanted to remind him of the girl she guessed he remembered, letting her hair fall loose over her shoulders. Then she picked up the key and went to meet her future, the man she hoped would be husband number two. He owed her big time and he was going to pay with sweat, tears and cold, hard cash. She cast a brilliant smile at Miriam as she passed reception on her way to the beauty suite, then finding the small doorway from the letter, she walked through and across a cobbled courtyard to the coach house building. She pulled the key out and opened the door before stepping inside.

Classical music wafted through the double doors ahead so she was drawn in that direction, picking up the scent of warm bread when she pushed them open. Her heels clicked across the deep mahogany floorboards and then she saw him. Lounging on the sofa, his golden blond hair gleamed in the weak winter sunshine that shone through the full height windows behind him.

"Felicity," he said her name, and every tiny hair on her body stood to attention in a second.

She tried to calm her beating heart as she hesitated in the doorway, letting him drink in her curves. She'd teamed her red wool dress with a wide black belt and her favourite heels so when he stood to close the gap, she was staring directly into his eyes.

"You've grown more beautiful," he said, lifting her hand to his lips. She hoped he wouldn't feel the tremor starting in her fingertips. He felt her wedding ring and glanced his thumb across it.

"So you went ahead then?"

"Needs must at the time, but they can change," she replied, pulling away slightly.

He poured them both a glass of whiskey and allowed her the choice of seat. She chose the chair next to the end of the sofa where she'd found him. He returned to that seat and allowed his hand to rest easily on the arm, so close to her.

"Quite an empire you've built up." She admired each photograph on the stark walls. Each was an aspect from one or other of his chain.

216

"Yes, from a small seed of an idea."

"And a large inheritance with the death of your father." Her gaze captured him, her eyes like headlamps trying to capture the startle. But he was good, poised as he took a generous swallow of the amber liquid.

"An unexpected and unfortunate turn of events," he replied, "but hey, that's water under the bridge now and we should look ahead."

"Ahead to what?" She smirked, her turn to bathe her flames in liquor.

He nodded and stood up, moving easily into the adjourning kitchen and returning with bread, olives and cold champagne.

"Let's eat and we can get to know about the intervening years."

The cold bubbles tickled her nose as she rejoiced in the decadence, trying to remain aloof and bury the simmering anger at what his actions and her own had created. Neither of them mentioned the night until Tony glanced at the clock.

"I had so many plans for our time together but the clock is ticking and I always get what I want."

"Do you?" she whispered, aware of his grip tightening on her arm.

"Yes, I still want you Flick."

With a swift tug, she was in his arms.

"Allow me to show you the bedroom."

As he carried her upstairs he didn't see her calculating look, taking in all the fineries of just this small discreet place. Setting her down she admired his masculine taste, stark but sumptuous.

"I'll just freshen up," she said, seeing a door to the side.

"Don't be too long," he replied, discarding his jacket on a small chaise longue.

Removing her dress Felicity admired the view in the full length, gilt-edged mirror. The sheer black body hugged her curves and hid the few stretch marks on her stomach. With a quick spritz of her perfume she was ready for act one, needing this to ensure act two and possibly an encore if she had time. She stood in the doorway and smoothed her hair over her shoulder, watching him gasp and then pat the bedcovers beside him. Like a puma stalking its prey she prowled to the bed, kicking her heels off so she could kneel beside him on the covers.

"Let me show you what I've learnt," she murmured, touching her lips to his, languishing as his mouth opened to allow her tongue entry.

The taste of whiskey mingled with the food, champagne and

undeniable taint of lust, spurring them on. Felicity made short work of the tiny pearl buttons on his shirt before sitting back to admire his muscular torso. The faint line of blond hair from his chest ran down and this time, she did trace it with her nail. He wriggled beneath her, allowing her to loosen his belt and peel of his trousers.

"Commando, eh!" she remarked, wasting no time in dropping her bright red lips over the end of his cock. Memories of the beach assailed her and she remembered his exacting needs. Her tongue licked and lapped while her hand gripped the base and squeezed his balls.

Feeling how close he was to the edge, she pulled back and Tony took charge. He grasped her wrist and wrestled her beneath him.

"How the fuck does this come off?" he growled, looking for a catch on her bodysuit. "Rip it off, it's old and you can always buy me a new one."

The lace netting yielded as he bit down over her nipple and pulled back, hearing the satisfying sound of the tear. Gripping the edges of the hole he pulled the rest of it from her body. It lay there stark and tattered against the snow white of the bedding. Tony paused and let his gaze travel her length, the breasts large and glorious topped with deep burgundy nipples. There was her pale skin and then, no longer a bush of black concealing her, just shaved and smooth. He wanted to go straight there but he also needed to savour her.

He licked across her nipples, letting her arch into his mouth so that his teeth could pull and pinch. But the sweet scent of her was entering his nostrils and he felt her hands in her hair.

"Please... do what you do," was her whimpering plea.

"Patience, you deserve to be savoured like a fine wine."

"Fuck the wine Tony, just fuck me." She yanked his hair tight and ground against him. He slid down her body and pushed her legs apart, opening her to him. He dipped a first finger into the folds, spreading them back to reveal the glistening, engorged pink. Her clit stood bold and proud for him as he leaned down and touched it with his tongue.

"God, Tony." Both her hands were on the back of his head, pushing him in deeper, making sure he didn't waver from the task in hand. She was exactly how he remembered, every lick or suck had her thighs trembling either side of him. Juice was seeping and slick amongst her folds and his finger squelched inside her while his tongue settled on the pace that was bringing her to climax. She shuddered on his tongue and before she had time to relax, he was pushing inside her. This was the one thing he'd not experienced in the past.

"Felicity, my sweet, sweet girl," he moaned before latching on to her mouth again as he pounded her into the covers. Deep inside Felicity, she felt the revulsion like a creature crawling through her veins. She kept her eyes screwed shut like her body was somewhere different, feeling while her mind struggled with the memories of his father. This was what she deserved as he filled her, pumping in deep before shrivelling away.

"Oh my girl, my Flick, it's always been you."

She felt him lie next to her, pulling her into his arms as he had once done on the beach. The silence cloaked them for a while before Felicity glanced at her watch. She had half an hour before she needed to meet James.

"I have to go," she said, untangling his arms and standing on slightly shaky legs.

"When can I see you again?" he said, following her body as she moved to the bathroom.

"Same time tomorrow, we don't leave until Tuesday morning."

When she returned, fully clothed and back to her polished self, Tony was still in bed, finishing off the remains of the champagne. Felicity blew him a kiss and then left before she could change her mind.

CHAPTER 42

Trying to smother her elation Felicity walked back into the hotel towards the pool. She slipped into her bikini and then stepped onto the cold tiles. She saw James ploughing up and down and waited for him to join her at the shallow end.

"Good day?" he asked.

"Yes, I'm enjoying this place." She joined him in some leisurely lengths before they dropped into the Jacuzzi.

"Out or in for dinner, I noticed a cosy bistro not far away."

"Yes, why not," she agreed, dropping a light peck on his cheek.

Over the next few days they spent time apart, indulging in their own favourite activities. For James it was cycling, archery and the gym. Felicity enjoyed every spare moment in the company of Tony as they played together and he indulged her expensive tastes.

Their last morning together felt bittersweet.

"So when will I see you again?" Tony asked, letting his finger glide down the curve of her spine.

"You tell me," she giggled. "I'm the attached one, remember?"

"Can't you become unattached?"

"Maybe, but not yet. I have a two year old at home." She resisted the urge to add, "and another on the way, thanks to you!"

"Yes, I'm not sure I was meant to have children, not after my father!"

"Because you are so much like him?"

He pushed her away and stood up, scrambling into his clothes. "You'd better go."

"Afraid to admit it?" she goaded, rolling onto her back and stretching her long legs in his direction. He turned his face, beet-red, his eyes dark. He caught her foot and held on tight, crushing the bones of her toes so hard she gasped in fright. Then as if in a trance he shook his head and released her.

"Just go."

She watched him walk away, hearing the door slam shut. She scurried to the window, despite the pain shooting through her foot, and watched him disappear back into his kingdom. She took her time, leaving a red lipstick mark on the pillow to remind him.

James was packed and ready to leave when she hobbled into the room.

"What happened?"

"Just a twist, teach me for walking too fast in these heels."

She sat down on the bed and slipped off her shoes. Black bruising was visible on three of her toes. James knelt down and gently touched her foot, but she winced and pulled it away.

"I think you should get that checked out, you might have broken something."

"When we get home, babe."

The doctor confirmed the breaks the next day, two toes in all but being the smallest ones, there was nothing that could be done except to elevate and rest. Felicity now knew what she was dealing with and as the weeks passed, she planned and plotted. After two months and no sign of any sickness, Felicity took her pregnancy test into the bathroom, fearing that the hotel time had been a failure. But she was delighted when the pink lines appeared and told her she was pregnant again. This time she sailed through the whole period. James was delighted but at the same time, resigned to staying with her for longer.

Felicity paced the private hospital room, the contractions getting closer, but all she had on her mind was the blood test she needed once the baby was born. Keith had been keeping tabs on Tony for her as he'd made no attempt to contact her since their tryst at his hotel. Her interest in Stephanie's small town life had waned and apart from the odd slip of his tongue in sleep, James had been attentive and kind. The sound of the door startled her walk and she turned to find James holding a glass of water.

"Is everything ok?" he asked, setting it down on the side.

"All good this time, I've had every available pain relief," she replied.

She let him help her back onto the bed.

"Any bets on if it's a boy or a girl?"

"Think the station has a wager on, so long as it's healthy that's all that matters."

With the midwife in attendance James held her hand as she pushed and strained, but this time the baby appeared much quicker.

Wrapping up the little bundle the midwife smiled at Felicity and James. "It's a boy."

Holding out his arms James stared down into the eyes of his second son, captured by the love he felt.

"He's beautiful," he gasped, passing him to Felicity.

She took a breath as the eyes of her son stared into hers, clear and emerald just like Tony's. In her mind there was no doubt but that piece of paper was important to her future. Stretching out she knocked the glass of water, sending it spiralling and into shattered pieces on the floor. James bent down and started to gather the shards, catching himself on a particularly pointed piece.

"Ouch," he exclaimed.

"Here's a cotton pad." The Nurse stepped forward. She'd been primed by Felicity for a large donation to the hospital funds. At the same time she picked up the glass with blood still on it.

"I'll sort it out," she assured.

Felicity watched her scurry out of the room and hid the smug smile behind her concern.

"Are you ok?"

"Yeah, bit sharper than I was expecting," James replied. "Hey, I'm going to ring my parents, let them know the news and find out how soon we can get home as I'm sure Darren will want to meet his brother."

Felicity nodded and cradled their new son close. "You can name him if you like?"

"Let me think about it," he replied, stepping out into the corridor.

Pam and Peter were overjoyed at the news, although Pam could detect his sadness at the situation. She had finally prised from him the truth and knew that he was looking for a way out that wouldn't hurt his children. With James out of the room Felicity studied her new son, he was perfect with his dark hair and apart from the colour of his eyes, enough of James' features to pass scrutiny. Now it was just down to her and another well-planned visit to one of Tony's hotels when she was back in shape.

On the way up the corridor James pondered names, he almost decided upon Christopher after his best friend. But now they were distant it didn't seem right. Then it struck him, he'd been watching *Top Gun* again the previous evening and allowing his memories of Stephanie to come alive whilst he was alone. He remembered her comment, "If we ever have a daughter we can call her Charlotte…" That sentence had floored him then, but now he wished more than anything to turn the clock back. Back in the room he found both his wife and son sleeping. He settled down to the film characters and when Felicity woke up, he'd chosen.

"He's called Mitchell," James said, standing to look over his sleeping son.

"Mmmh, Mitchell, is that a family name?"

"Nope, just one I like," James replied, watching the baby stir and look up at him.

"I've just got to have a check-up in the next hour and then hopefully we can get out of here."

Their conversation was interrupted by the arrival of the doctor so James left them to it. Cass was waiting outside and he gave her a hug.

"It's another boy," he said.

"Oh, is she disappointed? I think she wanted a daughter."

"Hard to tell," he replied, "he's called Mitchell and he's a beauty."

He let Cass go in once the doctor left. The nurse was just taking a blood swab but left quickly with just a nod.

"Something up?" Cass asked.

"They think I might be anaemic, just wanted a blood sample," Felicity lied, knowing that within a couple of weeks she would have written proof of her son's father. Cass plucked the baby from the crib and rocked him in her arms.

"He's smashing, such unusual eyes."

Felicity grinned at her comment, the first hurdle passed – in that Cass had not questioned it. And as usual James was smitten.

223

CHAPTER 43

Felicity smiled when a week later, the confirmation of her infidelity came through. James was not Mitchell's father.

"I'm going to pop into town and get the birth registered," Felicity said over breakfast.

"I'll come if you want, I'm not back in work until later."

"No, I'll be ok, if you can drop Darren at nursery then I'll do it before I pop in for coffee with Cass."

"Fine." James hardly recognised his new maternal wife. She absolutely doted on Mitchell in comparison with her indifference to Darren as a baby. Plucking Darren from his chair James whisked him upstairs to get ready for nursery.

Placing Mitchell into the pram Felicity walked out the door an hour later. It was a brisk walk into town but all the while she stared into Mitchell's eyes that were watching her, reminding her. In the town hall she filled in the form.

"Is this correct?" The clerk asked, looking at the different surnames of the mother and father.

"Yes, just register it, or do you need proof? I have a blood test," she snapped.

"Certainly Mrs Cooke," the clerk simpered and finished the paperwork quickly. "Do you need two copies?"

"Yes." Felicity turned away and chuckled to her son's beaming face. With the paperwork safely tucked away she strolled along to Cass' house.

"Hi Mummy Flick," Cass said, opening the door. "You're positively beaming."

"Hell, yeah life is great."

"So the spark is back with James?"

"Mmmh you could say that."

Back at home later Felicity got out paper and pen and set to work on her letter to Tony. It was just over nine months since she'd seen him but Keith had told her that he was mostly in residence in his London hotel, apparently with another project on the go. Licking the seal an hour later she tucked Mitchell into his car seat and then went to collect Darren from nursery and at the same time, she posted the letter. She'd set up a post office box for Tony to reply to if he wished. Now she just had to wait.

In his London hotel Tony opened his many bills and quotes. The work on redeveloping his father's old private club site was taking time but it would be worth it. Despite the bad taste that the Felicity incident had left him with, he was unable to deny his more distinct tastes inherited from his father. His club was to include two well-stocked dungeons as well as many different rooms, together with a restaurant and bar. It was registered under the pseudonym Madame Zee Zee and he just needed to employee his mistress as that person. No one would ever know that it belonged to him. At the bottom of the pile the pale cream envelope stood out and he slit it open.

Dear Tony,

It is so long since I last saw you and enjoyed our time together at your hotel in Manchester. I hope you will not be too shocked by the news I have to tell you.

I've just given birth to your son, conceived during our time together in the coach house. Before you deny this think back... you never asked if I was on birth control you just took what was on offer as I did. But it is I who have to deal with the consequence. I had a blood test to be sure that my husband is not the father and when you see the photo of our son you'll know my words are the truth. I have even named you on the birth certificate, of which a copy is enclosed.

I am willing to give up the stability of my marriage to be with you, the only true love of my life. I hope you will be happy to take us both into your heart and make me your wife? For my protection you may contact

me through my Post Office Box No. 3879
I look forward to being back in your arms soon!
Love Flick

He dropped the paper as if it was on fire. Horror bloomed in his chest and he struggled to grasp the glass of water on his desk. He drained it and then stood up to refill it with whiskey, not minding the early hour of the morning. His hand shook the ice making it clash against the cut glass of the tumbler. He'd never wanted to be a father, not after his own childhood. He'd always been careful with all the women he'd been with until Felicity. He shut his eyes and found her image there, his favourite from the beach on the last night of the holiday that had brought them together. She was still a siren and this letter and photograph had grounded him on her slippery rocks.

He paced the office, knocking back more alcohol until his mind was a blank. He wanted Felicity but not with a child in tow, so afraid that he would be just as cruel as his own father. In the end he did nothing and instead tore the letter, photograph and birth certificate up.

After a month Felicity sent another letter and each time, received no reply back. Each time this happened her anger grew, burning inside her until she had no choice.

"I'm absolutely worn out," she declared one evening, as she sat with James in the lounge. "I've booked a weekend away in that lovely hotel we went to but this time I'm going alone."

"Fine," James replied, looking over at Felicity and secretly feeling pleased to have a weekend without her dark mood. It had been hanging over the house for nearly a month and he'd even taken the boys over to his parents' to keep them away from her foulness.

The next morning she packed her bag and drove off for her showdown. Once again Keith had come up trumps and she knew Tony was in residence. Also she had never returned the key so unless he had changed the locks, she would be ready and waiting for him. The girl on reception was the same as before as Felicity booked into her suite, this time under her maiden name Jennings. She took a leisurely bath, moisturised thoroughly and slid into her new underwear and dress. Then she sauntered to the hidden door, across the courtyard and slotted the key into the lock. It swung open but hearing the music playing she knew she'd been rumbled.

"Flick, I've been expecting you," Tony said as he wandered into view. His dressing gown hung open and he held a champagne flute. "Come join me and we can talk."

"I think I gave you the chance to talk and you ignored me." Felicity stood her ground, hands firmly planted on her hips.

Tony smirked and turned away. "No one tells me what to do."

"Really!" Felicity turned on her heels but only took three steps before she felt his hand on her waist.

He grabbed her roughly and reeled her into his chest. She didn't even get the chance to move her arms that were now pinioned to her sides. She inhaled his pine tinged aftershave and the oak tones of the whiskey on his breath. She opened her mouth to protest but her words were halted by his dominant kiss. Claiming her to his will, yet still she struggled. Tony held firm, loving the fight in her as he reached for her hands and led her to his spare bedroom, the one that held his toys. Looking into her eyes he saw the sparkle of both anger and desire.

"Let me show you what I'm capable of." He let her go, circling her like a predator.

"You think I'm scared of you, scared of all this?" She sneered, slowly pulling at the zip on the back of her dress. It dropped to the floor leaving him gaping at her scarlet corset, barely there g-string and stockings that revealed only the tops of her thighs.

Felicity heard him catch his breath, ragged and coarse. "I know what you are Anthony, you are your father incarnate." She knew the comment would incense him further. He grabbed her wrist, squeezing it tightly so that she yelped. "Maybe I am… maybe I'm more than he ever was."

With his free hand he ripped open the ribbons that held her armour in place and revelled in the sight of her ripe breasts spilling out. She'd kept her shape despite two pregnancies but the lines were on her skin. He pushed her backwards to the wall and brought her arms above her head. He took the opportunity to press against her bare flesh with his own, feeling her bullet hard nipples soften as they touched his warmth.

"What do you want Tony?" she whispered.

"What do you want Felicity?"

Before she could say more he captured her lips and let his tongue push inside to tease hers. He locked her wrists into place above her, the cuffs of the finest soft leather, tightening the straps to just allow enough circulation. Then he stepped back to admire the sight of her alabaster skin against the black stockings. Her eyes blazed into his, her cheeks flushed red.

"I should have done this to you last time," he said, letting his dressing gown slip from his broad shoulders.

He was a fine specimen with his daily gym and swimming regime, his muscles firm and well defined. His cock stood alert and ready for action as he let his hand reach down to pull on it a couple of times.

"I'm going to take you to the point of just feeling, where you will beg me to both stop and keep going in the same breath."

He reached for the blindfold neatly folded on the cabinet and saw the sweat start to bead on her forehead.

"No, not that… please."

"Now, now Flick, they say the only way to overcome your fears are to embrace them!" The black silk slid over her hair and covered her eyes that she had involuntarily shut. She was spinning back in time to her frightened eighteen year old self, the one she hid deep inside.

Tony let his fingers slide over her cheekbone and then trace the outline of her lips before her mouth opened to the pressure. She licked and sucked each digit in turn, needing the simple action to take her away from the fear.

This would be different, this was Tony, and Malcolm was dead. DEAD! With his fingers wet with her saliva he trailed them down her elegant neck and over her shoulders. He let them graze the side of her one breast and felt the tremble run through her skin at his touch. He slid on past, knowing he had all the time in the world.

The scent of her perfume was heady on the heat of her skin but as he dropped to his knees a more potent, musky shade was added to it. This had never felt so good before and he'd had plenty of girls in the past. The difference was they simpered to his will and he saw the pound signs in their eyes. With Felicity he saw raw power, frighteningly intense.

He kissed her mound, still clad in the lace material. She whimpered and pushed into him, her body craving his touch. Felicity was spinning out of control on a mixture of fear and lust that was hard to fathom. One minute she was panting with desire the next it felt more like hyperventilating as her skin fluctuated between heat and cold! But she would not beg, she would not give in without a fight. Tony let his finger hook beneath the fabric, letting it glance over her folds. He let the fabric slide down her legs and he picked each of her feet up in turn so that he could hold them in his palm.

"Your scent is overpowering," he said, taking a deep breath before discarding them on the floor.

Then his nose nuzzled into her, parting her to his delicate but probing tongue. Immediately she was thinking about the night in the villa and trembles starting to resonate in the skin of her thighs. Damn she hated her traitorous body! The ripples were rolling into waves, waiting to engulf her in her first orgasm.

Tony sensed her turmoil and knew she was close so he pulled away and moved up to run his tongue in languid swirls between her two breasts. Feeling her nipples harden beneath his teeth, he nibbled and gnawed. Each small bite took her to a higher level of sensitivity. Tony left her with a single kiss on her perfectly upturned lips before finding his riding crop. He laced his hand around the handle, releasing an extra scent of leather next to the cuffs around her wrists, keeping her body taunt and straining.

"Let me see," she whined, missing his touch.

"Not yet my beauty, you've only had pleasure so far, it's sweeter after the pain," he growled.

With the blindfold on she had no idea what he was about to do, until she felt the flat end of something running up her leg. Tony started off slowly, running it over her skin before he tapped her right breast with it.

"Oh," she gasped, "is that the best you can do?"

"You want it harder?"

"Yes, do your worst." She gritted her teeth beneath the smile.

He would get his payback at a later date.

She felt the first strike of the crop against the topside of her breast before he ran it across to even out the sting to both sides. He licked across the marks he'd left, feeling her flinch but sigh. Tony let the crop slide down the curves of her hip and round so he could place some well timed thwacks on her ass, each one harder than the last as she panted and squealed. He was surprised, most women caved by this point.

In the shadows of the room Tony felt his private ghost watching, laughing and smugly saying, "You're just like me, son." He squeezed his eyes shut to the childhood pain he'd suffered at the hands of his father. When he opened them again he dropped the crop and slumped to his knees in front of her. His siren, his goddess. His finger jabbed into her, letting him hear her gasp. His tongue found her clit and he sucked her in, nibbling and licking. Felicity smelt his desire, intermingled with the distinct aftershave he wore. She could feel her first orgasm, held off briefly, return with depth. She circled her hips, grinding onto his face beneath her, allowing him no chance to breathe. He felt the liquid running down her thighs as he struggled to drink it all in. She slumped for a second but he didn't need to catch her.

He eased away and unfastened the cuffs before carrying her to the bed.

"Your turn now," he said, lifting her blindfold away. Her eyes took a second to adjust before she saw Tony lounging on the covers. His hand covered his cock and he was hard at work.

"Suck me," he demanded.

"What happened to manners?"

"Please fucking suck me," he grunted, his eyes glazed with desire.

His lips and chin dripped juice from her. Moving closer she ran her tongue over his face, enjoying the taste. Then he fisted his hand into her long hair, forcing her lower. Opening her mouth she took him in, right down so that he touched the back of her throat. She still hated the taste of spunk so when she felt him tense between her lips and tongue, she pulled her mouth off and angled the spray to meet the skin of her chest and stomach. It was her small act of defiance to his preferences. She watched him breathing heavily in front of her and let a glimmer of a smile light the corner of her eyes.

CHAPTER 44

Climbing off the bed she prowled around the room, letting her fingers glance over the bondage chains and the sturdy wooden cross on the other wall. She peeped into the small dresser draws, fingering the arrangement of floggers, crops and one just containing panties. She saw hers lying on the floor so picking them up she walked over and emptied the others into the nearby waste basket. She knew Tony was watching her as she placed the damp g-string into it before shutting it and turning to face him.

"You don't need all those now, only mine."

"Oh is that right? You certainly have a high opinion of yourself."

"Maybe I know that I was meant to be a spoilt bitch, your spoilt bitch."

He moved from the bed to capture her waist in his hands, bringing her tight into his body.

"Come let's relax in the main bedroom. I have champagne on ice and I can order some food from the restaurant for us to enjoy."

"Mmmh perhaps I can stay a little longer, it all depends…"

"On what?" he asked, guiding her through to the expansive master bedroom. The plush covers of red and gold glowed in the soft lighting. He released her so that he could pass her a silk robe.

"Why do I need to cover up?" she asked, her mouth forming her favourite pout.

"I don't need my staff seeing what is mine."

"Don't you trust them to avert their eyes?"

"Yes, but they don't need to feel tempted."

Pouring a glass of the chilled Bollinger he handed it over and then filled another. They clinked the glasses together and drank. Reclining on the bed he picked up the phone and ordered a platter of oysters and caviar for them.

Within ten minutes they heard the door open.

"Where would you like your food, sir?"

"Leave it on the coffee table, bring strawberries and cream in about an hour."

"Yes sir." They heard the footsteps retreat and Tony wandered through, pressing a button so the fake coal fire blazed into life.

"Hungry?"

"Yes, but first I need to shower." She could feel his sticky remains against the fine soft material.

"Later, I will run the bath for you but for now my spunk stays." He reached to pull open her gown, admiring the red scars from the whip and the sheen of his seed drying on her skin.

Tony fed her the oysters laced with lemon juice, followed by the caviar on thin water crackers. They had only just finished when the waiter appeared again. His eyes darted from his boss to the woman who sat beside him.

"Gerard, please bring some brandy later." Tony watched as the bowls of dessert were set down and the empty platter removed.

"Yes sir," he replied, before scurrying out. He knew what the brandy meant as it was always after his set working hours.

"You are spoiling me," Felicity said, picking at a strawberry, dipping it into the fluffy clotted cream before biting into it.

"I'm giving you a taste of life as my Mistress."

"But what if I want more than that?" She stared at him. "I want marriage and recognition as your equal business partner."

"Let's not ruin food with demands unless they are to satisfy other desires."

He left her to run the bath, adding in drops of pure rose oil that reminded him of his mother. The steam and scent filled the air.

"Join me Felicity," he called.

She stepped into the marble paradise in monochrome design. The bath tub was sunk into the floor and far larger than the standard size. He gently peeled the gown from her shoulders, allowing her the luxury of stepping in first. Then he joined her, allowing the water to surround and cocoon them in warmth. He watched the pink heat tinge her skin and the ends of her long hair float out around her. He knew that he loved her but he was not ready for the commitment of marriage and he didn't want anything to do with raising a child.

They were just drying off when they heard footsteps again.

"I have a surprise for you," Tony said, reaching for her hand and guiding her into the bedroom. Gerard was waiting for them, lying naked on the bed.

"Youth, beauty and virility," Tony declared, "and so submissive to my wants and needs."

The bath with Flick had revived his cock which was now back to full strength and ready for round two. Felicity watched as he strode to the bed and loomed over the young man, who looked barely legal. His mouth latched onto the cock he was offered while Tony reached down to fondle Gerard's balls.

"Watch if you want? Or join in," Tony said.

Felicity had never seen two guys together before so she took a seat on the end of the bed.

She realised that both were practised in their moves, each giving and receiving of each other before it became obvious that Tony was in complete control. She watched him squirt a liberal amount of lube on both his cock and the asshole now upturned and ready for him.

Felicity winced and wondered if she could house his cock in that way. The sight and sounds of the two men grunting away before her was turning her on as she spread her legs and let her fingers run down to rub at her nubbin. Tony was watching her at all times and as she pleasured herself, he seemed to move harder and faster. Gerard shot his load quickly onto the towel beneath them. Tony pulled out and the young man swivelled to capture the ejaculation in his open mouth before pulling Tony close to kiss and exchange the fluid.

Fucking hell that was a hot show.

Felicity tried to double her efforts to let her body experience release but in the end, Tony crawled across and dived between her legs. His tongue was far more effective than her finger in bringing her to the pinnacle.

"Come here Gerard, watch this woman come," he said, proudly licking and probing her pussy for the sweet spot that made her arch and splash against his fingers.

"Let me watch you lick her clean," Tony demanded as Gerard slowly lapped at the pussy juices flowing from her.

Felicity was sore but the touch of this softer tongue had her lifting and swirling back into the throes of another less violent orgasm.

Tony watched it all in ecstasy, she was truly his kind of woman.

Jealous of the last orgasm, he pushed Gerard away.

"Go," he whispered before he stretched out and let his tongue slide back between her luscious folds. Felicity was beyond speaking as she groaned and cried with another ripple breaking her apart before the room receded into blackness.

When she woke from her faint she was back in the warm waters of a fresh bath, Tony sitting alongside, just letting his fingers trail on the surface.

"Magnificent," he said, helping her out and then drying her with the towel. With legs still shaking he helped her into the bed and then slipped in beside her. Felicity had never felt so bruised and content.

He let her snuggle into his side and watched her fall asleep. This was new to him, he'd never let a woman stay beyond her worth to him. It felt nice to see her eyelashes flutter and move, her hand straying to touch his chest. Hearing Tony start to snore, Felicity woke up. She longed to stay but he needed to beg, plead and give in to her demands. Mistress was just not part of her plan! Pulling on her dress she tiptoed from the coach house and back into the hotel. No one saw her creep through the corridors.

Waking in the early hours Tony saw the side of the bed empty and the place in silence. Ah so she wanted to play hard to get? He wondered how long she would wait if he decided to not show up. He downed the last dregs from a champagne flute and then turned to inhale her faint scent still on the pillow.

Felicity strolled into the restaurant for the final serving of breakfast and smiled as a few late diners watched her sit alone at the table by the window. Smoked salmon and poached eggs filled the hunger left by the previous evening and then she went back upstairs to change for a run. Keith had informed her that this was what Tony did each day. Setting out at a gentle pace she followed the pathway around and between the trees at the perimeter.

She soon caught sight of a figure standing by a small summer house that looked out across the hotel and grounds from its higher elevation. Moving with speed she sprinted up the hill and came face to face with Tony.

"Hey," she breathed, smoothing back the tendrils of hair stuck to her forehead.

"Oh Flick, nice to see you. Didn't know you ran?"

"There's plenty you don't know," she smirked, before setting off in a jog down the other side.

She heard his footsteps behind her before he was level. He slowed his pace to match hers and she caught his gaze for a moment before she sped up. Again he let her escape for ten minutes, enjoying the view of her ass in the shorts she wore. Then as she headed into the tree-lined final stretch before the hotel came back into view, he caught her, pulling her off her feet with his forceful grip.

He propelled her back until she hit the rough bark on a tree and her breath was pushed out by the bulk of his body.

"I want you Felicity," he growled. "Leave your husband, be my Mistress."

"No." She pushed against him, trying to get free.

"Yes, you know you want me. You need me."

"Never, I can't be a kept woman."

"Not even mine?"

With a strong shove he released her and ran on down the path. Felicity watched him and stifled her laugh. She had seen the look in his eyes, the desire and despair that she had refused him. Refused Anthony Carmichael-Astaire.

She jogged the rest of the way back to the hotel and as she walked past reception, the girl behind the desk coughed.

"Ms Jennings?"

Felicity stopped and took a step back. "Yes, I am."

"Here, this is for you."

She took the cream envelope and sauntered to her room. She showered and shrugged on her dressing gown before opening it. Inside was a letter and a cheque.

Dear Felicity,

I'm afraid that urgent business in London has called me away. I hope you stay and enjoy the rest of your time at my hotel, your bill will be paid so feel free to indulge.

Marriage and fatherhood is not for me, all I can offer is my body, passion and enough money to keep you in every luxury you can imagine! Reconsider and you can be my Mistress for the rest of your life. Overleaf are my private numbers for each hotel and a rough plan of where I will be throughout the year. A room will always be provided for you, and of course discretion. The money is what I feel I owe you after that night!

I hope to see you again soon.

Your Tony xx

Shaking, she read the words again. The figure on the cheque swam in the angry tears that fell. She was not and never would be his whore to be bought and paid for! Ripping it up she found the hotel stationery in the bedside cabinet and she popped the pieces of cheque inside an envelope.

CHAPTER 45

1993

A year later, Felicity was leafing through the local newspaper during her lunch break when she saw a job vacancy for Leisure Manager at the local Carmichael-Astaire resort. She had resisted crawling to him but at night, lying in bed next to James, she thought only of Tony. Marriage was dull, neither of them earned that much and she still felt no real affection for her sons. Darren was meant to make her happy but he didn't and Mitchell just reminded her of Tony every time she looked at him.

With her CV and covering letter duly sent, she waited. Perhaps this would be her way into Tony's life, where he would see her as his equal? A week later and she was off to her interview and she hoped that Tony would be there. Walking into the office she was not disappointed when she saw him stand up and walk around the desk.

"Well, well, well. I just had to interview you in person when my assistant told me the candidates' names."

"I don't expect any favours," she replied, smoothing her skirt down before she stretched out a hand. He took it but brought it to his lips instead, letting the slight stubble on his chin graze her skin.

Refusing to let him fluster her she pulled it away and took a seat opposite. She watched as Tony leaned against the desk and plucked her CV from the top of the pile.

"You have very good credentials in the leisure industry," he mused, watching her intently over the top edge of the paper.

"Thank you, I've worked hard to get where I am but I'm ready for a new challenge."

"And you think I can give you that?"

"I think your company can. I noticed that aside from a pool, massage and gym equipment, you offer no specialist training or exercise classes. I could implement that. Your doors can then be opened for daily use, membership and more earning potential."

Tony nodded his head, he'd been thinking the same thing in the past year, along with tennis courts and even small nine-hole golf courses where he had enough land.

"And you can deliver this Mrs Cooke?"

"Yes, I know I can." She went on to outline potential figures based on the business she'd brought in at the local leisure centre, possible upfront costs and increased staffing.

Tony had zoned out and was admiring the line of her lower leg as it slid up and beneath her skirt. He wondered what underwear she wore and with every breath he inhaled her perfume, always the same and so tempting. The room was silent and he looked up to find her amused grin greeting him.

"Why didn't you take the money? Why did you never contact me? We have something, you and I."

"I don't settle for second best." She stood up and extended her hand once more. "I'll await your decision," she said, giving it a tiny squeeze before pulling away. But he was too quick for her as he cut off her exit and stood between her and the door.

"The job's yours, I have no interest in any one else," he said, catching her waist and finishing his sentence with his lips brushing hers.

She sighed and let her body submit to his as their tongues slid against each other's, reigniting the flames inside. His hand slid down the fabric of her skirt before lifting it to hook a finger in her panties.

"You do know that I can be a very demanding boss," he said, softly into her ear.

She nodded as the small scrap of material pooled at her ankles and he dropped to his knees before her, the tip of his tongue catching her clit in the first sweep. She trembled as he licked her to the point where she though her legs would crumple beneath her. He stood up and pushed her back to the edge of the desk.

"Turn around and bend over."

"Like this?" she simpered, playing along in the submissive role he'd cast her in.

"Yes, spread those legs for me, wide."

Letting her hair sweep against the oak surface she heard the zip on his trousers before his hands spread her buttocks. She felt the head of his cock nudging at her entrance.

"Fuck me Tony, fuck me hard," she gasped before she struggled for breath as the edge of the desk slammed into her stomach. His length filled her in that one swift move, pummelling with ferocity until she ached, throbbed and his heat stifled it.

Pulling out he watched her reach for the tissues to stem the flow before it hit her stocking top.

"I love leaving stains," he said.

"Yeah and I hate them," was her quick retort.

Tony let out a belly laugh as he watched her straighten her skirt, followed by her hair.

"So how soon can you start?"

"I'll be here in a month, have my office ready." Then blowing him a kiss she sauntered through the office door.

Getting home Felicity penned her resignation letter and left it ready on the side for her meeting the next morning. Then feeling slightly guilty about her assignation she showered, changed and ordered takeaway for when James arrived home.

Grubby after a vehicle collision and a small chimney fire, James was looking forward to a soak in the bath and bed, so when he stepped through the door he was startled to find the table laid and candles lit.

"Hi, I'm home," he called, "but off for a shower first."

"Fine, darling but don't be long as I've ordered your favourite."

On the landing James stopped at the first door and poked his head in.

"Hi Daddy," Darren said, holding out his arms. James crept in and wrapped his arms around his eldest. Kissing him on the forehead he settled him back beneath the covers.

"Night son, sleep tight and don't let the bed bugs bite." That always made Darren laugh. Then he opened the door of the nursery and crept towards the cradle. He stared at the sleeping form of Mitchell and pulled the blanket back up to cover him. Somehow he always managed to kick the sheets off or end up tangled in them every morning. Then after a quick shower he went downstairs, trying to work out what the occasion was.

"Can you open the wine?" Felicity asked, motioning to the bottle on the table.

"Sure, what are we celebrating?"

"I've just got a new job at the Carmichael-Astaire health spa as manager." She grinned, as James passed her a glass of champagne.

"Congratulations." He tapped her glass with his, racking his brain as to whether she had told him about applying or even the interview.

Felicity noted his puzzled frown.

"Oh, I never mentioned it as I was nervous I wouldn't even get an interview."

Over dinner James noticed the shine of happiness brightening her features as she told him her plans.

"Oh, I may need to sleep in every so often," she said. "I'm sure we can make arrangements for the boys if it ends up coinciding with your night shifts."

A month later, Felicity stepped inside her office, a new grey pinstriped suit hugging her curves. She'd spent the last month at her old job pounding the treadmill and working out so that all her remaining childbirth weight gain had vanished. She'd had her hair trimmed but it was still long so she wore it in her favoured high ponytail. Her signature red lipstick was the only bright colour in her sombre attire. She was still admiring the sumptuous décor of her domain when her nostrils prickled at his familiar scent.

"Morning Felicity," he said, his voice reducing her insides to a writhing mass of snakes. She heard the door shut before she turned to face him.

"Anthony." She smiled and stepped closer. "My compliments to your designer, this office is amazing."

"Plenty more time for you to admire more closely the sheen of the desktop or feel the pile of the carpet on your knees," he whispered, having closed the gap between them.

He let his lips linger on her cheek in a light kiss.

"But it's business first and I need to get you acquainted with all the staff, so when we are in their presence it must be strictly formal between us."

Felicity arched her eyebrows and smirked. "That won't be a problem Mr Carmichael-Astaire."

Tony smothered the need to laugh as he knew how close to the surface her temper lay. He was going to enjoy having her around. Perhaps this development was better than having her as his mistress? Employee was far more interesting and arousing.

Guiding her lightly through the door he removed his hand and then strode ahead, letting her follow his lead out into reception. All the staff were gathered and waiting. It was six in the morning and Felicity knew this was only half of them, the others were scheduled in for the same talk before their shifts began at two pm. Silence descended as they surveyed their boss and their new manager. Felicity watched a few guys dig each other in the ribs and she let her tongue slide over her lips to maintain the glossy red of her shade. Felicity noted that all the women were young and striking in various different ways. Tony obviously didn't have a type.

After the introductions Tony ordered them coffee and breakfast to be sent to the boardroom. Felicity smiled as all the staff hurried off in various directions to begin their working day.

"So this is my office when I'm here. I rotate between my four hotels and my project in London. I will ensure you have my full timetable and contact numbers."

"Yes Tony," she replied, watching his step falter, but they were alone in the corridor.

"Here is the boardroom, please check with my secretary should you wish to book it for staff interviews or meetings." Tony grabbed the two handles and pulled them wide to reveal the large oak table, fourteen chairs surrounding it and a tray waiting for them. A waiter stood so silently in the corner that Felicity almost missed him. But with her second glance she tried to stop the blush creeping up her neck – it was Gerard.

Pulling out the chair for her, Felicity sat down and then waited as Gerard stepped forward to pour the coffee.

"I hope smoked salmon and poached eggs will suffice?"

"It will Mr Carmichael-Astaire."

With the food presented Gerard left the room and they were alone.

Tony ate quickly but Felicity savoured the taste and the knowledge that her plan was progressing.

"You'll meet my secretary, Jane at the first regional management meeting." He reached into his file and handed her the programme. "Holiday will never be allowed if it clashes with a planned meeting and we alternate hotel venues. The next one is in London next week so I assume you can make it?"

"Yes, Tony," she said, after finishing her last mouthful. He pulled the papers from his file and pushed their plates away.

"So here are the plans for the tennis courts. What I need from you in the first instance is the best quote for speed and quality. I need these up and running for the summer."

Felicity glanced over the plans for eight tennis courts, a racket centre adjacent and a path to the main gym complex.

"If this works here then I will roll out the same at the other three hotels over the next eighteen months so the contractors need to be flexible and available to travel."

"Certainly Tony," she said. "Can we tour the grounds so that I know exactly the dimensions?"

He nodded and finished his coffee and waited for Felicity to stand up. They walked around the rest of the hotel, Tony filling her in on all the various staff and facilities they already had. She diligently made notes, nodded, smiled and occasionally got a grin in return.

The wind whistled around them as they walked across the grass. Felicity tried not to shiver but in the end Tony noticed her discomfort and shrugged off his jacket to drape over her shoulders. She watched as he took a quick glance back at the numerous hotel windows, probably to check that none of his staff were watching. Felicity knew that they would be and she also knew that she was bound to hear rumours. The job of a good boss was to quash these and she was more than capable of cracking the whip. Back in the hotel Tony left for his office, only returning when it was time for the next staff meeting.

By the end of the day Felicity's head was reeling and her desk was filled with papers stacked neatly beside the computer. All she'd used before this was a till so she had a steep learning curve to figure out how to use this. She was still staring at the screen when Tony knocked and entered.

"Getting started then?"

"Not really, I've never used a computer before and I was going to take the manual home with me tonight."

"Tell you what, if you can stay an extra hour I'll show you the basics now." He loosened his tie and removed his jacket. Opening one of the cupboards he revealed a built-in fridge and pulled out a chilled bottle of white. Felicity saw the glasses on a shelf and put them on the desk.

"I'd better ring James and tell him I'm working late," she said, her fingers dialling the number.

"Oh yes... Mrs Cooke, the dutiful wife," he snickered as she reached out to ssssh him. Keeping the call brief Felicity maintained her cool despite the feel of Tony's lips on her neck as his fingers lifted and held her long hair.

Dropping the receiver into its cradle she arched back as his hands slid around and opened the buttons on her blouse.

"I thought you were teaching me about the computer," she said.

"All in good time," he replied as she looked round and his mouth crushed hers.

Pulling his tie off, he stretched her arms behind the chair and bound her wrists together, the silk soft but the knot biting into her skin. Spinning the chair around he knelt down and stretched her thighs apart, hitching up her skirt to find her naked and dripping for him. Helpless to resist Felicity surrendered to his tongue and teeth, and on the verge of her orgasm, he backed away. Turning the chair to the computer screen he turned it on. With each step of his teaching he reinforced it with a tweak of her nipples or a kiss on her lips until she moaned and begged for completion. As she logged off he lifted her onto the desk and dropped his trousers, his cock needing release from its confines.

Two hours later Felicity smoothed her suit back into place, pulled on her coat and left for home. Tony watched her car from the office window and straightened his own suit. He took a quick walk down the corridor so that he could slip unnoticed into his personal suite.

CHAPTER 46

James heard the door open and close as he lay in bed and pretended to be asleep. Felicity crept into the bathroom and turned on the shower to rid her body of Tony's scent, then she slid into bed beside James. He turned away from her and Felicity for once didn't care, she had much bigger things on her mind. With work keeping her busy she hardly saw much of James and her boys as she knuckled down. At first Tony only stopped by every other month, then it was once a month and soon it was every week. The staff believed it was to do with him overseeing the tennis court construction but he was addicted to Felicity. All the while Felicity plotted and planned, keeping up to date with Tony's plans through Keith, who was also still monitoring Stephanie's life in Ross.

The most interesting information she had was on Tony's London project as he referred to it. None of the other managers knew what it was but thanks to Keith she found out he'd bought the land belonging to his father and was building another private members' club. She also had the opening night date in her diary and as it was a masquerade ball, she could attend in disguise, despite hoping Tony would invite her. But as the date got nearer he became distant and agitated if she even mentioned his London project. He was still trying to goad her into leaving James and moving into the hotel and she was still waiting on more, she wanted his surname and status.

It was Friday morning, the day before his grand opening, when Felicity's phone rang.

"Carmichael-Astaire Health Spa, Ms Cooke speaking, how can I help?"

"It's me, Keith. I have some information you might like to hear."

"Ok, meet me in the restaurant at lunchtime, Tony is not here to see us."

At noon Felicity took a seat at the corner table and waited for Keith to arrive. He was smartly dressed and he took the seat quickly.

"I've ordered for us, so what's the news?"

"Stephanie is getting married this weekend to that doctor friend of hers, the one she's been dating."

"Oh, that's brilliant news, in fact it couldn't be better."

Their food arrived and she watched him tuck into the tender steak.

"So do you want me to get photographs?"

"Yes, I need them for the following weekend if possible."

"Not a problem."

Hugging the information she struggled to contain her joy. She was looking forward to seeing Tony's face when she removed her mask and told him all the information she had on his father's affairs and the way Tony had played his part, possibly even telling him that she had lit the fire... But then again, maybe not that little secret! Leaving early she called in to collect her gown, wig and mask before a quick call to James.

"Hi hun I just wanted to check in and let you know I'm on my way to London for the conference tomorrow. I will be back on Monday morning so give the boys a kiss from me."

"Yes dear," James replied and was about to add something sarcastic like they didn't even know her anymore, but the line was dead.

The car sped down the motorway and Felicity was soon parked at the hotel. She always liked to use the one where she'd stayed with her father, especially now she could afford the top floor suite. On her way up in the elevator she stopped on the second floor and walked slowly past the door of Room 40. Tears brimmed on her lashes but she blinked them away, remembering all the years he had abandoned her and her mother. Would her life have been different if he had been there everyday?

A couple rounded the corner and Felicity turned on her heels and marched back to the elevator and away from her broken childhood. Stepping inside her room she kicked off her heels and savoured the feel of the soft pile on her instep. Walking through she ran a bath, determined to fully pamper and preen, ready for tomorrow night.

Alone in the house James watched *Top Gun* again, his favourite form of torture. Darren held his airplane aloft and ran around the room every time the planes filled the screen. Mitchell snuggled into the crook of his arm, struggling to keep his eyes open. Tears softly wet the hair on his son's head as James thought of Stephanie and the love they had once shared.

On the eve of her wedding to Mark, Stephanie tossed and turned in the spare room of Sarah and Chris's small house. She had been their maid of honour only a few months ago and it was her turn now. But every time she closed her eyes she could see only one set of bright blue eyes, a shock of short blond hair and smell the hint of her favourite aftershave. Sobbing Stephanie cried for her lost love, James was the one for her but he had thrown her away. Next door Sarah slipped from Chris' snoring and his grip. Opening the door of the spare room she walked across to the bed.

"Come here," she whispered, climbing onto the bed and enfolding Steph into her arms.

"I don't think I can do this," Steph whimpered, clinging to her friend.

"Yes you can, Mark loves you so much. He adores you, dotes on you and James is never coming back."

"I know, but he doesn't deserve this broken shell that needs pills to get through each day. Or these scars to forever remind him of what I did for a man I truly loved."

"Steph, he knows and he still loves you. Just give him a chance, let him heal your heart."

Slowly her tears subsided and Steph fell asleep. Sarah crept back to the arms of the man she loved. Snuggling into his embrace, Chris stirred and pulled her close, kissing her upturned lips.

Felicity enjoyed a day of shopping in the capital and found the perfect underwear to compliment her gown. Then she spent an hour having a manicure, pedicure and a hairdresser fix her wig into place. She'd chosen a dress that reminded her of the one she'd worn for her date with Tony but this time she was a blonde. Fixing her red mask into place and tying the ribbons she wrapped her black fur stole around her shoulders. Then with a quick taxi ride just around the corner, she was there. The car park was filled with parked money, a glaring yellow Ferrari next to a black Lamborghini. Her limousine pulled up by the red carpet that led to the open doors. A doorman stepped forward and opened the door for her.

She handed the other doorman her gilt-edged invitation and then entered the main dining and bar area. The place was full of elegant men and beautiful women, and she stood out as she was the only one not part of a couple. The staff were all dressed like geishas and the barmen in plain black mandarin collared suits. Felicity took an offered glass of champagne and found a table in the corner so she could look for Tony.

He was the last to arrive and on his arm was a stunning Chinese woman, in an ornate but sexy take on the traditional dress. Felicity noted that she was older than Tony and on closer inspection, her make-up covered a pock-marked complexion. They circulated the room alone and Felicity walked in his direction.

It didn't take Tony long to notice the mysterious blonde in a red dress, a dress that brought back memories of another night so long ago. Grabbing a tumbler of whiskey he knocked it back and as the band started to play, he walked across to the woman.

"May I have this dance?" he asked. "I'm Anthony, the owner."

"Thank you," she replied, sliding into his arms.

"Do I know you?" he asked, as they swayed around the dance floor.

"I don't think so, maybe you can show me around and get to know me."

"Certainly, but let's finish this dance."

"What about the woman you came in with?"

"Oh, she's just the manager of the place. Madame Zee Zee."

When the music died Tony took her hand and led her from the room.

"Let me show you the many rooms on offer, perhaps we can be the first to try a few?" Tony said.

Felicity watched him arch his eyebrows and squeeze her hand at the same time. She nodded and followed him away from the crowds. They peeped into decadently styled boudoir rooms in different colour schemes or themes.

"Do you have anything darker? More... you know." She gripped his

247

hand tighter and taking him by surprise, pushed him against the wall.

Pinned there he chuckled, "Oh, you like rough?"

Leaning in she brushed a kiss on his cheek on her way to nip at his earlobe.

"Steady now... I still don't even know your name."

"Well if you find a room to my liking then maybe I'll tell you." She released him and saw the stairs leading upwards.

"Let's go up," he said, letting her go first so that as she ascended the spiral staircase, he let his eyes linger on her legs to wonder what lay beneath the flirty dress.

On the landing she waited for him and then they walked to the door on the end. Letting her in he turned to lock it, he wanted no distractions or sharing. She looked around the room as she slowly crossed to a cabinet that opened to reveal various sized whips. Picking one out she stroked down the length of it from handle to tip and then back up again.

"Good choice," he said, "so how about I fasten you into some restraints and let you feel it?"

"I think not, how about I try it out on you first," she purred, advancing towards him and pushing him against the wall.

"Could be fun." He laughed but it sounded thin and strained.

Felicity touched her lips to his and let her tongue probe as he opened for her. As her lips occupied him, her hands deftly fastened his wrists into the handcuffs that dangled from some chains.

"I'll be gentle," she whispered, "but you'd best choose you a safe word so I know when to stop."

"Why not your name?"

Leaving him waiting she bent down and stretched his legs apart so that she could fasten his ankles too. Then she slowly slipped down the straps of her dress, revealing her creamy skin and the tight black corset beneath connected to dark stockings. She wore no panties and her pussy was smooth and shorn of hair. Tony sucked in his breath as his gaze travelled to her burgeoning breasts and then the ultimate prize between her legs.

"You like?" she asked, letting her fingers slide down over the outside of her underwear, before delving a digit into her wet folds.

Spreading her legs slightly she flicked her nail onto her clit and gasped as the first small wave of desire flamed through her skin. She watched the tell-tale tent of his trousers and licked her lips. Stalking over to the sideboard she found a thicker, stronger whip and watched his eyes widen as she returned to face him.

"If you answer my questions then maybe I will not need to use this," she said, letting it run over the material of his trousers, up his inner thigh. She rested the tip on the bulge constrained there.

"What questions? Who are you?" he asked, but his voice lacked authority as he struggled to contain his lust.

"You don't need to know who I am just yet," she murmured, stepping in closer and undoing the belt and zip to let them fall.

"Why did you build this here?"

"The land was cheap due to a fire."

"Wrong answer, this is a prime real estate plot in the centre of London," she replied, stepping back to aim a mark on the top of his thighs. She watched his face and he just winced slightly.

"Answer the question or the next one will be harder."

"It belonged to my father, I wanted to invest the money he left me back into a place he loved." He lowered his head and closed his eyes.

"Mmh, that's better," she murmured, "for that you get a reward."

She stepped towards him and brushed her body against his.

"Let me kiss you?" he asked, letting his eyes implore her.

She stood back again and shook her head.

"So why another gentleman's club? Why not a bar? Nightclub? Or a small boutique hotel that is your preferred business?"

"Why not a haven where men can fulfil their fantasies?" he replied.

She watched his eyebrows arch as his tongue licked across his dry lips.

"But just for men, you're losing half your potential business," she replied. To reinforce her point she laid some welts on his chest, relishing the sound the crop made on his firm flesh.

"Enough now," he gasped, feeling the sting. "It's my turn."

He strained against his ties. Felicity stepped closer again and kissed the marks she'd made.

"I have more questions for you," she replied, "if your answers please me then maybe you'll get your reward."

She paced back and forward in front of him, letting her hands sweep up through her blond wig as it was starting to itch.

"Have you ever been in love?"

"What sort of question is that?"

"Answer it, I need to know the real man behind your hard exterior."

"No, never." For an instant the image of an eighteen year old Felicity swam in front of his eyes. She spotted the tell-tale flush of a lie on his neck and gave his inner thigh a sharp smack.

"Not even in your younger years?" she enquired, watching his lips curl up at the edge.

"Well, maybe," he conceded. "I was young but we were constrained."

Tony watched her sit down on the bed, crossing her legs and allowing him a glance.

"Tell me more, I'm intrigued."

CHAPTER 47

Tony swallowed and watched the blonde stranger get comfortable on the bed. He longed to break her to his will but equally, she intrigued him by her direct questions.

"It was my stepsister. She had it all, a sultry innocence in a breath-taking body. I moulded her to my wants and needs and she captivated me," he sighed, "but my father had other ideas and to gain my inheritance, I carried out his plans even though I didn't want to. It broke my heart to walk away and leave her at his mercy and that's why I will never love again."

"Not even her?" As she uttered the words, Felicity removed her mask and then pulled off her wig, shaking out her raven locks, all the time holding his gaze as he watched her reveal.

"Felicity," he gasped, his eyes wide, a red blush staining his whole body.

"Can you love me again? Can you be my man, my lover, my husband and a father?"

Felicity curled her hand around the handle of the crop, letting the end travel up her leg.

"Lover yes, but never a husband and father. I can't be like him."

"But you are like him." She shrugged, moving to stand and walk across to her clothes. She pulled out the mini recorder and held it up.

"I have enough information of what you did and your loathing of your father. Perhaps with a little false evidence the arsonist and killer of Malcolm and my mother could be made to fit your profile. The case still sits there unsolved."

"What do you want? Compensation? An apology?" he demanded, angrily.

"I've already told you what I want. To be more than a mere mistress. I want to have your name and an equal standing in your empire, maybe then I might forgive you."

Felicity let a well-planned tear slip from beneath her lashes, letting it slide down her cheek before she wiped it away. The room was silent as she watched Tony wrestle with his feelings.

They heard footsteps outside as guests wandered to other rooms off the corridor. A hand tried the handle of theirs but finding it locked, the steps moved on.

"I need an answer Tony, I don't have all night and I'm sure your guests might be wondering where their host is? I'd hate to have to leave you exposed and chained up!" She laughed as sweat dripped and ran down his body.

"Ok, I'll do it but on one condition."

"What condition?"

"I just can't be a father to our son, it terrifies me beyond belief."

Felicity hid her delight and knew that with her new place in his life, maybe she could wear him down to the possibility of Mitchell as his son. She walked over to him and freed his ankles, then running her fingers up his body, she removed the cuffs at his wrists. He lurched forward and wrapped his arms tightly around her waist before pushing her backwards and down onto the soft bed.

She didn't struggle as his body parted her thighs and he plunged deep inside her. She wrapped her ankles over his back to hold him secure as he thrust into her in the measured way he knew she loved.

"Come for me baby," he moaned, his body tense for release but waiting for her to join him.

"Say my name," she moaned, "my full name."

"Felicity Carmichael-Astaire, would you do me the honour of your orgasm," he declared, staring into her eyes and pausing on his final stroke. He felt her ripples start to grip him, like a tight vice as she squealed, "Yeeesssss!"

Rolling off, Tony tried to relax but Felicity pinned him down with her stare.

"You mean what you said, I have it recorded so I need you to play your part. I have a very difficult week ahead, leaving my husband for you."

"Just do it and come to the hotel."

Leaning down she pressed her lips to his and kissed him with every fibre in her body. He had walked straight into her web and everything was going almost according to plan. Getting dressed she dumped her wig in the bin before getting Tony to tie her mask back into place. Before he unlocked the door he took her hand in his and pulled her close.

"I'm sorry for what I did," he whispered, "but I'm going to give you everything you can ever dream of and more."

Stepping back into the throng of the party crowds, he plucked glasses of champagne from the hovering waiter and handed her one.

"Here's to us," she said, her smile broad and bright.

"To us," he echoed.

***

In Ross-on-Wye, Stephanie also sipped from a glass as she looked across at the remaining few guests at her wedding. Mark walked over and slipped his arm over her shoulders.

"Penny for your thoughts Mrs Eden," he said, touching his glass against hers.

"Thank you," was all she could manage as the words got stuck in her throat. The tablet was wearing off and the bright surroundings were turning into shadows and making her panic. Sarah and Chris walked over to the newlyweds.

"It was a beautiful day, now just enjoy your honeymoon." Sarah reached out and wrapped Steph in her arms. She felt the tremble under her cool skin and hugged her tighter.

"You'll be fine," she whispered, "Mark will look after you."

Stephanie hugged her best friend back. "I hope so," she whispered.

***

On his way to bed, James opened the door of Darren's bedroom. A dark mop of hair was all he could see of his sleeping son. Soft snores and snuffles echoed through the room. James smiled and closed the door before he took a few steps to the next one. He tried to creep in but Mitchell was awake and staring at the patterns of his nightlight on the ceiling.

"Hey champ, you should be asleep."

Mitchell smiled as his dad knelt down by his bed.

"Dada kiss," he mumbled.

James popped a light one on his forehead and then tucked in his covers. He waited as Mitchell turned over and closed his eyes before he crept back out. Stepping into his own room he dropped his clothes on the floor and climbed under the covers. The bed felt cold and lonely which was how it felt even when Felicity was home. Turning the radio on low he let the music soothe him to sleep and dreams where he was once again happy.

***

Felicity spent the night with Tony but before he woke in the morning, she slipped away. She left him a message, written on a £50 note she'd found in his wallet, finishing it off with her red lipstick mark:

Tony, there is no escape from my bloodstained heart, Flick x

Before she left London she stopped at a small café, already open despite the early hour. Hunched in the corner was Keith, cradling his steaming cup of tea. She ordered a coffee and then joined him.

"Do you have them?" she asked, sitting opposite him.

He pushed the brown envelope towards her and she tipped out the contents. A happy, smiling bride and groom greeted her.

"Excellent work, just what I wanted."

"So everything is set then?" he asked.

"Oh yes, it is indeed," she replied, writing out a cheque and letting it dangle between her fingers. Keith plucked it out and folded it quickly before it disappeared into his coat pocket. Finishing his tea he stood up.

"See you soon."

"Undoubtedly." Felicity stood up too, leaving her coffee barely touched. With her foot on the accelerator she took off in the direction of the motorway and the Midlands. She glanced at the brown envelope on the passenger seat and relished the lingering scent of Tony's aftershave on her skin.

CHAPTER 48

James was making boiled eggs and toast soldiers for the boys when the front door opened. The draught swept her cloying perfume into the room before she appeared in the doorway.

"I'm just going for a shower, I feel all grimy from the drive," she called, before he heard her steps climb the stairs.

In the bathroom Felicity ran the bath instead and stepped into its warm, silky water. She listened as a car pulled up to take Darren to nursery and then she heard James approaching.

"I've brought you a tea, I'm going out for a quick jog in the park so I'll take Mitch with me in the pushchair."

"Ok," she replied, still luxuriating in the bubbles and the news she had for James on his return.

Stepping out of the water she dried, dressed and re-packed her suitcases. She loaded everything she would need for a week into the back of her car. She wanted to tell him the news and then leave for her new life. When James returned with a sleeping Mitchell she waited for him to put her son to bed before he joined her in the kitchen.

"Good weekend?" he asked, flicking the switch on the kettle.

"Yes, better than I could have imagined. But we need to talk."

"Talk about what?" he asked, noting the drop of her voice to the tone that normally meant an argument was brewing.

"About us, well about me really. I need more than this life, I need wealth and power."

James sat down and stared across at his wife, one that he'd contemplated leaving on so many occasions in the past.

"I think it's time we went our separate ways. I'm sure we can get a quick divorce if neither of us contest anything, like the fact that you will keep the boys with you."

"So, it's just over… just like that, because you say so!" James spluttered, angry at her dismissal.

"Yes, pretty much. This is my house so I'd like you and the boys out by the end of the week. I will sort out a payment to you and visiting access to Darren and Mitchell."

"Why now? I at least deserve some sort of explanation."

"I don't love you, in fact I've probably never loved you. You were just a stop gap in my ambitions."

James felt his hands shaking into tight fists and bile rose in his throat as he thought of who he'd given up for her. Felicity watched him, revelling in the power she wielded.

"So, just think you can go back to that sad little excuse of a girlfriend if she'll have you!"

"Well, maybe I fucking will, you bitch." James stood up and wrenched off his wedding band, letting it clatter on the table.

"It's been fun! So I'll just get going to my new life. My solicitor will be in touch. I will send the paperwork to your parent's place. I'm sure they will be overjoyed by the news."

Standing up she walked past him, picked up her handbag and left the house.

It took James a few minutes to regain his composure. He saw a brown envelope lying there with his name on it. He tipped it up to reveal a selection of photographs and a note:

Oops, looks like you're too late!

He turned over the prints and reeled back against the counter. It was his Stephanie, except she wasn't his anymore. Each of the four photos showed her gazing up into the face of a tall, handsome man. They were framed by the arched doorway of the church. His fleeting dream of happiness was dashed. On the back of one was written: *Stephanie March marries Mark Eden on Saturday 15th June*. The date of the previous weekend. How could she have known? Slumping into the chair he studied the pictures through the tears in his eyes. He'd fucked up big time. Mitchell's cries broke him from his own sorrow as he wiped his eyes and took the stairs.

Mitchell stopped crying as his dad entered the room and reached his arms up. Picking him up James cuddled him close before popping him down on the floor with his toys.

"Daddy's going to pack some things and then we're off on an adventure once we fetch Darren from nursery."

Mitchell looked up, his green eyes bright as if he understood every word. James smiled weakly and hurried to grab some clothes from his room, discovering that Felicity had cleared hers.

Then he returned to pack for his sons, enough for overnight. He could come back tomorrow before his late shift and get everything else he needed. After lunch with Mitchell, he packed the car and took the short journey to collect Darren. It took all his concentration as his mind kept showing him the photos of Stephanie in her wedding gown.

Pulling into the driveway, James saw his mum at the kitchen window, surprised by this unplanned arrival of her son and grandchildren.

"Nana," Darren shouted, as he ran the short distance to the front door. Mitchell struggled in his dad's arms, wanting to copy his older brother as Pam pulled the door open and scooped up her eldest grandson.

"So what are you doing here?" she asked.

"I've come to play with Grampy and his train set," Darren declared, as she put him down and he continued through the house.

"James, this is a nice surprise," his Mum said, reaching for Mitchell so he had a free hand for the bag.

"Felicity has left me, I hope you don't mind some guests for the next few days."

Pam's mouth gaped open at the news as she stepped back inside to find Peter on the way upstairs with Darren.

With tea in front of them and Mitchell in his highchair eating a biscuit, Pam looked at her son.

"Well, I can't say I'm unhappy about the news. I never took to her."

"Thanks Mum, it was a bit of a shock to me. I have to be out of the house by the end of the week. She says she'll reimburse me what she thinks I'm owed and will help towards the cost of the boys."

"She wants you to look after them?" Pam said, surprised.

"Yeah, guess her maternal instinct was never that strong in the first place. I just hope the boys will understand, even though I still don't at the moment." James shrugged and tried to stop the sob threatening to break free from his throat. Pam watched him struggle and laid her hand over his on the table.

"You have a place here with us, you all do."

***

Driving up to the rear car park of the hotel Felicity hoped none of the staff would see her. Tony had given her the key for his private flat at the rear and told her to wait there for his arrival. Walking inside she dumped her bags and walked across to the fridge. She pulled out a chilled bottle of Bollinger and found a glass in the cupboard. The liquid eased the butterflies in her stomach, not from nerves, but sheer exhilaration at her actions. She'd wanted to stay and see his face when he looked at the photos but it didn't matter now. She was free, she was going to become Mrs Carmichael-Astaire and be wealthy and powerful. She knew she could wrap Tony around her finger and then one day, when the time was right, she'd reap her revenge.

Giggling at her plans she stared out across the vast land behind the hotel that now held tennis courts and the beginnings of a nine-hole golf course. All this would soon be hers along with the three other health spa complexes and the club in London. She watched as Tony's Jaguar sped up the driveway and parked next to her car. He looked up at the window and she waved at him, licking her lips to renew the shine of her crimson shade.

"You were quick," he said, as he stepped into the lounge and she passed him a glass.

"To the start of our new life together," she breathed, as she tapped her glass against his.

"Absolutely," he agreed, letting the cool liquid try and soothe his worries.

"So I'm guessing you have a good lawyer I can use for my divorce. I want it quick, painless and relatively cost free."

"I will see what I can do," Tony said, "but there's no rush is there?"

"Of course there is, I want a Christmas wedding with all the trimmings and that's only six months away." She fluttered her eyelashes at him before taking his empty glass. "But first let's get re-acquainted in the bedroom…"

To be continued in…

Bloodstained Heart: Part Two – Revenge

COMING 2017

ACKNOWLEDGEMENTS

I'd like to thank Darren Hayes for the inspiration that I took from his song entitled 'Bloodstained Heart', please check it out as it's an amazing song.

As usual a thank-you to my other half, Steve, who continues to put up with my constant tap, tap, tapping away every evening as I fit writing in around work and life. It's always appreciated.

A big thank-you to Mike's Graphics and Dando's Delights for fitting my book cover onto some imaginative gift items. Don't worry I'll be back for more! And Fool's Journey for providing the music for my book trailer video that can be found on YouTube.

ABOUT THE AUTHOR

Audrina Lane lives with her partner Steve and two Labradors in Herefordshire where *The Heart Trilogy* is set. The first book is based on a diary the author wrote in 1992 and is inspired by her own experiences of first love.

To find out more about Audrina and her books, visit:-
www.audrinalane.co.uk or http://author.to/audrinalane.

Facebook: The Heart Trilogy

Twitter and Instagram: @AudrinaLane

Made in the USA
Charleston, SC
31 December 2016